D0730363

This is a work of fiction. All of the charact portrayed in this novel are either products or the author's imagination or are used fictitiously.

Author:

www.ByTiffanyCampbell.Com

writtenbytiff@gmail.com

Facebook.Com/AuthorTiffanyCampbell

Twitter/Instagram: @writtenbytiff

10 9 8 7 6 5 4 3 2 1

Publisher:

shauntakenerlypresents@gmail.com

Published in Charlotte N.C.

Edited by Nicole Scott

Cover Design by AMB Branding

ISBN: 978-0692480359

SCARED OF BEAUTIFUL
BY TIFFANY CAMPBELL

Bobbi.

"I'm not crazy," I defended softly as I rubbed my left arm with my right hand and stared at the patterns on the carpet. The goose bumps evident along my skin only confirmed that it was freezing in this doctor's office, and the cool leather from the couch I was sitting on was not making it any better.

"I never said you were Bobbi," Dr. Moss replied as she stared intensely into my eyes with her icy blue eyes over her thick framed glasses that I could see my reflection in. She was a middle aged woman, probably in her early 40s, with stringy blond hair and bags underneath her bottom eyelids. She seemed to have needed her own help more than I needed hers.

"I was just having a bad day. Everyone is entitled to have a bad day," I shot back; my voice harsh and brash as I rubbed my clammy hands together. Ever since being released from the hospital, people treated me like a cancer patient causing me to lack patience. I wasn't sick. I was fine, yet no one wanted to believe me.

"Taking twenty painkillers and washing it away with Vodka sounds like more than a bad day Bobbi. It sounds like a lot of built in resentment and anger. Enough to where you no longer wanted to be on this earth," she answered calmly not at all affected by the temper slowly increasing in my tone.

Hearing the sounds of my actions always made me feel a certain way. Made me really analyze the events and emotion that led me to that moment, the moment where I just couldn't take it anymore.

"I just wanted the images to go away," I admitted softly trying to avoid her stare. "Every time I close my eyes, I see my best friend on top of the love of my life. Do you know how painful that is? To be betrayed by two people who were supposed to love you the most?"

"They didn't love you Bobbi. Nothing in that demonstrates love," she corrected as I stared up at her blankly, swallowing hard before taking in a deep breath.

"They continued to tell me that they did after that day you know? Kept calling and texting talking about how sorry they were and didn't mean to hurt me. I don't know who they were trying to convince. Me, or themselves," I paused for a moment.

"I just wanted to know what I did so wrong?" I choked feeling the emotion stuffed in the pit of my throat causing my voice to tremble restraining myself because I hated crying.

"For the last 18 months, I've just been trying to figure out what I did to them? I gave Jo everything I had; everything. Every bit of me there was left to give, he had it," a tear escaped as I sniffled and wiped at my nose with the back of my palm.

"And I was always there for Tashay. Regardless of all the people that could care less about her. I always had her back and was there for her through it all. I just never thought my kind heart would come back to bite me."

"18 months is a long time," Dr. Moss commented as she jotted down notes on her pad, "I think it's time for you to move on from all of this. Let it go and start your healing process. The worst is behind you, and your future rests before you. You're graduating with your nursing degree in the spring, and you've endured a very traumatizing experience. It will be so good for you to rise above all of this."

I shrugged my shoulders slightly while sniffling. I was able to contain the tears like I had grown so accustomed to, "I've tried, and it still feels fresh. It still hurts. It's turned me into someone that I never thought I'd be. Cold, disconnected, heartless...I used to be so full of love and life. They robbed me of that."

"You've allowed them to."

I felt my blood boil at the sound of her words and I couldn't hide my offensiveness, "I didn't allow them to do anything!"

"You've allowed yourself to become a prisoner to the pain."

I sat back hard in my seat leaning back with much attitude while tapping the soles of my feet against the floor trying to calm myself down. Her words were as cutting as daggers. *Who did she think she was telling me this?* I threw my hands up in defeat no longer desiring to continue yet continued, "I really don't want to talk about this. The only reason why I'm here is because the hospital made me schedule an appointment before I could be released. Like I said, I'm not crazy. Was just having a bad day and wanted to forget about it all. I was hoping the painkillers would actually do what they said they would; take away the pain. I experimented and they didn't. Now I'm over it and ready to move the hell on."

She smirked before removing her glasses, "Why won't you accept what you were trying to do? You were trying to do more than just take away the pain for a moment Bobbi. You were trying to take away the pain permanently by committing suicide."

"I didn't want to die," I retorted; the attitude clear in my voice at this point.

She furrowed her brows, "Are you sure?"

My nose instantly turned up at her question, "Are you seriously asking me if I'm sure of something I just said?"

"You didn't want to die, but you had gotten to a point where you couldn't tell the difference between being alive and just living. What difference would death have made to how you already felt?"

I was silent.

She continued, "I see a hint of who the old Bobbi could've been in your eyes. I can tell she still lives within you, and you want so badly to let her free, but you're scared. You've been hurt, and you don't want to feel that again. We've all had distasteful moments in life, but it's how you recover from those moments that show your inner strength. You're stronger than this situation. You always have been. You just continue to play victim to it. You can't remain the victim forever. Eventually, it becomes self-inflicted pain."

I sighed as I looked at my watch before grabbing my book bag, "You're wasting your time Dr. Moss. I hope you still get paid for this session."

"We still have thirty minutes left Ms. Cochran," she said sweetly as I rolled my eyes.

"I guess the hospital ignored my class schedule when they made this appointment. I have to make it across campus in fifteen minutes for my Biology class. Sorry, but I can't stay to talk about feelings," I spat as I flung the strap to my bag over my shoulder hurriedly making my way to the exit.

"You should come back and see me Bobbi," she pressed as I just slammed the door on my way out.

I pulled out my headphones, connected them to my phone, and jammed the ear buds into my ear drums as I quickly left the campus Psychologist's office. Even going to that appointment reminded me of what a foolish and careless decision I had made from taking all of those pills that night.

Nobody understood what I had gone through the evening everything happened. What I had witnessed as I saw Jo. He didn't see me, but I saw him. He was smiling and happy. His eyes were full of so much light and joy, completely unaware of the misery he had caused me for the past year and a half. He had moved on from the heartache he had inflicted and was casually showering some woman with affection - the same love that he once showered me with. She was grinning from ear to ear: excited for this new found love. And here I was, depressed, heartbroken, and laying in a puddle of tears every other night because I couldn't let go.

Seeing his face instantly brought back the painful reminder of the day I came home on my lunch break. It was the home we shared together full of our pictures and other memories. I just had a hunch. Something in my heart just didn't feel at peace. I didn't want to be right but I was. I came home to find my best friend and him in bed together. I saw them and blacked out.

Chills came over me as I reflected over the tragic events that had transpired in what seemed to me like a short period of time. The way Dr. Moss was describing it; you would think it's been longer than that. In my mind, everything still felt real, like it happened yesterday. I hated her because she was right about the things she said. I had lost a grip on reality in the midst of everything. I needed to stay focused on what was important.

I caught my breath as I jogged lightly up the steps to the building my Biology class was held in. I breathed in through my nose and out of my mouth as my heart rate slowed while approaching the classroom door. Walking in, a few eyes glanced in my direction before returning idly to their phones. Class hadn't started yet.

I took my usual seat in the back and began to unload my book and notebook for this class while smiling softly at Monica who smiled brightly at me as she walked into the classroom. She was a classmate turned acquaintance. She was in the nursing program too, and we always found ourselves ending up in the same class.

Her petite, 5'4" frame made its way to a seat next to mine. She dropped her bag down next to her and turned to face me flashing her infectious smile that was filled with dimples, and her light brown skin seemed to glow more than normal.

"You need to come out with me tonight," she demanded versus asking me. I raised a suspicious brow at her as I opened my book to the last chapter we were on.

"That sounds like it involves people," I responded flatly hearing a small groan escape her lips.

"Because it DOES involve people. I met this really cool guy the other day, and he really wants to kick it with me, but he has a roommate and..."

I quickly stopped her. "No. Hell no. I am not playing wingman for the ugly roommate."

She chuckled before smacking her lips, "You don't even know if he's ugly!"

"Yeah, but I'm sure you do..."

Her facial expression led one to question.

"Actually I don't. Let me see if he has an Instagram," she said pulling out her phone and quickly texting away.

I looked through my folder to pull out our assignment that was due as I awaited the verdict.

"Okay, he's not *that* bad," she said squinting at the phone as I quickly snatched it from within her grasp.

"Wait, let me find a better picture!" she begged as my mouth dropped at the sight. The man on the screen was midnight black, with acne, crooked teeth, and unmanaged facial hair. I couldn't believe Mo would try to set me up like this.

"Are you kidding me? I can't even do it. If he tries to touch me in any way I'm calling the cops. He looks like he stinks Mo." I frowned handing her the phone as she couldn't stop laughing.

"Come on man! For me! If you do this, I owe you big! I swear," she pleaded as I rolled my eyes. So much of Mo reminded me of Tashay. She was always needy of me and wanting me to do things for her, but she never returned the favor, not once. Tashay's world revolved around her just like Monica's. That's why she couldn't become more than an acquaintance.

"He doesn't have any other roommates? Like one that actually gets his hair cut and washes his face?" I asked as she giggled and shrugged her shoulders.

"I don't know, but the friend is really cute!" she said quickly tapping away on her iPhone. She turned the screen towards me moments later. I turned up my nose. He didn't look any better. Monica liked ugly men.

"He aight," I shrugged as she smacked her lips in disapproval of my response.

"Well excuse me for liking tall dark and handsome!" she defended.

"You mean skinny, black, and ugly?" I corrected as she rolled her eyes causing me to laugh. I had to go now simply because I knew I hurt her feelings, "I'll go, but get your business over with so I don't have to pretend to be interested for too long." I sighed as she turned to look at me excitedly. Our teacher walked in at the same time.

"Thank you so much Bobbi! I owe you!" she said as she turned in her seat and pulled out her notebook for class. I watched as the teacher closed the door and smiled at everyone in the room.

"Sure."

Donovan.

"Ain't nothing but ugly hoes in here," Shane groaned as I looked down at his short stature and laughed.

My business partner and I stood in the crowded Graystone Manor; a club in downtown Los Angeles. We had spent a long day at the shop doing tattoos and piercings and made our way here to relax and unwind: the typical 23-year-old, young entrepreneur, and bachelor life.

"Relax little one. You have to keep your eye out for the right chick," I assured him while taking a sip of my Crown Royal and Coke.

"Aye, chill with that little shit," he said deepening his voice as I let out a chuckle. He hated when I teased him about his height. It wasn't my fault he was only 5'6" and I was 6'1".

Shane shook his head at my amusement before running his hand through his short cut even all around hair. I didn't know why he complained. Girls always gravitated towards his short frame, hazel eyes, caramel brown skin, and straight smile. He had no problem charming women, not to mention, women in LA were into men with tattoos. Shane and I both had sleeves full of body art. Mine extended to my neck.

I sported a short haircut like him, but I was lighter. I had the type of skin that got pale in the winter time, but my eyes stayed brown. Women liked me for the tiny freckles plastered from the right cheek, across my nose, and on my left cheek, and I was a slim with a sleekly build. I didn't have muscles, but I was in shape, and because Shane got braces in high school and I didn't, my two front teeth slightly overlapped. It never stopped me from getting chicks though. They rocked with my crooked smile.

"Let's just go by the bar and post up. I'm sure we'll see somebody bad," I suggested as he shrugged a little and followed me.

"Man I should've got ol' girl wit da fat ass that I tatted today. She wanted me," he smirked arrogantly while we stood against the edge of the bar.

"I'm sure she did with her boyfriend hovering over your neck," I joked as he smacked his lips.

"You think I care if she gotta man? Once I told her I co-owned the parlor with you, I saw a little glitter in her eyes. She was flirtin n'shit. I know she wanted it."

"You think everybody want you. Only person that want you is Joi," he gave me the blankest facial expression ever causing me to burst into a fit of laughter.

"Come on man. What I tell you about bringing up the baby mom when we're out? We having a good time. No need to bring up her thirsty ass."

"I told you she was trouble when I first met her."

"That's the first problem. You were never supposed to meet her. It was never supposed to be anything serious. Next thing I know, she pregnant."

"Doesn't matter. I have a beautiful god-daughter because of it," I said as I killed the last few swallows of my drink then turned my attention towards the bar so I could order us a few shots.

Shane and I had been boys since we were young. Me, him, and my god-brother James, all grew up together. You couldn't tear us apart back then and couldn't tear us apart now. James went to college though while Shane and I became apprentices at a local tattoo shop because we were both artistic. Once his business went under, we hustled enough money to open our own shop, and business had been pretty good for us. We opened in a popular area in West Hollywood. We started getting a lot of celebrity clientele, and social networking sites like Instagram and Facebook, were really good to promote our business.

"Asshole!"

I heard a small voice screech as I looked to my right to see the prettiest set of green eyes I had ever seen. She was short and petite and about my complexion with dark red hair. Her full pink lips were perfect, and I could tell a beautiful smile lied behind her scowl.

"Sheesh what I do?" I asked pretending to be hurt as she looked over at me and rolled her eyes.

"Not you. The bartender. He keeps walking right passed me!" she huffed as I instantly wanted to help. As if on cue, the server looked in my direction, and we locked eyes. I motioned for him to come our way.

"What can I get you man?" he asked resting his hands on the countertop.

"Um, I'll have four Crown Royal shots and whatever the lady wants," I said as I smiled in the beautiful stranger's direction.

"A Corona please," she ordered with attitude as the server nodded politely and went to fix me and Shane's shots.

"This doesn't mean I'm just going to offer you my number or anything," she said randomly to me as I looked at her confused.

"Never asked for it."

"You were going to," she said confidently as I chuckled lightly while pulling out two twenties as the bartender returned with our drinks.

"Keep the change man," I slapped the bill into his hand, and he took it gratefully.

"Enjoy your Corona beautiful," I said sweetly to the girl as I grabbed the shots carefully and took them over to Shane. I could feel eyes burning into my back.

"Aye, ol girl fire," Shane commented looking past my shoulder then I shrugged.

"She knows," I said lightly crossing my eyes and inhaling my first shot. Shane followed suit. We made ugly faces as we swallowed the liquor.

"What was her name?"

"I ain't ask for it. I need her to humble herself first."

Shane rolled his eyes, "Man here you go. That don't always work Don! Especially not with chicks like her. She look high maintenance. Like dudes be all over her."

"And I'm sure they are which is why I've already piqued her interest. I didn't respond to her like she expected. She wanted me to kiss her ass and pry more into why I couldn't get her number without asking for it. She thought she had me figured out, and now that she realizes she doesn't, she can't stop sneaking looks at me to see if I'm just some guy here to get girls."

Shane looked past my shoulder quickly before disappearing out of her view, "Shit. She was looking."

I smirked. He hated when I was right, "Now watch. These two chicks approaching us that I'm about to turn down. Watch what she does after this."

As I finished, two attractive women approached. Shane drooled all over them while I remained cool coming off as disinterested. I made sure to make it clear in my expressions.

"You two wanna come to our table in VIP?" one girl asked staring sensually at me as she lightly bit her lip.

"We're good here. Thanks though," I politely declined as Shane looked at me as if I had two heads.

"Hell you mean?" He turned back towards the women, "Aye, I'm down. Come find me in a minute Don!" he finished excitedly as he swiftly followed the two women off leaving the extra shot I bought him.

"More for me," I sighed turning back to my drinks. A few moments later I felt her presence approach. She was an open book– easy to read.

"Looks like you could you use some company," she softly said as she sat on a stool next to me. I looked down at her and smiled. She was going to be fun.

"He had a nice opportunity. Couldn't turn it down," I told her sliding Shane's abandoned shot in her direction.

"Then how could you?" she asked while pulling the cup closer to her as we both prepared to shoot.

"I liked my view," I smirked slyly before quickly gulping the liquor as she smiled doing the same.

"Sorry about earlier. I just get annoyed with so many guys always hitting on me," she bragged as I shrugged.

"Not every girl I buy a drink for I hit on."

"Oh, so you're just a nice guy," she said sarcastically.

"I ain't say that. Just looked like you needed a drink," I said flatly as I turned to walk away. I counted down from five in my head...*two...one...*

"Wait!"

I turned around and looked at her with question.

"I'm sorry. I can come off as a bitch. I didn't mean to just assume like that. You're different."

"I'm Donovan actually," I replied as she giggled before extending her hand.

"Stacy."

"It was nice talking to you Stacy. I better get going though. I gotta find my friend," As I attempted to walk away for the second time, she gently rested her hand on my arm to stop me.

"I have a better idea."

****

"I don't normally do stuff like this..." Stacy panted as she pushed me backwards onto her bed. I just nodded as I rested on my elbows and looked up at her. She was stripping her clothes off as fast as she could.

"I don't judge," I answered as she bit her lip before crawling on top of me.

Her lips inched towards mine, and I gently turned my head causing them to collide with my cheek.

She looked at me strangely, so I chose to give her an explanation, "Not a fan of kissing."

She nodded in understanding before resting her hands on my chest and swirling her tongue against my neck. I lifted my elbows up to lay flat on the bed as I let her get to work.

Several hours later, both Stacy and I laid breathless while staring up at the ceiling. She was by far the freakiest one night stand I had ever encountered. She was willing to do any and everything to me, and she honestly had me tired as hell.

I looked over at her, saw her eyes were still closed, and found this the perfect opportunity to catch my cut.

As I was making my way out of the bed, she softly wrapped her arms around my waist attempting to cuddle closer with me. No way was I doing this shit.

"Where are you going?" she cooed as her legs attempted to intertwine with mine.

"I gotta work in the morning. Can't stay here tonight," I lied. The shop was closed on Sundays.

"Then just stay with me a little longer. I'm not ready for you to leave yet," she pleaded as I gave her an apologetic look before carefully removing her arms.

"I can't tonight Stace. Maybe another time," *Shit*.

"I can see you again?"

Dammit Don, I thought.

"Put my number in your phone," she said as she sat up wrapping her sheets around her naked body.

My t-shirt was still on and my boxers were down at my ankles. I sat up and slid the used condom off and held it by my fingertips as I lifted my boxers up with my free hand. I walked to the bathroom connected to her room and disposed of the soiled plastic in the toilet before flushing. I looked over myself briefly in the mirror and checked to make sure she didn't leave any marks on my neck. I wasn't trying to look crazy in front of whatever girl I picked up tomorrow.

After splashing a little water on my face from her sink, I walked back into the
room and noticed she was standing up wearing nothing but a small white tank that barely covered her pierced nipples and her bottom half was completely bare. She rubbed herself gently with her manicured index and middle finger, before inserting them all the way inside of her, allowing a moan to escape.

"Don't leave me yet baby.." she said in a voice that caused me to get rock hard.

"Maybe I'll stay for a few more minutes,"

Bobbi.

"You're back," Dr. Moss smiled as she watched me walk into her office a week later. I rolled my eyes as I sat across from her while setting my purse down next to me.

"Figured I owe you thirty more minutes," I answered dryly as I sat with my arms crossed.

She gave a small smile, "Me or you?"

"Stop trying to get deep. It really isn't that deep. You wanted me back here now I'm back."

"How was your week Bobbi?"

I shrugged my shoulders in response.

"What did you do?"

"I went to class, studied, hung out with a chick from school, and kept to myself," I answered placing my chin in my palm and looking out of the window. I watched as students walked past the building heading to their next set of classes.

"That's all you did? What did you do for you? No hobbies?" she questioned as I shrugged and thought about it for a moment.

"I like to take pictures," I admitted shyly as she instantly beamed.

"Oh! Photography?"

I nodded a little, "Yeah, I know how to edit them real good too. It's something I do in my free time. Take pictures of shit."

"Why didn't you study that in school then? If it's something you like to do?" she wondered.

"No stability in taking pictures. I'm interested in Nursing, and it's a good career move. If I take a nice picture and am able to sell it down the line then cool, but it's something I forever want to enjoy in my free time. Sometimes when you make your passion your job it can force you not to love it as much anymore."

"What made you have a passion for taking photos?"

"I like what they represent. Each photo represents a new memory. Reminds you of where you were and what you were doing in that moment. Each time you look at that picture you can go back and relive that memory."

"You became more interested after the incident happened, so you could forget that memory and create new ones," she assumed.

I didn't argue with her. "I did."

She nodded as she jotted down some notes. "You called your friend, 'a girl from school', a moment ago. Why?"

What a dumb question, I thought, "Because that's what she is."

"You're afraid to use the word friend."

"I don't fear anything."

"Do you always lie to yourself like that?"

"Who said I was lying?"

"I did."

"Well, I'm not."

"I see a scared individual; someone who fears getting hurt and letting people in because of the past. I see someone afraid to move on."

I shook my head as I tuned her out. "Why did I come back here?" I asked aloud stopping her mid-sentence.

"Because you want my help."

"I really don't. I'm not sick okay! I can't go around my family or people that know because everyone treats me like I'm sick! And I'm not! I'm HURT! Can no one see that?! I'm *hurt*! There's a difference." I stressed.

"Does sickness not come with pain?" she asked rhetorically.

I crossed my eyes.

"When you look in the mirror Bobbi, what do you see?"

I stared at her blankly as I thought about what she asked. I wanted to be a smartass and tell her my physical appearance. I was 5'6", with rich mocha brown skin, and long natural wavy hair that I inherited from my Native American grandmother. My nose was small, yet pudgy, and rested underneath my almond shaped eyes. I had a skinny yet toned frame; 27 inch waste with my 'C' cups resting up top. I clasped my long fingers together as I stared back at her, "I don't like to look at my reflection."

"Why is that?"

"Don't like what I see."

"You're beautiful."

"Eh. I'm okay."

"You don't have to be difficult. Let someone help you."

"How are you helping me by challenging everything I say to you? How is that helping me?"

"I'm just trying to figure you out. You don't give me much to work with."

I let out a sigh of frustration as I ran my hands over my face and then through my hair. We stared at each other for a moment before she spoke again.

"What's your plan after graduation Bobbi? It's coming quickly."

"I don't know yet. My mom thinks I should go stay with my Aunt Lisa."

"Where does she live?"

"In Los Angeles."

"Oh my, that's definitely a change from this small city. Have you considered?"

I raised my shoulders slightly, "I have. I told my aunt we'll talk more about it when her and my cousin comes up to see me graduate."

"I think you should do it."

"I don't care what you think", I replied rudely as she frowned a little.

"If you don't then why are you here?" she asked innocently as I asked myself the same damn question.

Why did people actually choose to come and talk to these people? This didn't help. All we were having was a pointless conversation about things that made no difference to her. She could sit here and pretend she cared all day but it won't have any impact. My life would still be the same, and I'd still feel how I felt. I didn't need her help to realize that.

Without another word, I snatched my purse off the floor and stood to my feet to make my exit.

"Miss Cochran..." she called, but I ignored her, while once again slamming the door on my way out.

Donovan.

I bobbed my head to the sounds of Future while cleaning around the front of the shop. I wiped down the glass tables and counters and also sprayed Lysol on all of the couches. Preparing to wipe down our laminated picture books with Clorox wipes, I heard the front door chime.

"Sup peanut head!" Tierre sang obnoxiously in her Harlem accent. I smiled at the beautiful short red bone girl with a full head of long wild curly hair as she made her way towards me.

"Sup booty," I greeted as she hugged my waist before setting the bags of food she had in her free hand down on our coffee table.

"Shane told me he wanted Roscoes so that's what I got us," she said smacking on her gum while rubbing her hands together; her full lips glistening with lip gloss. Tierre was what I liked to call a sexy tomboy. She could hang with us guys, and even dress like us, but at the same time get dolled up and get any man she wanted. She was beautiful in every right.

"That's coo. You get me some chicken?" I asked sitting on our love seat and reaching for the bag.

"You know it. Always look out for my bros," she said grabbing the other bag and pulling out a container filled with a burger and fries.

She took a large bite of her burger, flopping down next to me. She stopped mid chew and looked at me closely with her almond shaped eyes before flicking me hard in the side of my neck.

I jumped before rubbing the spot she just hit, "What you do that for?"

"Noticed the little shiner on your neck buddy. Did you at least know this one's name?" she asked continuing to eat her food.

I chuckled out of embarrassment while scratching my head a little. I forgot about that hickey being there.

"I did as a matter of fact," I smirked grabbing a leg out of the box.

"I swear you need to get a girlfriend before your dick falls off," she huffed rolling her eyes. I was fixing to respond, but Shane walked out with his client capturing both of our attention.

"Sup Ti Ti!" Shane called across the room putting his arms in the air. She gave him a head nod in response as he went to ring out his client.

"Thanks boss," his client said with appreciation as Shane escorted him out.

"No prob man. Remember to keep it moist with ointment and wash it out with cool water. Should be fully healed in about a week and a half," he instructed while holding the door open for him. He was thanked once again before he excitedly made his way over to us.

"Man, I couldn't wait to get him finished. All I could think about was this food!" we chuckled as he sat down and grabbed the containers that hadn't been touched yet assuming they were his.

"Shane, tell this dude to get a girl before his penis fall off," Tierre told him picking our conversation back up.

"Man, you're pleading the wrong case. As long as I've known this fool, he's never had a girlfriend," he replied as he cut up his waffle with the edge of his fork.

"Thank you, and I don't plan on getting one either," I said with confidence as Tierre stared blankly at me.

"But why not though? Why don't you want some stability?" she questioned as I shrugged.

"Just never been my thing. I like what I got going now. I can do me with no feelings involved."

"But feelings *always* get involved though. That's why you end up with these crazy ass girls most of the time."

"She *do* gotta point D," Shane interjected as I shot him a look of bewilderment, "You always wind up with some crazy ass broad."

"That's why I don't ever sex where I lay my head. Don't have time for all that," I said proudly as he gave me a facial expression that seemed as though he thought, *Yeah Right*.

"You just had Stacy at your house last week. Quit stylin,"
he busted me out as Tierre looked at me with her mouth wide open.

"Who the hell is Stacy?" she asked.

I smacked my lips while mugging my dumb ass partner,
"Nobody," I replied lowly.

"Stacy. The chick he been with for like three weeks
straight."

"Shane bro!" I yelled at him as he laughed and continued
eating. I could tell he was amused by this knowing Tierre was
about to get on me.

"Ok, she sounds the most consistent out of everybody. Why
aren't you making her your girl then?"

"Why are you so obsessed about me finding a girlfriend?" I
questioned as she sighed.

"I just worry about you sometimes Don. You do your best
to stay disconnected from anything that could potentially bring you
happiness like having one woman. I swear ever since that stuff
with Ashley after your mom.."

I quickly cut her off, "Drop it Ti. Respect me enough not to
go there of all placcs," I scolded as she quieted down. She knew
she was heading towards a very sensitive subject.

"Welp. This just got awkward," Shane commented in the
midst of our weird silence as Tierre and I both let out a laugh.

As we continued to eat, the front door chimed and I looked
up. My smile and appetite instantly disappeared.

"Stacy?" I asked aloud watching her look around the store
holding my beater that I left over there last night. I didn't mean to;
I was just in a rush to get out of her crib.

She smiled when her eyes finally landed on me but soon
frowned when she saw Tierre sitting so closely next to my side.

"Hi baby. You left this.." she grinned not taking her eyes
off of Tierre as I quickly stood and walked up to her.

"Um, Stacy," I spoke lowly while gently grabbing her arm
and leading her out of earshot, "How did you find out where I
worked?"

She shrugged a little playing with the chain that hung around my neck, "I was bored so I entered your name on Google and this came up. I didn't know you worked here, so I just thought I'd come and check it out."

"That's weird," I said staring at her strangely before sensing the sadness in her eyes.

"It's weird that you just didn't want to tell me where you worked like it has to be some big secret. You know where I work and everything Don, and I barely know shit about you," she spat dropping her hands and becoming emotional.

"I'm just a private person."

She quickly smacked her lips, "Forget that. Is it because you're really with her?!" she roared openly pointing at Tierre. I quickly put her hand down to avoid any unnecessary confrontation.

"Man, chill out. That's my home girl."

"Then why does the bitch keep staring at me?" she asked crossing her arms and staring angrily at Tierre. I looked behind me noticing her and Shane laughing and talking amongst themselves. Not paying any attention to Stacy's crazy antics.

"Come back to my office," I ordered angrily snatching the shirt out of her hands. It was just an excuse to pop up on me.

Shane and Tierre both snickered as I walked past but I tuned them out. Once I reached my office door, I held it open for Stacy to enter first.

"Wait in here for a second. I'm going to grab my food," I told her as she nodded while watching me close the door.

"Aye man, tell that hoe to watch who she point at all willy nilly next time. You lucky Shane was here to calm me down," Tierre said nonchalantly as I grabbed my container full of chicken.

"My fault, Booty, I ain't know she was just gonna pop on me. I never even told her where I worked," I admitted as both of their eyes widened.

Shane just shook his head, "Always find you a crazy chick man. She lucky she cold or else I would tell you to drop her."

"Man, I don't give a damn if she cold or not. Poppin up on me is some crazy shit. It's too early for all that. I'm about to go in there and tell her I'm done with her. I don't care how good it is."

Tierre turned up her nose, "Gross."

I laughed a little as I turned making my way back to my office. We had to end today. Just from her actions I could see how clingy, possessive, and jealous she was. I knew seeing her more than once was going to get her caught up with me. That's the last thing she needed to do.

I walked in with my head tilted down towards the floor, "Look Stace.." As I spoke, I looked up in surprise seeing her butt naked sitting on my desk holding a condom wrapper with her legs wide open.

"Just tell me how you want me Daddy.." she whispered seductively as she opened her legs wider and I could see the wet pink flesh of the inside of her vagina. At that moment, I mentally decided I was going to get this quick nut off and then tell Stacy's crazy ass I was done with her.

Bobbi.

"Honey, I am so proud of you," my mom repeated once more as she wrapped her arms around my neck kissing my cheeks repeatedly. It was the phrase I heard from my family all day after finally receiving my nursing degree from The Ohio State University.

I smiled awkwardly as I looked around our dining room table. My younger sister and brother sat there along with my Aunt Lisa and my cousin Jay. The rest of our large family was all over the house eating food and talking amongst themselves as music played from our flat screen.

"What's next for you honey?" my gorgeous Aunt asked as she sat down across from me. I felt small avoiding the stare of the beautiful caramel toned woman whose make up was laid perfectly bringing out her features.

"Well, I have to take a test to register as a practicing nurse and then after that I can pretty much work anywhere," I explained as she nodded in understanding.

My cousin flashed a goofy grin, "Like California?" he quizzed.

I rolled my eyes.

Aunt Lisa instantly beamed her bright smile, "Yes! Oh baby, you would love it out there. Me and Jay have already been getting the spare room together for when you come."

"I haven't even decided if I'm really going to come yet.," I replied softly messing with a napkin; anything to distract me.

"I don't see why not cuz? There's seriously nothing to do here, and it's cold," Jay frowned as I chuckled. He's been saying it's cold since he's been up here. It's been in the 40s all week due to winter approaching.

"I have a life here," I defended. He instantly started laughing and auntie quickly smacked his arm.

"What? Ma, you know that was full of crap," he chuckled as I crossed my eyes. Jay and I had a love/hate relationship. This was one of those "hate" moments.

"Bobbi, I really think you should go stay with Lisa. You need to get away from this city. Nothing here makes you happy anymore," my mother spoke as all eyes fell on me.

"But I'm used to everything here."

"That may be the problem sweetie," Auntie added as her eyes looked sadly at me. I hated that they knew about the 'situation' that happened a few months ago. Everyone knew I was doing much better. I didn't need to still be treated like this.

"I'll think about it," I said in a low tone as I rose up from the table. I grabbed my keys that laid on the kitchen counter and made my way out the front door. I needed space. Ever since my family got here they were all trying to pick my brain and see what was next with my life. All wanting me to move on.

"Yo Bobs wait up!" I heard Jay call as I was halfway up the street; my arms wrapped close around me as the wind blew harder. I didn't know where I was walking to just wanted to get away.

I continued my pace as I heard steps getting closer, "I know you heard me girl!"

I growled as I halted suddenly before feeling Jay's body smack into my back.

"Damn, wasn't expecting you to stop," he said out of breath while I turned to contain my laughter. I gave him a good once over as the street lights illuminated his figure. His skin complexion was a soft mocha like mine, and he wasn't much taller than me: maybe about 5'10. He had a Caesar cut with waves, and a chin strap connecting his side burns to his chins hairs. He took another deep breath running his tongue quickly across his pink lips while scratching at his large biceps. His father always made sure he kept in shape even as a little boy still growing.

"What you want man?" I asked while walking again except slower so we could walk together.

"Why you get all dramatic and storm out? Everyone in there wants what's best for you."

"Yeah, but what everyone in there fails to realize is, regardless of where I go, I'm taking *me* with me. Just because my surroundings change doesn't mean I will."

"That's a messed up way to look at things," he said bluntly while shoving his hands in his pockets, "This whole pity party is starting to get pathetic Bobbi."

I shot him an evil expression at him while stopping, "Are you serious?" The attitude was clear in my voice.

He nodded with confidence, "Yeah, I'm serious. Look, I understand you went through a bad break up and it gave you a hard time, but hell, everyone goes through that shit. It's been almost two years. Let it *go*."

"Easy for you to say."

"Yeah it is, and by now, and after all this time, it should be easy for you. I don't feel sorry for yo ass no more, and I thought it was selfish and weak as hell what you tried to pull. You just need to get away from this city and everything that reminds you of that worthless ass dude. Get some friends I mean, damn. You couldn't think of one person you wanted to invite to your graduation party?!" he questioned as I instantly became more annoyed with his presence.

"Fuck you Jay."

"I'm serious."

"I don't want or need friends."

He let out a sigh of irritation as he rubbed his hands over his face, "Man. Please move in with us. Please. This is just sad as hell. Your whole being is just *sad*. I get it now man because talking to you makes *me* wanna kill myself."

My heart dropped. "That hurt," I admitted as he looked over at me with apologetic eyes.

"I'm sorry. I know that was a low blow but sometimes I forget you have feelings because you try so hard to hide them."

"Yeah well, I do…" I said barely above a whisper. Jay turned to stand right in my path stopping me from moving an inch further.

He pulled my body into his and held me close, "I'm sorry. I took it too far. I just really want you to get out of here. You're not the Bobbi I used to know. Me and you used to be the best of friends. You were always the one keeping me in high spirits, and seeing you so broken really pisses me off because I feel like you're doing this to yourself now. I don't want this for you."

I finally wrapped my arms around his waist returning his embrace as I felt a tear make its way down my cheek.

"I'm doing this for you."

He rubbed my long straightened hair as he held me tighter, "Don't do anything for me. Do this for yourself."

****

I pressed my head against the cab window looking at the palm trees and sunny California sky. My brain couldn't wrap around the decision to move out here against its better judgment. It didn't understand what was going to make California isolation any different than Ohio isolation. I had no desire to meet anyone or get close to anyone; just wanted to live in my peaceful little shell. As we turned into the neighborhood, I had visited only a number of times before, my stomach instantly wanted to escape through my throat. The feelings of unease and nervousness about this decision were becoming even more apparent.

My eyes rolled at the goofy grin plastered across my brown skinned cousin's face. He rubbed his low fade and squinted his eyes while watching the taxi pull up. Once the driver parked, Jay walked up and opened my door for me. He frowned when he noticed my blank expression.

"You definitely look too 'busy' to come and pick me up from the airport, asshole," I growled as he smacked his lips.

"Man, you just got here. Don't start so early Bobs," he replied closing the door behind me and meeting the driver at the trunk to pull out my bags.

He scrunched up his nose at the sight, "You only brought two bags?"

I nodded running my fingers through my hair, "Yeah. One's life shouldn't be filled with meaningless possessions. I gave most of my stuff away to charity before coming," I answered watching him lift the bags out of the trunk then pay the taxi driver.

"Here you go with that hippie shit," he said breathlessly while placing both bags on his shoulders, "We got so much work to do to get you back to normal."

I shrugged, "I am normal. Maybe it's everyone else that's different." I could imagine his eyes rolling as I stared at the back of his head and followed him into the nicely built two story brick house. My Aunt Lisa always made sure Jay lived comfortably even with his father being a lieutenant in the Navy and traveling frequently–she made sure he always had stability.

"Where's Lisa?" I asked while closing the front door behind me then followed him up the stairs to what I assumed to be my bedroom.

"She's with my Dad in Hawaii. He was close so she flew out to stay with him for a couple weeks," I frowned a little. I really wanted to see my Auntie more than my cousin at the moment.

I followed Jay into the nicely decorated room that was well lit from the open blinds and windows. In it was a queen size bed that rested on a princess like canopy, a desk with a new Apple Macbook resting on it with a bow, a tall dresser, walk in closet, and my own personal bathroom. My eyes widened at the sight.

"Spoiled as hell," my cousin commented while setting the bags down on the floor next to my bed.

I continued to walk around admiring the room, "I seriously am. This is a lot."

"She said all of this is your graduation gift. You're like the daughter she always wanted, so enjoy it and be comfortable until you want to leave," he said as he sat in my desk chair and spun around a little.

"Now I see why you're 23 and never left," I teased as he slightly chuckled.

"She's hardly home and gives me my space when she is. My girl is allowed to stay here whenever she likes, so why leave? Got it made," he bragged.

"Momma's boy, and you say *I'm* the one spoiled?" I asked rhetorically while sitting on my comfortable bed.

"Whatever. Look, I'm having a little party here tonight, so you need to look through these bags and find something decent to wear to it," he said looking at me seriously as I shot him a crazy stare.

"Um. No. I'll just stay up here in my room," he instantly groaned.

"Man, come on Bobbi. I want you to meet my people and hang out a little. There's going to be plenty of liquor and you need to loosen up."

"I don't like being around a lot of people, especially a bunch of people I don't even know. I'm not tryna get close to nobody like that," I rejected.

"Come on man. I thought we talked about this when I was up there. You need to make steps to move forward. Being a prisoner in this room is not gon help shit. My friends are cool, and they may like you if you're not having a bitch fit tonight."

"I don't even have anything to wear," I said coming up with another excuse.

"That's fine. We'll go to the mall. It's not too far from here."

"You're really not going to let me *not* go to this are you?"

"In your own damn house? Hell no. You're going to get cute, whether you want to or not."

I let out a sigh giving up the fight, "Okay, let me at least take a shower and wind down from my flight before we head out."

"Deal."

Donovan.

I stepped out of the bathroom after taking my morning piss to the smell of something burning in my kitchen. I stretched a little before making my way down the hall and into the kitchen to see Stacy there attempting to cook what looked like eggs.

"What the hell Stace?" I asked aloud as she looked up and smiled at me continuing to scramble the browned mess in the pot.

"Hey baby."

Baby?

"I was trying not to wake you. I wanted to surprise you with breakfast in bed."

I sighed scratching the top of my head thinking of a response. Stacy was not supposed to spend the night last night. No woman has ever slept over here simply because I never wanted to give them the wrong impression. Sleeping over was something significant in their mind. I was just way too faded last night to think clearly; I think she did that on purpose.

"I'm not really hungry. Plus, I gotta leave for work in a little bit."

Her face quickly changed from one of happiness to anger in seconds, "Bullshit." She spat before picking up the pan and dumping it and her eggs into my trashcan then stormed past me.

"Yo! What the f-?!" I asked quickly going up to the trash and pulling the hot skillet out of it. I knew she was going to be pissed. After setting the pan in the sink, I walked into my bedroom to find Stacy angrily dressing herself.

"What was that all about?" I asked while staring at her as her dark green eyes looked into mine. She was surely upset.

"Fuck you Don! You prove every day that this isn't going anywhere! Lying to me acting like you gotta go to work. You and I both know the shop doesn't even open until 11:30! Lyin ass," she said pulling her jean shorts up onto her waist.

"You've just been wasting my time the last three months. Where are we going huh? Are we going to be together? Or you just gonna keep screwing me and treating me like shit?!" she asked throwing a pillow at me as I ducked. Thank God there wasn't anything heavy on that side of the room.

"Stacy, you knew what this was. You staying the night last night didn't change anything. If you ain't trynna be here, you don't have to be. It won't be hard to find someone else," I replied nonchalantly while lying down on my bed and turning the TV on.

"You seriously just say that to me?! Like I'm replaceable."

"You are Stacy. Ain't nothing you do, that's different than anyone else. We had sex on the first night and you really thought you were going to be somebody's girl? Fuck outta here." I began to channel surf unmoved by this conversation.

"I hate your bitch ass!" she yelled at me.

I chuckled, "I don't care." This was a usual argument with us. Every other day she told me she hated me and called me a bitch. Nothing new.

As she continued to cuss me out, I looked over and saw Shane calling my phone. I was actually happy to see him calling during a time like this. I needed a distraction.

"What's good bro?" I answered hearing small cries on the other end.

"Hey man, I got Shai, about to drop her off. Don't worry about opening this morning. Can you stop by the mall and pick up the shoes I put on hold with Erick?" he asked as I looked up seeing Stacy straddling me. I knew she was going to calm herself down eventually.

"Yeah, I guess I can do that. You pay him, or do I have to?"

"I paid him. I'm trynna wear them to the party tonight when we get off."

"Aw, I forgot all about that. I should pick me up something too then before I come in. I got you," I answered as Stacy pulled down my basketball shorts.

"Kiss my God baby for me. I'll see you after I pick em up."

"Aight man. Thanks."

We got off the phone and I looked down at Stacy as she prepared to place all of me in her mouth. "I'm sorry baby," was all she uttered before she went to work.

****

I walked into the mall heading straight for Footlocker where our connect Erick worked. He always got us all the new shoes out and would let us purchase them with his discount. He was a cool dude just tried too hard to be down with us. We always rocked with him for the connect though. As I strolled through the mega store, not paying attention to my surroundings, I suddenly bumped into something or *someone* rather.

"Aw damn. My fault," I apologized eyeing the stranger. She was a shorter, mocha brown skinned girl with long black hair and a nice little figure that was evident behind her sweat pants. My eyes widened a little when I noticed a fresh pair of Jordan's on her feet. Hell, she would probably be even cuter if a smile was present on her soft face.

"Watch where the hell you're going next time," she shot back as I furrowed my brows. Wasn't expecting that response. Normally we would already be flirting by now.

"Uh..I said it was an accident. I wasn't paying attention."

"That much is obvious, asshole," she said looking down at her things that fell onto the floor.

In an effort to reconcile, I kneeled down to help her with her purse and shopping bags that dropped from her hands. I didn't even understand why I wanted to assist, especially with her attitude.

"I got it," she growled snatching a bag from my fingers.

"Look, I was just trying to help."

"I didn't ask for it," she snapped, cutting me short, angrily grabbing the rest of her things, and storming off.

I watched as she walked to the other side of the store and shook my head. *Bitter bitch.*

Brushing off my run in with the rude stranger, I walked towards the register where Erick talked to a familiar face.

"What up bruh." I smiled dapping up my God brother James.

"Yo! Wassup man. I ain't seen you since before I went out of town," he smiled as I laughed a little.

"I know, yo broke ass finally gets a job and goes ghost. How was your trip? You went to a graduation or something right?"

"Yeah for my cousin Bobbi," I nodded remembering him talking about that dude.

"Yeah, they live with you now right?"

"Yep. Ya'll will meet at the party. We actually at the mall together now. I don't know where.." he started as he looked around for his family member.

"Aye, it's coo. We'll meet tonight like you said. I'm sure we'll be coo."

He chuckled, "You don't know my cousin man."

"Come on. I get along with everybody," I grinned before turning to face Erick. "You got Shane's shoes?"

He nodded as he leaned down behind the register pulling out a bag, "You ain't see nothing you wanted?"

I shook my head, "Nah, I ran into a rude ass shorty a minute ago. Took me out the shopping mood," I frowned as I mentally relived the situation.

"What? Somebody actually dissed yo ass?" Jay questioned sarcastically as I smacked my lips. I saw the girl across the room and nodded my head towards her as Jay and Erick both looked in the same direction.

"Aye she cold," Erick commented eyeing her.

I interjected, "Yeah, cold hearted. Ain't nobody tripping over that girl. I wasn't even trying to talk to her. She just got all crazy on me for accidently bumping into her ass." Jay made a strange look before looking in the girl's direction.

"Hey that's my.."

I tuned him out looking at my watch. My first client was going to be at the shop in twenty minutes.

"Aye, ya'll I gotta go. I'll see you at the party," I rushed dapping Jay and Erick up before grabbing Shane's shoes.

"Aight man," Jay said tossing me the deuces and continuing to check out.

As I was heading out, Ms. Rudeness and I locked eyes. She rolled hers as I did the same. I was hoping to never have to see that chick again.

Bobbi.

I sprawled all of the clothes I bought at the mall today onto the bed trying to decide which outfit would be best. The party was already underway downstairs, and I was still back and forth about even attending. My thoughts were interrupted by the sound of my phone ringing, and I smiled when I saw it was my mother calling me through Skype. I quickly accepted the call and smiled brightly at her warm expression, "Hey Mommy." I greeted as she grinned.

"Hey baby. You never called me after you landed this morning, so I just wanted to make sure you were okay," I sighed and ran my fingers through my hair before responding.

"Yeah, I'm fine I guess. Jay is doing everything he can to make me feel at home. Auntie got me a lap-top and decorated my room nice. I can't wait until she gets back."

She nodded taking in my words, "She'll be home soon. Where is Jay at anyway?"

"Downstairs hosting his house party. I'm up here trying to find something to wear," Her eyes widened at the word *party*.

"Lisa knows about this?"

I laughed and nodded, "Of course Ma. Jay ain't crazy. He said he throws a party every few months. She lets him when she's out of the country visiting Uncle Vince."

"Ok, well show me your clothes; let me see!" she squealed as I giggled and turned the camera towards my clothes.

When I used to go out back home, my mom would always help me pick out my outfits, seeing as how she worked from home for a high end fashion magazine. It was a cherished moment between the two of us.

"Very cute Bobs! Hmm, let me see what I would tell you to wear..." she pondered out loud as I looked over my selections as well.

"It doesn't have to be anything spectacular Ma. I'm not trying to impress anyone downstairs. I just want Jay to leave me alone."

"Well you should still be cute honey. Jay is cute, and I'm sure he has cute friends. You need a man. I'm sorry but you do," she said honestly, as I laughed and shook my head.

"You think I'm playin. It's been two years since you left Jo's sorry behind. Now I know you don't want to hear this, but I miss seeing you happy with someone. You let Jo steal every bit of joy and happiness that possessed in your soul and I want you to have it back."

"Can't get that back through a man," I explained as she quickly added to her previous point.

"And I understand that but at least make a friend then. Anyone that can help you heal baby. I gave you your space to find it on your own, but you shut out any and everything that brings you a slight bit of joy. The happiest I saw you is when your Dad and I bought you that camera for graduation. Whatever that will find you peace that's what I want for you."

I sighed turning the phone back towards me so we could look at each other, "I know Mom. I wouldn't have taken this risk of moving out here if I didn't want to find peace somehow. Do I think that will come from a man? Probably not. I have to find it within first."

"Are you even trying though honey? Are you seriously digging deep to find the underlying issue?" she asked as I thought long and hard.

"I am going to now. I promise you. Just give me some time to get adjusted out here. Being isolated is a perfect time for discovery and growth. That's what I plan to do."

She forced a smile signaling that she understood, "Go with the camo jacket, white crop tee, high waist shorts and Jeffery Campbell heels." She changed the subject as I looked over the outfit she suggested. Cute yet comfy.

"Hair straight or curly?"

"Straight but feather the layers," she winked.

"I miss you mommy," I admitted as she blew me kisses.

"Miss you more baby, but I know you need this. Your Dad and I will be out to visit you soon honey. Hopefully we'll meet a special man in your life by then," she teased before beginning to laugh at the displeased expression on my face.

"I'm kidding. Sort of."

I rolled my eyes.

"Ok Ma. I gotta get ready for this party. I'll talk to you later." We ended our call, and I put away the clothes I wasn't going to wear when I heard a soft knock at the door.

"Come in," I called assuming it was Jay. He walked in with a very pretty caramel colored woman. She had long natural wavy curls with big full lips and almond shaped eyes. She stumbled a little as they walked further into the room; both of them looked under the influence.

"Hey, Bobbi I want you to meet my best friend Tierre," he introduced as she stuck out her hand to greet me.

"Hey, I've heard a lot about you. I figured you're not going to want to be around this fool all the time, so me and you should hang out or something. Get some food," she offered as I smiled and nodded glancing between the two of them.

"That sounds cool I guess," I replied awkwardly as she looked down at the clothes on the bed. Her mouth dropped as she went to pick up the camo jacket I found today.

"Yo, this is *fly*! We hella gotta go shopping too. You have good taste girl! Wear dis!" She handed me the jacket as I chuckled a little at the New York accent.

"I was planning to," I explained as Jay grabbed her hand so they could get out of my room.

"Ok, well hurry up and get ready cuz so we can turn up. You're missing everything and I wanna introduce you to more people," he told me, as Tierre gave one final wave before they disappeared out the door.

I sighed and instantly felt butterflies in my stomach. I was nervous about being around a lot of people at once, but it was time I started conquering the small fears that had developed over the years.

Donovan.

    I walked into Jay's house with Shane trailing close behind, greeted by smoke and loud music. We said wassup to a few people we recognized while making our way to the kitchen. Once reaching our destination, the first thing I noticed was Jay standing there with his shirt off pouring shots in a chick's mouth.

    "Yo, where ya shirt at?" I teased playfully grabbing his shoulders. He turned and smiled at me before dapping me up and then Shane.

    "Sup ya'll! Didn't think ya'll was coming through. Ya'll late as hell," he slurred, as I grabbed a plastic red cup to fix my drink.

    "We had a few late customers. We here now though," Shane answered as I handed him a cup.

    "Let's take a few shots before ya'll fix those," Jay suggested setting up a row of Dixie cups and pouring Hennessey in each one.

    "Damn, we going dark tonight?" Shane questioned out loud as I passed a worried expression in Jay's direction. He grinned like a fool.

    "You already know. The blacker, the better. Let's po' up," he said grabbing the first shot as we mimicked his actions. We swallowed the liquor and made ugly faces as it burned down our throats. Before we knew it, we were on our fifth shot.

    "Man forget this, I'm sipping the rest of the night. You about to have me messed up and we only been here five minutes," I complained pouring a cup of Hennessey and apple juice. Apple juice was great for hangovers.

    "Ya'll some bitches," Jay teased as Shane and I shot him a look.

    "Watch who you calling a bitch, ol' bitch ass," Shane warned as Jay and I laughed. He was the shortest of the group, but always talked like he was the biggest and toughest.

"You have to be this tall," Jay started using his hand to suggest a height taller than Shane, "To talk any type of shit in this circle."

"Man, fuck you Jay," Shane whined as he walked towards the den where people were dancing. Jay went back to entertaining company and I decided to make my rounds around the house to greet a few of my homies, and a few girls I had messed with back in the day.

As I walked, not really paying attention to my surroundings, I bumped into a small figure. I looked down and noticed the same girl from earlier at the mall. She wore the same scowl but was dressed differently. Earlier, she was just wearing sweats and a beanie, but tonight I could see every curve that rested upon her small frame. She was a lot prettier than I remembered.

She peaked up, but the second she noticed who I was, she smacked her lips and crossed her arms, "Seriously? Do you ever watch where you're going?" she spat as I looked down at her surprised. How could someone so pretty be so hostile?

"My fault, I'm a little drunk," I said chuckling lightly, as she found no humor in my response.

"Bullshit. Were you drunk earlier too?" she questioned as I laughed some more.

"Man, what is your problem? Why can't you ever just accept my apology and just be my friend?" I asked resting my hand against the wall and looking her up and down. She turned her nose up at me, feeling self-conscious.

"I don't want to be your friend."

"You don't think its fate that I see you the same day at the same party? Do you live around here or something?" I asked as she squinted her eyes in confusion.

"I live here," she answered pointing towards the floor as I tilted my head back in question.

"No you don't. My brother lives here, and I ain't never seen you here," I challenged as she just crossed her eyes.

"Jay is my cousin you dumbass. I just moved here today."

"Jay's cousin isn't a chick. He told me a dude named Bobbi was living here," I retaliated as she huffed.

"*My* name is Bobbi."

I could hear the irritation but I wanted to press further, "Oh. Well I'm Donovan." I introduced hoping to finally get on her good side.

"I never asked nor do I care. Now can you please move out of my way?" she requested rudely. I was going to continue to press but decided to give up. I never tried this hard with females and damn sure wasn't going to try hard with her.

"I see right through you. Know that," I said shaking my head before turning to walk away not even waiting for a response. I've encountered enough women to know when I've met a bitter one. I wasn't wasting any more time with her.

I walked back in the kitchen to reunite with Jay and Shane who were laughing about something. Both of their expressions fell when they noticed the displeasure written across my face.

"What's up with you?" Shane asked as I sighed looking at Jay.

"Just met your mean ass cousin. Why ain't you tell me she was the same b...I mean chick from the mall?" I asked as Jay laughed.

"I tried to, but you banged out after you copped the shoes. She's a piece of work ain't she?" he asked rhetorically as I nodded and rolled my eyes.

"Who is? Where she at?" Shane asked as Jay pointed her out standing against the wall. His mouth dropped as he looked back at Jay.

"Bro, why ain't you tell me you had fine ass cousins?! Put me on!"

Jay looked at him as if he had two heads, "Yeah. Hell no." he answered as Shane smacked his lips.

"You don't wanna fool with her anyway bro. She's mean as hell. A woman scorned."

Jay interjected, "I know you not talking. All the stories I hear about that crazy ass hoe you been messing with."

"Yeah! How the hell she get *my* number anyway Don? Got her blowing up my phone looking for you. Joi was looking at me crazy one night," Shane said as Jay and I both looked at him.

"You still hitting ya baby mom?!" we said in unison as Shane looked around to see if anyone heard us.

"She just something to do when there's nothing to do..." he replied as I kissed my teeth.

"Ok Drake," I said realizing he quoted the famous rapper's lyric.

"But aye, don't ya'll judge me. It was just a onetime occasion that Don's hoe happened to interrupt."

"Stop linking her with me like we together or some shit. Stacy is just good at what she does. That's it. She ain't even the only one."

Jay turned up his nose and shook his head, "Tierre was right. Your dick bound to fall off."

"I'm always strapped," I said confidently.

"Well you better hope that psycho doesn't start poking holes in the condoms while you sleep," Shane warned as we looked at him.

"That's what happened to you?" I joked as Shane's face remained blank causing us to laugh. He shook his head before looking past me and then smirked.

"I wouldn't be laughing Don. The red headed devil herself has arrived," I looked at him strangely before turning around and seeing Stacy walk through the crowd with some girl that we used to go to high school with. *Small ass world.*

Bobbi.

I stood against the wall watching everyone dance and enjoy their intoxication while talking to friends and strangers. I felt like an outcast in my own home. I knew none of these people and nothing in me wanted to get to know them. A few guys, including that Damien guy or whatever his name was, had tried to say something to me, but I blew them all off. I saw lust in each of their eyes; not one genuine person. I sighed as I looked around and searched the room for Jay or even Tierre. I spotted the two of them in the kitchen and smiled slightly making my way over to them.

"Hey boo. You not drinkin?" Tierre asked as I shrugged. A short boy with hazel eyes smiled at me as he stood next to Jay.

"Nah, you about to drink. Let me fix you something," she said walking past me to the counter to get my drink together. I looked back at my cousin and his friend.

"Oh, Bobbi, this is my homie Shane. Shane, this is my cousin Bobbi," he introduced as I extended my hand.

He frowned at my gesture before opening his arms, "We hug around here girl!" He said playfully as he squeezed me tightly. I giggled a little when he released me.

"Nice to meet you," I smiled before I felt a tall presence next to us. I rolled my eyes at the sight of who it was.

"Whoa. Wait a minute. He gets the 'nice to meet you' and I get the fuck off?!" Damien asked. There was a red head girl standing behind him watching me closely. *Must be the girlfriend.*

"Don't be mad cause she like me better than you. You need to be told to fuck off more often anyway," Shane teased his friend as I laughed. Damien looked at me in shock before he was suddenly pulled away by his girl who clearly had an attitude.

I turned my attention back towards Shane and Jay when Tierre walked up with my drink.

"Where Don go?" she asked while looking around. I sniffed my drink before I took a sip.

"Ol' crazy ass yanked him up," Shane said motioning towards the two who were now arguing. She was openly pointing in my direction.

"Did I do or say something to piss her off?" I asked the group looking around as they all shook their heads.

"You ain't do nothin B. Don't worry about her," Shane assured as I furrowed my brows.

"I was never worried. Just wanted to be clear," I shrugged then gulped down the mixture of Hennessey and Coke. I was already feeling its effect and felt relaxed when I noticed the red head brush passed me to fix herself a drink.

I paid no mind to her as I continued to listen in on the mindless chatter between my cousin and his friends. They seemed like cool people. As I was chuckling at something Shane said, I felt a hard bump and cold liquid running down my shirt. I looked down at the mess and then up to the smirking red head as she looked on as well.

"Oops. My fault," she said nonchalantly as I felt myself jumping in her direction. I was held back by two strong arms that belonged to Jay.

"You did that on purpose bitch!" I spat trying to get Jay to let go of me so I could rip her head off. We claimed the attention of everyone in the kitchen.

"And if I did?! So the fuck what?!" she snarled back before Damien came and dragged her away.

"Kick her ass out!" Jay yelled as I aggressively released from his grip, "You alright?"

I said nothing to anyone as I stormed out of the kitchen and out the patio door to get some air. It was already embarrassing for me to approach everyone, and then to have that hoe challenge me in front of them, that took me to a new level of anger.

"Stupid bitch!" I yelled angrily towards the sky before being startled by a voice.

"Damn. What I do to deserve that?" I turned to look where the voice came from and my eyes widened a little at the handsome stranger. He was tall, chocolate, and chiseled. Every feature of his seemed perfectly in place as he flashed a smile full of beautiful teeth in my direction.

I laughed from nervousness, "Oh. Not you. Some red head inside spilled her drink on me because she thought I wanted her boyfriend," I explained as he smiled and nodded.

"Sounds like you met Stacy," he chuckled causing me to cross my eyes.

"You know her?" I asked.

"Met her a while back. Saw her when she walked in. That girl is nuts," he shook his head as I smiled.

"I'm Aaron by the way," he introduced reaching out his free hand that didn't contain his beer.

"Bobbi."

He turned his nose up at my response, "Bobbi? That's an ugly ass name for a girl. What's it short for? Roberta or some shit?" he questioned as I laughed. He was the first person to question my real name.

"Don't judge my nickname and no it's not for Roberta," I giggled as he smiled.

"Happy I got you smiling. I've been watching you. You looked mad in there."

"Just wasn't comfortable. I'm new here. I live here with Jay and my Aunt," I explained.

"Welcome to LA," he flashed his perfect smile as I admired his facial features. He had a thin mustache that connected to his tamed goatee with thin side burns coming from the sea full of waves in his hair. His chocolate skin was smooth and clear. He was extremely handsome to me.

"Why are you out here and not in the party?" I asked changing the subject as he smirked a little.

"A lot of people don't really mess with me in there."

"Like who?"

"Like Donovan and his little circle. I'm only here because Tierre is my cousin, and she wanted me to be her designated. Me and Jay cool for that reason alone," he shrugged as my interest in him rose.

"Why don't you get along with them? If you don't mind me asking?"

"Over petty shit. Donovan was cool with this girl named Ashley back in like high school but he always played it to us like they were just friends and nothing more, so I guess she was fed up with that and came crying to me, one thing led to another, and we had sex. He found out and we fought. Guess he thought we knew he was in love with her. She wasn't shit anyway," he told me as I took in the story.

"I don't really care for him either."

He smiled at me before taking a small sip of his Corona, "So what do you do? You move out here for work or something?"

"I have a nursing degree, but I moved out here for a fresh start. Looking for a job. You?"

"I sell drugs," he said in a serious tone as my face fell. He laughed at the expression, "Legally. I'm a pharmaceutical sales rep. I go to different doctor offices and sell them new drugs on the market."

"Impressive."

"Yeah, majored in Biology, and I have a way with words. Works out. Looking to go back to school and be a pharmacist, but the money is good where I'm at."

Aaron and I talked some more as we continued to get to know each other. He was the most genuine guy I had met thus far.

"Hey so about earlier when I said Bobbi was ugly. I ain't mean it. It's cute on you actually. Fits," he confessed earning a blush from me.

"Thank you."

"We should uh hang out some time? I could show you the city. Open you up to some new things since all of this is a different experience for you. I don't want you to regret your decision."

I nodded in response, "I'd like that. Put your number in my phone," I said smoothly handing him my iPhone as he graciously accepted it. Our little moment was interrupted by the back door opening.

I looked up at the tall, tattooed figure and rolled my eyes as he began to speak, "Hey, I just want to apologize for Stacy's actions earlier. I kicked her out right after," he explained as I shrugged accepting my phone back from Aaron. They didn't even acknowledge each other's presence.

"It's coo Damien. Just control ya hoes," I shot back standing up and dusting the back of my shorts off of any debris.

He looked annoyed, "It's Donovan," he corrected as I gave him a blank expression signaling that I didn't care.

"I know what I said," I turned back in Aaron's direction as his eyes met mine, "I'll hit you up later okay?"

"I'll be looking forward to it," he flirted purposely. I smiled before turning to see the disgusted look on Donovan's face. I simply brushed past him and walked back inside.

****

It had been a couple days since the party, and I sat at the dining room table filling out applications online when I heard the doorbell ring. Auntie was still out of town and Jay was supposed to be on his way home, so I hopped up from the table to answer it.

I was kind of surprised to find Tierre standing there wearing a Bulls fitted cap to cover her long thick hair, leggings, and a loose fitting crop top; she was a little startled to see me too.

"Yo wassup! Bobbi right?" she asked walking in as I nodded and closed the door after she walked in. I understood why she was questioning my name; she was extremely intoxicated at the party.

"Yeah, Jay hasn't gotten home from work yet," I informed her sitting back down at the table. She decided to join me.

"Whatcha doing?" she asked popping her gum as I looked up.

"Oh, filling out applications," she smacked her lips.

"Man, Jay's ass ain't tell you! You're a nurse right?!" she asked earning a nod in response, "I work at a hospital in West Hollywood. I'm a receptionist there. We need nurses badly. I told him to have you send me your resume, and I can get you on with no problem," My heart began to race with excitement.

"Seriously?!" I questioned for reassurance.

She nodded, "Yeah. I got you. You fam now. Even though you come off bitchy." Her tone was flat.

I released a small sigh, "I wasn't always like this..." I admitted.

"Yeah I know. I can see deep down you want to be yourself, but you're not allowing yourself to. Thing is. We're all strangers. None of us have done anything wrong to you, and we don't rock with ill intentions. Leave whatever happened at home, back at home. If it's going to be a fresh start, have a fresh attitude as well ya know?" she advised as I took in her words.

"I'm not saying don't have your guard up because if I had been through what you've been through, I would have mine up too, but be open minded at least. We're good people...well most of us," she said leading my mind to instantly think of Donovan and Stacy.

"What's up with that Stacy chick?" I questioned turning my nose up. She groaned at the sound of her name.

"I can't stand her! I've been telling Don not to even mess with her crazy insecure ass since the first day I met her," She spat while pulling out her phone.

"Is that his girlfriend or something?" I questioned wondering why the hell I even cared.

"Nah, as long as I've known Donovan, he's never had a girlfriend," she said, in a matter-of-fact tone, piquing my interest.

"Why not?"

She shrugged her right shoulder a little, "I don't know. He doesn't get emotionally attached to people like that. He cares about me because I'm his friend, but nothing deeper than that. I've never even heard him tell anyone he loves them...ever."

"I don't blame him though. Why love? It causes nothing but pain," I sighed.

She looked up grinning at me, "Love is beautiful Bobbi. Your last boyfriend and your friend didn't love you. You'll know when someone truly does. It'll overtake your whole being, and your whole world will consist of you wanting nothing more than to be the reason for that person's happiness. Don't give up on it."

Donovan.

"Stacy has not stopped blowing up my damn phone!" I growled ignoring the 20th call from her while sitting behind the register. Mondays were always slow at the shop. Shane and I were just bullshitting.

"Man what happened? I saw you actually kick her ass out," Shane said attempting to throw his trash in the trashcan basketball style; of course his weak ass missed.

"Nothing happened. She asked why I ain't go with her when she left, and I told her she's childish and needs to grow up, and I don't want to rock with her anymore," I explained rubbing the back of my neck with the palm of my hand.

"Bout damn time. You need to find you a real woman and quit dealin wit these hoes. I know your whole objective is not to catch feelings but they always do," Shane said sitting on one of the couches.

"They just be too bad. Stacy would be cool if she wasn't psychotic. I won't be surprised if I wake up and my tires are slashed tomorrow. It's just her sex is amazing."

Shane just looked at me and shook his head, "I'll tell you who's bad. Jay's sexy ass cousin."

I turned up my nose, "Man, fuck her."

"Shiiittt, I wish I could," Shane stretched earning a laugh from me.

"She is cute but her attitude isn't. I'd end up choking her," I huffed causing Shane to laugh.

"Ya'll seem perfect for each other. Two stubborn people stuck in their ways."

I gave him the blankest stare ever then said, "Never. Not even my type. She was talking to bum ass Aaron anyway."

Shane started cracking up, "You still bitter from that man raw doggin the love of your life?!"

I smacked my lips at his comment, "I ain't love that girl."

"If you didn't then why you still mad? That shit happened in high school," Shane questioned while I just fanned him off.

"It doesn't matter. She got 3 kids with 4 baby dads now any way," I growled as Shane busted out laughing.

"Sure do know how to pick 'em Don. What was so special about her back then anyway?"

I looked up to the ceiling to think, "I don't know. She was just different than the other girls we came across back then. She was my friend and truly cared about me for who I was, and I cared about her too. Plus when mom was sick...she was the only person I could really talk to because she understood," I answered, an awkward silence filling the room short after.

"Did you ever hit?"

"Yeah. Like one good time then I stopped calling her and started ignoring her in school," I chuckled thinking about my actions.

Shane laughed too, "Why bro? Was she that bad?"

"Nah. I just felt different, vulnerable, and I didn't like that. I didn't want to shut her out completely. I just wanted space because Mom died right after, so when I finally talked to her, she confessed that she had sex with someone else after me."

Shane was quiet knowing exactly who it was. He was fixing his lips to say something else until we heard the front door chime.

In walked two gorgeous biracial women. They were both laughing and talking amongst themselves when they walked up to the counter. Shane and I were awestricken.

The shorter of the two spoke up as she looked around awkwardly, "Um. Do you guys do piercings?" she questioned while glancing around finally letting her slanted eyes meet mine. She smiled a little allowing her deep dimples to reveal themselves.

"Yes we do," I answered as Shane couldn't stop looking at her friend.

"Uh...do you do them anywhere?" she asked biting her lower lip a little as I raised an eyebrow.

"What do you have in mind?"

She looked towards her friend as they shared a small laugh before she used her index finger to point down.

"You mean?" I asked looking down below her belt.

She giggled and nodded, "If you're up for it." She gave me a flirtatious smirk as I chuckled.

"What's your name? Freaky girl."

She giggled even more, "Call me Lynn."

****

My new friend Lynn rolled from on top of me and flopped down onto my bed, breathless from our third round of sex. She was my replacement for Stacy. Ever since I gave her the piercing on her clitoris, we instantly clicked, both of us wanting the same thing from each other and nothing more. After a few moments of lying there, she sat up, stretched, and got out of bed searching the floor for her clothes.

"Hey uh...you trynna go get some food?" I suggested grabbing a freshly rolled blunt from my night stand.

She chuckled while pulling up her panties, "Sounds like a date don't you think?"

I shrugged, "Sounds like two hungry people going to grab some food." She laughed a little more then nodded her head in understanding.

"Thanks but no thanks."

I lit the blunt then peered over at her strangely, "Why? You're not hungry?" I questioned passing her the drug after she slid her tank back on.

She took in a puff and made little O's with the smoke, "I didn't say that. It just sounds like a lot. What me and you have is just sex..we don't need to like hang out. That's how you get caught up."

"Nah, when people make getting food a big deal is how people get caught up," I replied as she giggled some more passing me the blunt.

"Don listen. I know you're just using me for sex. You don't want the relationship and all that. I get it, so I'm not gonna waste my time doing anything else with you but that. Imma grab lunch with the guy that sees a little more in me than just what I can offer him physically but actually wants to offer me something in return. Getting food may not be a big deal to you but to some girls it is. I'm one of them, so I'll go grab me something alone, and the next time I need some, I'll hit you up," she said flatly grabbing her purse from the floor.

"Just know when you're getting used too sweetheart."

She smiled before kissing my forehead. She found out early I didn't kiss.

"I gotta head to work. Talk to you later ok?" She left without even waiting for a response as I sighed. It wasn't that I necessarily wanted to hang out with her today; I just didn't want to be alone. I had no appointments at the shop and no errands to run. Suddenly I remembered one little lady that would never turn me down to kick it. I made the decision then to go pick her up.

Bobbi.

"How you think it went?" Aaron asked me after I adjusted myself in his passenger seat. I had just had the interview Tierre set me up with at Cedar Sanai Hospital in their General Medicine clinic.

I wiped my sweaty palms against my navy blue scrub pants. "I really don't know. I think it went good, but I was stuttering and stumbling over words trying to remember everything I learned. They're just going to start me on something part time, until I pass my registration. I have to register for classes to take before California will allow me to take the test. Once I become a Registered Nurse, then I can become full time."

He nodded taking in my words, as he pulled from in front of the hospital building, taking me back to my house. I was grateful that he agreed to pick me up and take me to my interview. Auntie was finally back in town, but her and Jay both had to work.

"I bet you did fine. They understand you're a recent graduate. Nervousness is expected, and since they told you their future plans with you upon hire, I'm sure you got it. My cousin wouldn't set you up like that," he assured as I smiled.

"Thanks for picking me up and waiting. I really appreciate it. I'm happy that I found somebody here that I can talk to and depend on so early," I told him as he grinned and quickly glanced at me making sure he was still focused on the road.

"No big deal. You my homie, and I got you," he answered turning onto the expressway.

"Do you have plans later? Or do you think you can hang out with me for a little bit...?" I asked softly causing him to make a remorseful frown.

"I gotta get ready for work right after this shorty, but aye, Tierre was saying something about how she wanted to take you out tonight to celebrate your first interview."

I furrowed my brows, "What? I haven't even gotten the job yet. There's nothing to celebrate."

"Don't think negatively. You're going to get the job but it will just be us and Jay. Not a big thing. Show you a few of the clubs here. They're actually pretty dope."

He wasn't doing a good job of convincing me.

"The party was a lot for me. I'm not sure if I'm trying to be in the club scene," I sunk back in my seat.

"Come on Bobbi. You gotta live just a little. We're not gonna throw you to the wolves. Just want you to loosen up and relax. Get some drinks in your system and unwind. A night of fun is what you need to break you into LA life. It's a good step to move forward and appreciate your singleness," he rubbed my thigh a little at the end of his speech.

I still wasn't feeling it.

"I'll talk to Jay when I get home, but I guess I can go. It's the least I can do, since you took time out of your day to take me," I sighed as he instantly started to smile big. He had the prettiest set of teeth.

"Tierre is gonna be shocked I actually convinced you to go."

"Just barely," I corrected as he shrugged.

"A win is a win."

We let the music take over the conversation and rode in a peaceful silence to my house. Once we pulled up in the driveway, I got sad knowing I would be home alone. I couldn't wait to start working again just so I would have a purpose during the day.

"Ok, so I'll see you tonight?" he asked as I nodded reaching over for a hug. After our embrace, and one last "thank you", I exited the car and headed up to the front porch. Before I could reach the first step, Aaron had taken off back up the street.

I walked inside and headed upstairs to my room, so I could grab my camera. During the day, I took pictures of inanimate objects so I could edit them later. Today I thought would be a good day to take some outdoor pictures. After placing the camera around my neck, I went back downstairs to grab my tub of Cookies n Cream ice-cream out of the freezer and a spoon then sat on the front porch. I ate my frozen treat in silence as I studied my surroundings trying to decide what I would capture first. My serenity was interrupted when I heard loud music coming from an all-black 2009 Dodge Charger with tinted windows, which soon made its way into the driveway. I squinted my eyes at the vehicle and waited for the mystery person to park. I instantly groaned at who stepped out. He gave me a strange look before opening his back door. He disappeared inside the car for a few moments before popping back out with a small curly headed little girl. She was adorable.

He walked up, clutching the baby girl tightly in his arms while frowning at me. I returned the favor.

"Can I help you?" I asked looking up blocking my eyes from the sun with my hand.

"No. Jay in there?"

"No. What's with everyone always popping up on him like he's always home. He has a job you know?"

He smacked his lips at my response, "He didn't always have one, so we're used to just coming over here. You ain't doin shit anyway."

My mouth dropped as I stood up to become eye level with the little girl, "Do you always use such foul language in front of your daughter?" I asked smiling and making silly faces at her. She blushed and hid her face in his shoulder. She couldn't have been older than two.

"She's my god-daughter, and she's heard and seen worse," he defended as I lifted my spoon full of ice cream to her lips.

"Doesn't mean you should continue to talk that way in front of her. She's observing everything," my spoon was getting closer to her lips, and I looked up at him for approval, "Can she have some?"

"I don't know where your mouth has been," he said rudely as I brushed him off and fed her some anyway.

"You just get off work or something?" he asked me as I shot him a crazy look.

"How you figure that? You stalking me?" I snapped.

He chuckled and pulled at my scrub top a little with his free hand.

"Just observant. Chill. Ain't nobody pressed for your ass."

I smacked his arm then pointed to the baby.

"I'm sorry Shai Shai," he cooed placing playful kisses all over her neck and cheeks causing her to giggle.

It was a cute sight.

"Well, we were about to head to the park until Jay gets off or something," he announced as he turned and walked down the driveway. Shai and I locked eyes the whole way down.

"You can come you know! Take some pictures or whatever," he called not looking back. I smirked a little to myself before quickly removing it from my face. He thought he knew me so well.

I ran inside the house to put my ice-cream up and went back outside after locking the door to catch up with the two.

****

I sat on a nearby bench watching Donovan chase Shai all over the park. I was surprised to see him have just as much energy as she did. He was so patient and loving with her like she was his own. It was sweet.

I pulled out my camera and took pictures of the scenery at the park. The lens quickly found its way on Donovan and Shai. I admired his features through the camera. He had a genuine smile with a small dimple on his left cheek, and his arms were both covered in a sleeve full of tattoos. He was more attractive than I was willing to give him credit for.

He looked up and caught me staring, and I quickly looked away. I didn't know what made me on edge around him; I didn't want him to know I was having any nice thoughts in his direction.

"You're not slick," he snickered walking up to me with Shai trailing close by.

"What are you talking about?" I spat back as he chuckled and rolled his eyes.

56

"You can't never be real about shit and just put up a front. Why is that?" he asked sitting down next to me and reaching for Shai's bag. He pulled out her sippy cup, handed it to her, and she giddily took it from his hands.

"What's the front? What if I just don't like you?" I snared as he smiled.

"You're not the sweetest rose in the dozen either sweetheart. Don't get that confused. You just got this vendetta against me and I ain't do shit to you and personally...I don't think it's fair because I'd like to say that I'm a good guy," he said placing his hand on his chest earning an eye roll from me.

"I just know your type and don't care for it too much," I said simply as he looked at me intrigued.

"Tell me about myself then beautiful stranger. It's cute you think you know so much and this is the first real conversation we've ever had," he said with attitude in his voice.

"Oh, and you don't assume the same about me? One of the first things you said to me is that you see right through me," I responded causing him to grin a little.

"Because I do. Look, I can't say I know specifically what you've been through, but I can see that you live out your pain. Some dumb ass dude hurt you and that's obvious, so you rule off anybody that comes your way. Well except..."

Before he could finish I cut him off, "Forget that. Tell me why you've never had a girlfriend?" I asked as his eyes widened. I was tired of his ass trying to always get on me.

"Tierre told you that?" he asked as I nodded. He shrugged slightly, "Never wanted one."

"Who wouldn't want someone to emotionally connect with?" I asked him as he shook his head.

"Just don't," he said simply.

I pressed on, "There has to be a reason..."

"No reason. Just don't," he lied as I looked for the truth in his eyes. They were too blank for me to read. I didn't know him well enough.

"Anyway, what's up with you and punk ass Aaron?" he changed the subject as I smacked my lips.

"Aaron is cool. Why don't ya'll like him?" I asked. He picked up Shai and set her on his lap.

"He's cool but not loyal. I don't fool with that," Donovan said as I watched him make goofy faces at his god-daughter.

"You love her," I blurted. He turned and looked at me before looking back at Shai.

"I adore children. They're the most innocent beings on the earth. They see the world through unfiltered lenses. I envy that at times," he expressed.

I smirked a little, "You love her as if she was your own," I said again wondering if he would admit that he even loved his god-child.

"Yeah, as you say," he replied tickling Shai before picking her up and carrying her off to the swing set.

Tierre was right. He couldn't express his love even for a baby. That was scary...yet... relatable.

Donovan.

I carried a sleepy Shai in my arms as Bobbi and I walked back in silence to their house. I had tried to make conversation but she rejected every attempt made. I never kept trying with people and didn't understand what was making me try so hard with her.

As we walked up I smiled at Lisa in the garage getting groceries out of her trunk. She smiled at the sight of us and gave a small wave in our direction.

"Hey, can you lay her down in the house while I help Lisa out?" I asked Bobbi as she nodded then grabbed Shai from my arms. I gave a small grin watching her walk into the house before heading towards the garage.

"Hey Miss Lisa. Let me help you with those," I said walking up behind her causing her short frame to jump.

"Ooh, Donovan you nearly scared me half to death!" she chuckled softly grabbing her chest. I laughed too beginning to reach for the groceries.

She placed a hand on my shoulder stopping me in my tracks, "How are you baby? How's your grandmother?" she asked.

"She's as okay as she can be. Last week she knew my name. This week she doesn't," I said flatly as she sighed.

"I feel your pain honey. My father suffered from Alzheimer's as well. It's just a sad thing to watch somebody so strong become so weak and frail and then not even know who you are when they've been such a crucial part of your life is heart breaking," she said softly rubbing my back as I swallowed hard.

"Just know I'm here for you Donovan. I don't want you shutting everybody out just because you feel like you don't have anyone. I promised your mother the day of the funeral that I will always be here for you," she added, choking up a bit as I just shook it off.

It was always stung when people reminded me that my mother was no longer here on this earth, "Well let me get these inside." I forced a smile and she did too giving me a soft kiss on the cheek.

"Okay. You and Shai should stay for dinner. I'm making lasagna," she smiled before we both walked into the house.

I set the groceries down on the kitchen counter and walked towards the living room to find Bobbi holding Shai on her chest and rubbing her back. She was sound asleep.

"Thanks..You didn't have to put her to sleep," I told her sitting down next to them on the couch. She smirked a little when she looked over at me.

"Who said you can sit here?" she questioned as I smacked my lips causing her to giggle. It was the first time I heard her laugh; it was kinda cute.

"You smile and laugh? I'm shocked," I responded sarcastically as she forced her smile to disappear and looked back at the TV.

A few moments later Jay walked through the door and looked at the two of us strangely. His face was funny the way he looked between Bobbi, Shai and I with question.

"Uh..what is.." he started waving his finger around at all three of us while walking in the living room.

"Not what it looks like. This creep was stalking you outside of the house," Bobbi said, crossing her eyes while I huffed.

"I was taking Shai to the park and stopped by to see if you wanted to come. That's it." I said to Jay before turning and giving Bobbi an evil stare.

Jay shook his head at the two of us and plopped down in the chair, "Work was stupid today. I'm ready to turn up tonight."

I shot him a look, "Turn up where?" I questioned as Jay hesitated a little to tell me.

"We're going to Supperclub," Jay started before Bobbi cut him off.

"And you're not invited," she added as I just blew her off and continued my focus on Jay.

"Why ain't you want me to come?" I asked him slightly offended. Jay and I were like brothers, simply because Lisa is my god-mom, so for him to try to play me, pissed me off.

"Cuz Tierre is coming with Aaron and I'm just over the bullshit. Ya'll act like ya'll can't be civil every time we're all around each other."

"I don't ever bother that man, and you know it. I've been bored all day and want something to do too," I said to him hearing Bobbi smack her teeth.

"Didn't I just say you weren't invited? Why do ya'll keep missing that key aspect of this whole thing?" she asked looking at the two of us as we both ignored her still.

"Man yo cry baby ass can come. Just know I ain't breaking up shit between the two of ya'll this time. Aaron cool, and you know I only fool with him cuz of Tierre, so if it comes down to it, I got yo back. Just don't put me in that position man. Seriously," Jay said sternly as I nodded. I was going to tell Shane to come anyway.

I heard Bobbi let out an irritated sigh before she gently placed Shai down on the couch and stormed out of the living room. Every time I think I'm getting decent with that girl, she reminds me that we've gotten nowhere. I didn't care regardless.

"Man seriously, what's her problem? She cool with everyone but me," I asked Jay as he laughed and shrugged.

"She just doesn't like you. I don't know," he reached down and grabbed the remote off the coffee table.

"Yeah, but I haven't even done anything to that girl. I'm normally not even bothered by this type of shit. She just gets under my skin," I sighed sitting back on the couch.

"She just been through things, so she's weird with certain people. Just ignore her ass. Girls like when you ignore them," he suggested as I nodded instantly thinking about Stacy.

"Man, I do that to girls I'm trynna smash. I'm just attempting to be cool with your cousin because she's family."

"You don't have to be cool with her. I'm telling you. Ignore her ass and she'll come around."

Bobbi.

"One last curl and I will be done," Tierre said, as she looked at me close before tending back to my hair. She had come over after we had dinner to help me primp for tonight's festivities. For some reason she was really excited about this.

"How am I looking?" I asked nervously hearing the smile in her voice.

"Gorgeous. You're going to have my cousin drooling tonight," she encouraged as I crossed my eyes while laughing.

"You keep saying stuff like that. We're just friends. Nothing more."

"I see the way you check him out Bobs. You ain't got to lie. My cousin is handsome. He thinks you're cute too," she said while sitting the curling iron down, standing in front of me, and running her fingers through my hair to get the look she wanted.

"He...he said that?" I questioned as she nodded nonchalantly.

"Of course he said that. You're beautiful girl. Don't ever think different. Shit, the way you're looking tonight you're going to have to fight off every man in the club, including those knuckleheads downstairs."

"Um no. Definitely not Dam...I mean Donovan. We hate each other."

"You hate practically everyone so Don is just going off your vibe. You should ease up on him a little. He's a cool guy. Fun to be around," she stood back looking satisfied with her work.

"Damn, I'm good. Check yourself out," she suggested, as I stood up and turned around. My eyes widened at the sight. The dark blue dress Tierre brought over for me hugged my shape perfectly, and the makeup caused my face to look radiant and evenly toned. The curls in my hair fell softly way past my shoulders. I couldn't believe it was my reflection that I was looking at.

"Wow, I've never looked like this before," I said admiring myself and turning to see different angles, even my ass looked bigger than normal.

Tierre smiled at me through the mirror, "Get used to it baby girl. Makeup and hair is my hobby. Anytime we go out, I will definitely hook you up." She walked towards my bed and reached into her bag to pull out a bottle of Patron.

"Come on. Let's take a few shots before we head out. It's always good to pregame," she advised as I sighed before shrugging.

I had nothing to lose, and I looked great. I wanted to enjoy every moment of this night without being self-conscious of my appearance or worried about anyone else around me.

She smiled while pulling out two shot glasses, and I couldn't help but laugh, "You just knew I was going to agree to this huh?"

"If not, I was going to go with the 'it's the least you can do' line since I helped you look sexy as hell." She winked as I shook my head while receiving my shot.

We took three shots together before gathering our things to meet Jay, Shane, and Donovan downstairs. Aaron had told me he would come through later tonight.

I strutted down the hall hearing my heels click against the hardwood floor as I stepped foot in the dining area where Jay, Auntie, Shane and Donovan all sat. They were in mid conversation before stopping; all eyes fell on me.

"Well...damn," Jay said in astonishment as Auntie smacked his arm before smiling warmly at me.

"You look beautiful baby."

I grinned bashfully before thanking her. I then locked eyes with Donovan before we both looked away.

Donovan.

"Yo...Bobbi is *cold*," Shane said shaking his head as I looked over at him in the passenger seat. We followed Jay's car up to Supperclub for Bobbi's interview celebration.

I shrugged my shoulder as I adjusted my body in the seat, "She was coo."

I could feel Shane looking at me out of the corner of my eye before he laughed, "You're full of shit Don. I saw you looking at her when she wasn't looking."

"I mean she cute, but she mean as hell to me for no reason," I huffed speeding up a little.

"She prally see right through your manipulative ass. You know you treat these women like shit," Shane commented as I blew him off.

"Ain't never met one that deserved more," I said flatly causing him to smack his lips.

"Yeah you have, and she played your ass right after mom passed away. It ain't Aaron's fault tho," Shane started as I turned up the music louder.

I was trying to be in a good mood and this dude wanted to talk about things that didn't matter anymore. I heard him sigh in defeat as he sat back in his seat and took a sip out of the Ciroc bottle that we had in the whip. I just zoned until we reached the club.

****

We were getting eye raped by girls as we made our way inside of the packed club. I had lost Jay on the freeway so I looked around to see if I saw them anywhere.

Shane tapped me on my arm and pointed, "They over by the bar." He said as I immediately saw Tierre's big head urging Bobbi to take another shot. She was always trying to get somebody drunk.

"Damn, ya'll taking shots without us?!" I complained walking up and putting my arm around Tierre while both Jay and

Bobbi smiled at us. I smiled too. When she did smile, it was infectious.

Bobbi handed me one of the many shot glasses on the bar counter, "Pour UP!" She screeched as my eyes widened looking at her. Shane and I both gave each other a weird glance before I turned and took the shot from her hands.

"I'll take one witcha!" she chuckled reaching for a shot and tapping it against my glass. We both swallowed the liquor and she quickly went for her cup of orange juice and took a sip.

"Ugh, I hate shots," she cringed fanning her face as I kept staring at her. She made the cutest faces sometimes.

I instantly shook my head to snap out of it. I never complimented women in a sweet manner. Plus she didn't deserve for me to think kindly of her, not with the attitude she possessed. Bobbi was inching to hand me another shot when Shut it Down by Drake came on and her eyes lit up. She put the glass down and grabbed my hand.

"I love this song Don!" she yelled as I allowed her to drag me to the dance floor. She pressed her butt against my pelvis and began slow grinding to the beat. Our bodies were moving together perfectly; I never felt this way dancing with a chick before. I was feeling this...desire for her.

"I didn't know you could dance," I whispered in her ear as Drake's second verse started on the song. She smiled as she slowed her hips down as I gripped them.

"I can tell you could...that's why I wanted to dance with you," she slurred a little from the alcohol as she ran her fingers through her hair revealing her neck. I had to shoot down the burning urge to kiss it. This dance was making me want to do all kind of things to this girl.

"How could you tell?" I asked biting my lip as she turned her head and gave me this sexy ass smirk. Who was she? Under the influence she was calmer and more natural. This must be who she really is: young and free.

She giggled and stood up straight as the song switched to a more upbeat tune. She blushed a little looking at me and made her way back over to Tierre. I couldn't even believe I was starting to soften for her mean ass.

As I stepped to follow her, I felt a gentle tap on my arm. I turned to look down and was taken aback by who I saw.

"Lynn?"

Bobbi.

I was slightly embarrassed I had allowed myself to dance so sexually with Donovan. I just wanted to have fun and show him I'm not always mean. Plus, Shane was too short to dance with.

Tierre snickered at me as I made my way back to her and nudged me in my shoulder.

"I saw that! What was that between ya'll? Had him shook for like two seconds," she laughed as I did too, mostly because of all the Patron she had snuck in my system.

"I just wanted to dance. Let me live," I chuckled as she just shook her head while handing me a glass of a blue concoction.

This was the most relaxed I had felt in years.

Something in me wanted to bother Donovan again, so I searched the room for his head. A small smile formed across my lips until I saw him talking to some Asian looking girl. I suddenly remembered that judging by the red headed demon chick, and this new girl he was canoodling with, I wasn't exactly his type.

"I wanna dance some more," I pouted turning to face Tierre. She looked at me strangely before looking past me and noticing the same thing I had moments prior. She rolled her eyes a little then grabbed my hand.

"We'll find some guys to dance wit. Don't even worry bout dat!" she said waving her hand in Donovan's direction. I wasn't worried. Just wanted a dance partner. Something about the way he moved made me feel some kind of way. A weird connection. I brushed it off though.

As we walked through the crowd, I felt a small tug at my waist and looked up to see a smiling face belonging to an attractive stranger.

"Smile beautiful," he said sweetly causing me to blush.

"I'm Trevor," he introduced reaching out his hand.

I hesitated a little before I shook it, "Bobbi." I replied as we continued to stare each other down.

Tierre saw our little exchange and turned her attention towards him and his homeboy.

"Ya'll wanna dance?"

Donovan.

"I peeped you making love on the floor wit ol girl," Lynn smiled as I grinned a little and shook my head.

"Just dancing that's all," I told her as she put her hands up slightly.

"Aye, you ain't gotta explain shit to me. I'm not ya girl. Just wanted to come say what's up since I saw you," she said stepping closer to me.

"What you doing after this?" I asked with a hint of seduction feeling her wrap her arm around my waist. I didn't make my action obvious by removing it. Public displays of affection were a negative for me.

"Coming over to your place," she replied not taking notice that her arm was now removed from my body.

"Coo...I'll be back at the crib by three."

She continued to make small conversation with me, and I pretended to listen searching the room for Bobbi. I couldn't even understand why I was looking for her.

I spotted Tierre's poufy hair first before I saw Bobbi talking to some guy. He kept making her laugh, and I noticed her playfully hitting his arm a few times. For the first time in as long as I could remember, I felt a hint of... jealousy.

What was that about?

Bobbi.

I sat down at the bar listening to Trevor talk about... himself. He wasn't asking me a single question, and I was too drunk to even comment on it. He was cool at first, at least to dance with, but now I was becoming bored and irritated by his presence. I just kept nodding, sipping my drink and roaming the room with my eyes. I wanted someone to put me out of my misery.

"....what about you?" I finally heard the magic words and looked up at Trevor wide eyed.

"Uh...huh?" I asked completely lost about where this conversation had taken a turn to.

He flashed his beautiful smile before he spoke again, "I was asking you where you work beautiful," he said as I felt a flush of embarrassment.

"Oh! I'm a nurse." He wasn't about to find out my future place of employment. For some reason, I thought he was going to stalk me or something.

He continued to tell me how his sister was a nurse and *blah blah blah* before I saw Donovan and Shane walk up smiling like idiots. I couldn't help but laugh at their expressions.

"Baby!" Don yelled opening his arms, "I've been looking all over this club for you!" He pulled me into a hug and I gave Shane a strange look behind Don's back.

"Yea sis," Shane spoke up placing his hands in his pockets, "I told him you were around here somewhere."

I giggled a little picking up on their game before Don placed a kiss on my cheek, "You look gorgeous tonight."

I flashed him a small smile before he directed his attention towards Trevor and stuck out his hand, "Yo man, thanks for keepin my lady company while I was on my way. I can take it from here champ," he said smoothly as Trevor scoffed at all three of us and stood up to walk away.

The minute Trevor did Shane and Don busted out laughing.

"Y'all so wrong," I chuckled shaking my head as they both looked at me.

Shane placed his hand on my shoulder, "Nah your ass is wrong for even getting that man's hopes up like that!"

"Yea. You were over here bored as shit. We rescue Tierre daily at the bar with that same line," Don added taking a large swig of his drink.

I was a little saddened to know that they didn't do it special for me.

"Oh...well thanks. He couldn't dance anyway. Tierre was just too caught up in his friend. I had to play wing man."

"Couldn't dance like Don huh?!" Shane teased as Donovan nudged him hard.

I locked eyes with him and bit my lip a little, "Nah...he couldn't."

I was inching to talk to him some more until I saw a familiar face in the distance not too far behind him. My face instantly lit up.

"Aaron!" I yelled calling his attention as I stood up from the bar and walked passed both Shane and Donovan.

Aaron saw me and smiled opening his arms for a hug.

"You made it," I said breathlessly in his ear as I wrapped my arms around his neck. I couldn't even explain why I was so relieved to see him.

"Of course I did," he said before removing himself from our embrace, "Tierre told me how hype you were."

"Yeah...I'm drunk as hell," I laughed as he did too.

His smile slightly faded when he noticed Donovan and Shane looking our way.

"You seem to be better around them," he commented as he put his arm around my shoulder and walked me in a different direction.

"Yea they're not so bad I guess. Just wish y'all wasn't fighting," I said looking up at Aaron. He looked really cute tonight.

"Trust me babe. It's not me with the problem," he replied nonchalantly as I peaked back at Donovan. He was watching me too.

Donovan.

I locked eyes with Bobbi and quickly looked away directing my attention towards Shane.

"What is it about that dude?" I asked downing the rest of my drink.

Shane chuckled before he took a sip of his, "Knew you liked her."

"I don't like her. I'm just wondering why she's so nice to Aaron and nobody else," I said looking in the direction of the two of them watching Aaron whisper something in her ear causing her to giggle. I blamed the alcohol for being so in touch with my feelings that I didn't even know I had, "I really hate that I care. I don't even understand why. She's always a jerk to me." I growled turning away.

"I don't know. I may not know her too well, but I would like her for you," Shane commented as I shook my head.

"I'm good."

****

About an hour later, our night was winding down and everyone was ready to leave. Currently, Jay was begging me to take Bobbi home as my irritation rose. I wanted to get home to link up with Lynn, not to be bothered with Bobbi's nonsense.

"Yo, where the hell Aaron go? Why you asking me to take her home?" I asked Jay as he shrugged.

"I think he has to take Tierre home and Bobbi doesn't wanna go over there. Man please, you know Felicia live way up north, and I need to get me some," Jay begged as I growled a little.

"Dawg, me too! I had something lined up for me at the crib."

I sighed watching Jay look at me with pleading eyes. I smacked my lips and searched the room for Bobbi. She was saying her goodbyes to Tierre and Aaron.

I waited for them to hug before I decided to approach her. I tapped her arm, and she jumped a little before she looked at me then smiled.

I had to look away before my ass started smiling too. I hated when she did that sometimes, "You ready to go?" I questioned keeping my hard exterior.

She nodded and grabbed my hand. I looked down at her fingers intertwined with mine and gripped her hand tighter escorting her out of the club with Shane close behind me. I never held hands with a woman before, and this was a foreign, yet comfortable feeling to be holding hers; guiding her through the crowd and protecting her from any harm or danger.

We got closer to my car, and I opened the passenger door for Bobbi to get inside. Shane looked at me strangely when I closed her door before he opened his.

"When the hell you start opening doors?!" he asked wide eyed as I fanned him off and walked to the driver's side. It was out of my character to open doors for women, let alone, ride front seat in my whip. I was just doing all of this off of natural instinct.

We rode to the sounds of the new Wiz Khalifa back to the crib and I caught myself peeking looks at Bobbi nodding her head to the music and looking out of the window. She was so different to me. Everything about her. I was feeling connected to her natural side and not the Bobbi that constantly puts her guard up.

"I can feel your eyes," she said without looking in my direction. I smirked to myself before shifting my eyes back on the road.

When we pulled up, Bobbi looked at me strangely when I put the car in park and took off my seatbelt, "What?" I asked her as she continued to admire me.

"What are you doing?"

"I'm making sure you get inside cool. Is that a problem?" I asked her raising my brows.

She quickly shook her head and smiled getting out of the car heading towards the front porch to unlock the door. I took the keys out of the ignition and decided to stay back and say bye to Shane before he took off.

"You gon try to hit?" Shane asked dapping me up.

I shook my head, "Can't do that to Jay's cousin bro. What I look like?" I questioned.

He gave me a look like he didn't believe me, "You fucked his other cousin on his dad's side." He reminded me as I thought back for a second then laughed.

"Aw. That was different," I chuckled along with him.

"In other words...you respect her. I got you G. Never thought I'd see the day when Don actually respected a chick," he replied shaking his head before turning to walk towards his car.

"That's not it either. I'm just chilling," I called out hearing him laugh.

"Yeah. Call it what you want. I'll see you at the shop tomorrow."

He chucked me the deuces and hopped in his car. I shoved my hands in my pockets and walked into the house to say goodbye to Bobbi and to make sure she was straight before I headed home.

I walked into the living room to find her sitting on the couch taking her heels off.

"Hey, I'm going to go," I started.

She poked out her bottom lip in response. "No one is here," she said softly as I looked at her not fazed by her statement.

"Can you just sit with me until I fall asleep or something? I don't like being here alone," she confessed. I released a conflicted breath. I knew I had to meet up with Lynn, but I could see the genuine fear in her eyes.

I reluctantly walked into the room and sat down on the couch with her. "You wanna watch TV?" I asked as she nodded, and I grabbed the remote off of the coffee table. I turned the channel to the first movie I saw and sat back. When I looked over, I saw Bobbi looking down and playing with the tips of her hair. I liked the way Tierre had curled it tonight. It made her face seem more defined.

"What's wrong?" I asked as she looked up at me with her soft brown eyes.

"There's something about you...I'm rude to you sometimes because I try to prevent myself from feeling the way I do," she admitted as I raised an eyebrow, "Do I feel that alone?"

I debated on whether or not I was going to lie or tell the truth. All rules went out the window when it came to her. I kept quiet unsure of how to answer, and she scooted a little closer to me. The room slightly spun forcing me to realize how intoxicated we both still were.

"This feeling is new to me. It scares me in a sense. That's why I keep trying to protect myself from it. I can see that women to you are simply just bodies. Nothing more than just space and time. I don't want to be that."

I watched her lips the whole time she spoke.

I leaned closer rubbing my thumb against her cheek. She brought her face closer to mine and our lips were inches away from touching. I studied how soft and full they looked waiting to be interrupted. I ran my tongue over my bottom lip before she pressed hers against mine. It was a gentle and tender kiss that sent my hormones in a rage. She spread her lips allowing me to slip in my tongue to deepen it. A moan escaped her mouth into mine, and I felt my member jump at the vibration it sent through my body.

I started to lean her body back on the couch before she quickly stopped me placing her palms into my chest breaking away from our intimate moment. She looked at me before she stood up from the couch and ran her fingers through her curls.

"Um...I need to go to sleep," she said in haste before picking up her shoes and heading up the stairs.

I pressed my fingers against my lips as they were still tingling from the sensation of hers. She was the second woman I had ever kissed in my life.

Bobbi.

I yawned stretching underneath my covers before blinking my eyes open. I searched the bed to look for my phone and sighed when it read 7:52AM. Even on drunken nights, I could never manage to get a good night's rest. I sat all the way up in my bed while scratching my hair and looking around the room. I couldn't even remember how I got home last night. Those shots of Patron had me tore off and made me hungry as hell.

After changing into a white tank top and olive green cheerleading shorts, I walked to my bathroom to wash my face and brush my teeth. Afterwards, I looked in Jay's room and noticed him missing then did the same with Aunties. They were both gone on a Saturday morning. I wasn't surprised. Auntie liked spending time with our grandmother on the weekends and would stay to help her clean and wash clothes.

I made my way downstairs towards the kitchen and saw Donovan sleeping shirtless on the couch. I rolled my eyes before reaching my destination and pulled out the contents I needed to make us breakfast. I didn't understand why he was here, but since he was, he could at least eat.

I put out all of the items to make cinnamon pancakes, cheese eggs, bacon, and grits and got to work. Cooking was therapeutic for me. I always did it when I had a lot on my mind.

The biggest thing picking at my brain was how attracted I found myself to Donovan last night. Dancing with him and feeling this sense of closeness felt strange to me, especially since it was with him of all people. I barely could stand being around him half the time and here I was attracted to him physically. I tried to force the same connection that I was feeling with Don onto Aaron but it wasn't the same.

I wasn't ready to feel anything for anyone just yet. Even though my last relationship was two years ago, I still couldn't find myself in a place to let someone back in; definitely not a womanizer like Donovan. He clearly wasn't interested in me either, and I was at peace with that.

Once I finished cooking everything, I set out two plates and fixed his first. I heard a noise and looked up to see him scratching his stomach making his way towards the kitchen. He leaned against the counter looking at me softly.

"Morning," he yawned as I smiled a little admiring his bare chest and the many tattoos painted upon it. I loved that he expressed himself through body art.

"You hungry?" I asked as he nodded. I picked up the plate I just finished preparing and handed it to him. He looked shocked.

"You fixed my plate?" he questioned looking between me and the food. I chuckled a little while nodding.

"Yeah. Go sit at the table, I'll bring you some orange juice," I smiled as he did as he was told.

I finished my plate, poured both of us something to drink, and skillfully made my way to the table to sit next to him. I noticed he hadn't touched his food yet.

"Are you afraid of the food or something?" I asked as he looked at me and shook his head.

"No. I was waiting for you to sit down, so we could eat together," he replied innocently.

I made an "Oh" shape with my lips. I was preparing to dig in until he cleared his throat.

"You're not going to wait until I bless it?" he questioned as I looked at him weirdly.

I barely ever prayed over my food. I set my fork down and bowed my head.

"Dear Lord, thank you for this food we're about to receive and bless the hands that made it. May it nourish our bodies, in Jesus name, amen," he said quickly.

I giggled and cut up my pancakes.

I watched him begin to devour his meal out of the corner of my eye while I ate slowly. I was always a slow eater, but Don on the other hand, looked like he was fresh out of jail.

"You were definitely hungry," I commented reaching for my juice.

He stopped mid chew and chuckled, "I'm not used to breakfast in the morning. I don't really make it. This is good." He complimented blushing at me as I smiled.

"Thanks..." I said then took in a fork full of my eggs.

"This reminds me of when my mom used to cook me breakfast. I think that's part of the reason why I stopped eating it," he said softly.

 I looked up at him.

I remembered Auntie said something about how Donovan's mom passed away from cancer a while ago when I asked about a picture of her and another woman in the living room. She was a beautiful woman and was smiling bright in the photo with my aunt. I just didn't know how to handle him opening up to me. I could barely handle my own feelings; wasn't sure how to deal with his.

"Well," I started running fingers through my hair out of habit, "I'm glad you're eating it again." I smiled watching him admire me from head to toe. Normally I would feel uncomfortable, but with Don, I didn't. He never made me feel uncomfortable, and I think that's why I constantly had my guard up.

"Listen, Bobbi..." he started before we both jumped at the garage door opening.

Jay came in holding a McDonald's bag smiling at the two of us sitting at the table.

"Sup ya'll," he said taking a seat as Donovan and I both mugged him, "What?"

"You went to McDonald's and ain't say shit?!" Don asked speaking my thoughts exactly.

"I mean...yeah. I had to take Felicia to work this morning. The hell ya'll mad at me for?! Ya'll eating!" he screeched as I shook my head.

"That's not the point. You ain't even shoot anybody a text to see if we were hungry. You wasn't the only one looking for hangover food this morning," I snapped at him as Donovan nodded in agreement pointing to me.

Jay leaned his head back at the both of us, "Ok listen Bobbi and Whitney. I'm too hungover to deal with the bullshit ya'll trynna give me, so I'm going to take my food and make my way upstairs," he said standing up and snatching his bag off the table. We were quiet for a moment until Donovan scrunched up his face.

"Wayment bitch you just call me Whitney?!" Don asked, as Jay and I busted out laughing.

He was growing on me...just didn't know how I felt about that yet.

Donovan.

Never hit me up…

I looked at the text from Lynn while putting my plate in the sink. I ignored it and shoved my phone back in my pocket. I had to diss her last night since I ended up staying here. What was throwing me off is that Bobbi is acting as though she doesn't remember what all happened. Kissing her was outside of my normal character and it all made me feel some type of way. We needed to talk about this before I lost the courage to mention anything at all.

I snapped out of my thoughts and walked out of the kitchen and back towards the table where Bobbi was still eating her breakfast and reading the comics out of the newspaper.

"I thought I was the only one who still reads the funnies," I chuckled as she looked up at me and half smiled.

"Only reason why I hold on to the Sunday paper. This is from last week; I didn't get a chance to read them yet," she said taking a small bite of her bacon while she continued to read.

"Aye, about what I was saying before Jay came in. I think we should talk about last night," I started hesitantly as she looked up at me blankly.

"What about it? The club was fun! Is this about Aaron?" she asked.

I raised an eyebrow before quickly shaking my head. Nothing I ever had to say concerned Aaron, "Nah. It's about...you know...the kiss?" I asked as she contorted her face in confusion. *Shit.*

"Kiss? Who kissed?" she asked confused.

I pointed between the two of us.

She let out a laugh, "Don, why on earth would the two of us ever kiss?"

"What do you mean? You were the one coming on to me last night. You were telling me how you was feeling me and-"

80

She cut me off, "What?! I couldn't have possibly said any of that! We barely get along. The only reason why we were cordial last night is because we were both drunk." She scoffed.

"Uh. I wasn't that drunk. You were," I spat back as she continued to look at me with disbelief.

"Oh, so you're saying you took advantage of me?" she asked as I quickly became offended.

"Hell no! What I look like taking advantage of you when you my bro's cousin? Like I said, you were in your feelings and told me you were starting to like me then we just kissed. It just happened. Now, I regret even allowing the shit to go down," I groaned mad as hell. *Bobbi was impossible.*

"I'm mad it even went down myself, but happy I don't even remember the shit! And somebody must've slipped something in my drink for me to even tell you those lies last night," she snapped as I felt my irritation rising.

"Man are you serious? If you was so far gone then why yo ass wake up and fix me breakfast?"

"Correction," she said waving her little finger, "I woke up to fix *me* breakfast. I decided to be nice to you for once since I saw you passed out on the couch and didn't want to be rude. I'm realizing now that I should've been since you forced your lips on me."

I smacked my lips, "Man I would *never*! I don't even kiss b-" I started but quickly stopped myself. I wasn't going to refer to her as a bitch...in front of her face.

She crossed her arms, "You don't kiss what?! You don't kiss *bitches* Damien?! Is that what you were going to say?"

She made my blood boil when she called me by that dumb ass name, "That's not my fuckin name." I gritted through my teeth as she grinned. She knew she pissed me off.

"Well, my fuckin name ain't bitch!"

"Quit acting like one then! Damn! I swear I'm done trying to be cool with your ass!" I yelled pointing in her face as she got in mine.

"Nobody asked you to try to be cool. I'm cool if I don't talk to you. I like Aaron over your dumb ass anyway!" She argued back stepping even closer to me.

I couldn't help how sexy she looked. It was pissing me off even more that I was attracted to her during a time like this.

"Is that right?" I asked my voice lowering. It was my hormones talking.

"Yeah, that's right," she answered.

I placed my hands on her hips and aggressively pulled her close. She was taken aback by my force but didn't budge. I couldn't even explain why I was doing this, how we were just arguing, and now I wanted nothing more than to kiss her again.

We started leaning in until I heard Jay begin to make his way down the steps. I quickly backed away and she did too. I made my exit towards the living room to grab my clothes and keys.

"Forgot my phone," Jay chimed as he walked towards the table grabbing it. Once he did, he looked between the two of us. I put on my shirt while simultaneously sliding on my shoes, and Bobbi was picking up her plate and cup from the table.

"Uh...was I interrupting something?" He smirked.

We both quickly answered, "no".

"Haha, yeah okay..." he teased as I huffed and chucked up the deuces before walking out of the front door.

****

I arrived at the shop about an hour later after going home and getting myself together for the day. I was happy to see a good number of people waiting for tattoos and piercings when entering through the doors. Shane was at the front ringing out a couple and gave me a light head nod when he saw me.

"We're busy. Time to get to work," he said as I nodded in response. Working always kept my mind busy.

After four hours of back to back tattoos, we were finally able to catch a break and straighten up the messy shop. Shane put away picture books as I wiped down the tables and chairs with disinfectant spray.

"Yo, how'd last night go? You smash Lynn?" Shane called out to me while I shook my head as if he could see me.

"Man hell no. Ended up staying at Jay's last night," I groaned.

He popped his head into the room I was in with the slickest grin on his face.

"Woorddd? You smash Bobbi then?!" he asked as I rolled my eyes.

"Nah fool. I already told you I wasn't on that," I answered with attitude debating on whether or not I was going to tell him what really happened, "I kissed her though."

Shane pretended to pass out on the floor as I laughed and threw the roll of paper towels I had in my hand at his head.

He chuckled opening his eyes and getting off the floor, "You *lying*! You kissing somebody? I ain't never seen you kiss nobody in *life*," he said in disbelief as I shrugged.

"Bruh, I can't even tell you what came over me. She was cool last night, but woke up to the same ol' bullshit wit her man, and yet, I still wanted to kiss her again. I don't know what it is about that bitchy ass girl. She's mean as all hell, yet I find myself doing things I don't ever do. I swear I'm about to start treating her like I do the rest. She's starting to take my kindness for some weak shit," I complained as Shane just smiled at me.

"I like Bobbi already. Got yo ass on some sucka shit," he clowned as I crossed my eyes.

"She don't got me on nothing. I'm good on her from here on out. Back to the real me," I said with confidence as Shane just shook his head.

"The real you ain't really you dawg," he said, before we both heard the door chime. He looked out at the door and rolled his eyes. "Aww shit. WE CLOSED!"

"Don't act like you're not happy to see me Shaney Pooh Pooh!" I heard her say as I cursed in my mind.

Moments later, I watched Stacy walk into the room I was in.

"Hi baby."

I looked her up and down. She wore jean shorts with a white crop top that fell off her shoulder revealing the tattoo I gave her there. She looked really good, and I needed to get the release I had been holding in since last night. She bit her lip as she placed her hand on her waist. She knew exactly how to lure me back in even after all of this time of me blowing her off.

"Let's go to my office."

Bobbi .

Donovan and I hadn't spoken in two weeks since that morning. Anytime he was around, we would avoid each other like the plague. I know I came at him crazy when he said we kissed and that I had told him how I truly felt about him, but I honestly didn't remember...then. Later on that day my memory hit me like a ton of bricks, and I recapped the whole night in my mind. The hand holding, the smiles, the affection...and the kiss. I hadn't felt that kind of intensity with someone in years even before Jo, and it terrified me.

"Hey hoe," Tierre said walking up to my work station popping her gum. It was my first week on the job, "Where we going for lunch?" she asked.

I shrugged a little and continued to sign off on some more patient charts, "I don't know. I haven't really thought about it today," I said in a nonchalant tone before looking up to see her smirking.

"Still thinking about Donovan huh?" she quizzed as I smacked my lips. She had strangely switched from Team Aaron to Team Donovan once she heard we kissed and it wasn't from me.

"Chill. He's not thinking about me, and I'm not thinking about him," I said with attitude clear in my voice.

"You're half right."

She smiled as I wondered which one of us she was referring to. I bet Donovan couldn't help but bad mouth me. I actually don't blame him this time though.

"There's a place across the street that has good burgers," she continued as she leaned against the counter and looked over at me, "Let's get some from there."

I nodded in agreement, "Okay. Let's go in thirty. I have to finish this up first."

Forty-five minutes later, Tierre and I waited to the side after we ordered our food. She had ordered two extra meals on top of hers and she wanted to drop them off before we went back across the street to the hospital.

"Where do we have to go to drop the food off?" I asked stuffing my hands into my scrub pockets as she grinned a little.

"Just right next door. I told my friends I'd bring them lunch real quick. I normally eat with them, but I wanted you to join me today. You been looking hella lonely taking your lunches all late," she commented as I laughed a little.

"I'm not lonely! You just go too early and I have a lot of work to do. They run me like a slave at that place."

Tierre chuckled, "They treat all of the nurses like that. Especially the new ones. Ya'll get paid for it though, so I ain't mad," she said taking a sip of her drink.

They called out our order, and we both walked up to the counter to collect our bags. We walked out to the warm California sun, and I followed Tierre down the street. I was intrigued to meet her daily lunch friends.

We approached a tattoo shop, and I smiled to myself. Hopefully her friends could get me the hook up on my first tattoo. I had been meaning to get one ever since I decided to move out here especially after being around people with plenty of them.

I followed Tierre inside and instantly felt my heart drop to my stomach when I saw Shane smiling from behind the counter.

"TiTi! Bobbi! What up tho!" Shane yelled putting his arms in the air. I was glad it was just him and not his big headed friend.

"Sup boy. Got your food," Tierre greeted placing the two bags on the counter.

"Thanks. He finishing up," Shane said instantly opening the bag.

I looked around the shop and admired all of the body art plastered on the walls trying to decide what I wanted my first tattoo to be. I definitely wanted it to be symbolic and special.

"Aww shit! You trynna get tatted Bobs?!" Shane asked as I turned and smiled before nodding.

"Yeah, just not sure what to get just yet. I'm definitely going to come back though," I said turning back around and continuing to admire the art.

"Oh word? You should have Don do it for you. He's sick with the tattoos."

I furrowed my brows before turning to face his direction, "Don..?" I questioned aloud before I saw him appear out of the back with a young man who was admiring the freshly inked tattoo on his shoulder.

"Good look D! This shit is hard cuz!" the guy exclaimed excitedly as he started to pull some money out of his pocket. Donovan looked up, caught my stare, and instantly rolled his eyes.

He walked up to Tierre and placed a soft kiss on her forehead, "Hey booty. You get me the number 5?" he asked walking up to the extra bag of food on their counter.

Tierre smiled proudly. "Yup. Your fave."

Don continued to look in the bag and popped a fry in his mouth before directing his attention towards his customer.

"Aye, that'll be $125 boss," he said to him as the guy counted the money and handed it to Don.

"That's $150 bro. Keep the change as a tip. I'll be back to get the rest of my sleeve," he said dapping Donovan up with his un-tatted arm then making his way out of the shop.

Donovan finally looked back up at me, "Sup mean girl."

I gave a small wave before looking at Tierre and Shane who were both looking between the two of us. It was the first time any interaction had taken place in weeks.

"Aye Shane, can we eat this in your office?" Tierre asked as he quickly nodded picking up his bag.

"Hell yeah. Let's crack the door open a little. I wanna hear this shit," he cheesed as she giggled before they disappeared out of the room. I just shook my head. They weren't slick for that.

"They're childish as hell," Don said shaking his head as he plopped down on one of their couches and took his food out of the bag. He looked up at me, "Sit down."

I wanted so bad to react, but I chose not to. I simply just sat down on the chair across from him and crossed my legs with my bag of food clutched tightly in my hands. He looked up at me and chuckled lightly.

"Eat weirdo. Quit looking mad. You know you're happy that I'm talking to you again," he teased as I rolled my eyes. I could honestly care less if he was talking to me again.

"You just think you know me so well," I huffed shaking my head in disbelief as he sat up and looked at me close.

"You wear everything on your sleeves. You don't hide as well as you think you do," he replied smoothly. This was the second time he told me something like that.

"Or maybe, no one pays attention to me as much as you do. Creep," I shot back as he smiled.

"Maybe," he answered taking a bite of his burger. I debated back and forth in my mind on whether or not I was going to tell him that I remembered. I eventually decided against it.

"Bobbi's not your real name either," he said randomly after he finished chewing.

I shrugged, "You're not the first person to figure that out."

"Yeah, but I bet I'm the first one who knows what it's short for," he smirked as I cut my eyes in his direction.

"You have no idea what it's short for. It's not obvious."

His smiled widely, "Oh it's not? Barbara-" He uttered as I quickly jumped on top of him to cover his mouth. *How the hell did he figure that out?*

I was resting in his lap and my hands were clamped over his lips as he laughed on the other side of them.

"How did you know that?!" I gritted as he continued to laugh. Him thinking this was funny irritated me. He finally found the strength and will to remove my hands from his mouth.

"Relax! Why you get all jumpy with that name?" He chuckled as I calmed down a little not even realizing I was still sitting on him. He placed one hand over my legs and the other arm was draped on the back of the couch.

"It was my great grandmother's name. My mom named me after her because she died a week before I was born. My dad gave me the nick name Bobbi. It's just old sounding and ugly," I confessed looking him in his eyes, "How did you figure that out?"

He moved some hair from out of my face as he looked at me, "That's for me to know." he said innocently biting his bottom lip. This connection we had to each other was so strange. I wanted to punch him but give him a hug at the same time.

We both jumped when we heard the front door chime and yelling right after.

"The hell is this?!" she yelled as Donovan and I both let out a sigh of irritation.

Stacy.

We didn't budge as she continued to look at us crazy; acting like we were sitting here having sex on this sofa.

"Don. Seriously?" Stacy asked with a hurt expression resting upon her face.

She had potential to be very beautiful; her attitude was just so ugly.

"Stacy chill the hell out. Ain't nobody even in here doing shit," he said with aggression as I decided to stand up. It was nearing the end of our lunch break anyway.

"What do you mean?! She's sitting in your lap Donovan! You don't find that disrespectful?" she asked pointing to me.

My eyes traveled from her and onto Tierre and Shane coming from the back. They were both looking at the scene questionably.

"Uh. No, I don't find it disrespectful. You and I are *not* together Stacy. Get that through your big ass head! I already told you what it was between me and you..."

I started drowning out their argument looking over to Tierre. We both made the "I'm ready to go face" and headed towards the exit.

"Hit me up later Donovan," I winked at him just to piss her off even more. I wasn't going to give her the satisfaction of me reacting to this. Don and I weren't anything just as much as they weren't.

She looked angrily at me before looking back and getting all in his face. I just laughed at the whole thing while we exited the shop.

"She's stupid," I said shaking my head.

Tierre agreed with my statement.

"She's desperate and pathetic is what she is. Don makes it clear to her every time that he doesn't want her. He's never even taken the girl on a date. Yet, she makes a fool of herself over him every gotdamn time. That dick must be *bangin*," she said while our feet came to a halt at the stop light waiting to cross the street.

"Mm. I'm good on that. He got too many crazies around him," I said shrugging nonchalantly. Tierre looked over and smiled at me, her long natural waves blowing in the wind.

"When's the last time you had sex Bobbi? Two years ago?" she asked as I affirmed. She laughed, "Don would turn yo little ass *out*!"

My mouth dropped, "No, the hell he wouldn't. I may not have had sex in a minute, but I'm freaky as hell. I would be turning him out. I run shit in the bedroom."

She shook her head, "Looks like you don't do nothing but talk shit. I like ya'll though. Ya'll cute whether you realize it or not." She smiled.

I gave a small grin not wanting to confirm or deny.

"Hey...do you know what happened between him and Aaron? Neither of them really get in depth about the situation," I asked as we were given the signal to cross the busy intersection.

She frowned a little, "Um... Donovan was really close to this girl in back in the day. They used to play the whole "we're best friends" card, but the whole crew knew better. At least, so I thought. He was really head over heels for the girl. I think mainly because he lost his virginity to her. I don't think they meant for it happen but it happened." she explained while I listened intensely, "Well, needless to say things got a little awkward after that because he had stopped calling her for like weeks and would avoid her any chance he could and out of nowhere he came trying to be in a relationship with her. She turned him down because she had fallen hard for Aaron after they messed around. That girl was a hoe anyway. All Aaron did was have sex with her, but once Donovan found out, he snapped. They got into a little fight and never talked after again. Donovan has been heartless ever since, especially because all of it happened around the same time his mom died. I haven't seen him connect with someone...until now," she finished looking up at me as I looked at her confused.

"You think, me?" I asked pointing to myself.

We walked through the hospital parking lot at this point.

"I know you and honestly I couldn't tell you why. Maybe because you reject him or it may just be a simple connection, but he's...soft with you. You may not see it, but I see the way he acts towards women constantly, and he could give a care-less. With you...he tries. He doesn't want to be on your bad side, yet he just always ends up there and it frustrates him," she told me as I took in her words.

"No one irks me the way he does. I'm normally good at just blowing people off, but he takes me to ten so quickly sometimes. I usually don't even care enough to get mad at someone," I sighed walking into the front of the building.

"Ya'll are more alike than you think. You should really give him a chance simply because for whatever reason he wants one."

"Well, until he fully expresses that to me, on a sober night then I'm not pressed."

Donovan.

I got a little sad on the inside watching Tierre and Bobbi walk out. Stacy always gotta come and ruin shit for me. I was tired of her.

"Why don't you look at me like that huh?! Out of these last four months, I've *never* seen you look at me the way you just looked at her. Not even in the bedroom! You really don't give two shits about me do you?!" she cried as I crossed my eyes. She was making my head hurt.

"Stacy. You have to stop popping up on me dude. This shit is getting old. I'm really tired of this," I said shortly. Her face softened and she reached out to grab my arm. *Here we go.*

"I'm sorry baby. What do you want me to do? What do I have to do to be good enough for you huh? All I want is to be enough and you reject me at every turn. I've never acted like this with anyone, and I've never wanted anybody as bad you. Why won't you just accept me? Why am I not enough?"

She looked pathetic pleading for my affection like this. I couldn't continue to keep doing this to this girl. She had gotten too attached, "Find somebody better than me Stace. I don't want a relationship. I don' see myself wanting one for a while. What I want you to do is move on. Stop calling me, stop showing up to where I work, stop popping up at my house. When I first met you, you were so strong and confident, and now you're selling yourself short. Chasing somebody that doesn't want to be chased," I explained in the calmest way possible. I didn't want to hurt her feelings, but she had to know the truth. This was a dead end road.

Her green eyes were piercing into mine as she let my arm go, "So. That's it. You're pretty much telling me I'm wasting my time?" She asked.

I hesitated a little before nodding. I wanted to apologize, but I couldn't force the words out of my mouth; not once did I lead her on to believe different. This was the choice she had made. I couldn't feel remorse.

"You're a piece of shit Donovan! A worthless piece of shit! I hope I'm allowed to see the sad day when a woman breaks your heart," she said coldly before flicking me off and storming out.

Shane walked up placing his hand on my shoulder, "Thank Heavens you let that psycho bitch go." He said while shaking his head.

I let out a sigh of relief, "Yeah. Just hope her crazy ass stay gone this time."

"But uh...what's up with you and Bobs though?! What you gonna do about that?" I shrugged walking back to the couch to finish my food.

He looked at me funny. "What? Anybody with eyes can see that ya'll feeling each other." he said sitting in the chair across from me.

"I ain't finna chase Bobbi. I don't chase girls, and she barely wanna be chased. She can't even admit that she remembered that we kissed, and I know her ass remembers. I'll be around. Just only when she's ready to be real."

Shane nodded before he spoke again. "Ok, and what are you gonna do when that happens?"

I took a bite of my burger and thought about it, "I honestly...don't know."

Bobbi.

I was in my room bored as hell editing photos and preparing for work the next day. I looked at the time on my phone and saw that it was only 8 PM.

"This can't be life," I sighed to myself aloud lying back on my bed staring up at the ceiling. I wanted company, so I decided to go and bother Jay knowing he probably wasn't doing anything but playing video games in the basement.

I walked down the steps to the basement and was instantly greeted by smoke and loud music. I waved the smoke out of my face a little while making my way downstairs. When I reached my destination, I saw Jay, Shane, and Donovan all concentrating hard on the TV. Shane and Jay played the game while Don just watched.

I walked further into the room and all three men looked in my direction. Jay kissed his teeth, Shane grinned, and Don just looked at me quickly before looking back at the game. I was disappointed in his response.

Jay paused the game before looking up at me, "What you want chump?"

I shrugged before sitting down on the couch next to Jay. Donovan and Shane were sitting on the love seat.

"I'm bored," I pouted.

Jay groaned and started the game back up, "Nobody gives a damn that you bored B," Jay commented.

I crossed my eyes before sneaking a peek over at Don who was still focusing on the game. I wondered why he wasn't paying any attention to me. I wondered even more why I wanted his attention.

"How's the new job Bobs? You should come and have lunch with us more often," Shane said making conversation as he furiously pressed buttons on the controller.

"Oh, uh it's good. Learning a lot, and I don't know. Don't want to impose on ya'll," I said looking in Donovan's direction who was now texting on his phone. His attitude was irritating me.

94

Shane turned up his nose, "Impose? Yeah right. Don was asking when was the next time you was gon' shoot through," he smirked before receiving an evil look from Donovan.

"You talkin shit. I ain't say that," he responded rudely as I looked at him weird. He caught my stare but dismissed it continuing to text on his phone.

"Ha. Told you," I smiled at Shane who was too into the game to even respond. He was losing to Jay at this point.

I felt awkward, so I gave a small sigh and got up. I was happy to see Don at first, but now, I just didn't care.

I made my way upstairs and into the living room to turn on the TV. Guess I was just going to cuddle up on the couch, in my lonesome, like I do every night. This was quickly getting old. I could've had this life in Ohio. I didn't need to come out to California to realize things weren't going to change.

I flipped through the channels and stopped when I saw Family Guy. I laughed at a joke when I felt someone plop on the couch next to me. I looked over instantly rolling my eyes.

"What are you doing up here?" I asked with much attitude receiving a shrug from Donovan.

"Looked like you needed some attention," he smirked looking over at me. It got under my skin that he could pick up on me so well.

"Well you're wrong," I replied making myself more comfortable on the couch.

"Am I? You come all the way downstairs where you knew your cousin would be to announce you're bored. See no one's really paying attention to you, so you cop an attitude and march up the steps. That wasn't a cry for attention?" he asked as I looked over at him.

All I could focus on were his lips. His bottom lip was so full and plump with a couple tiny freckles scattered across them mirroring the ones on his cheeks and nose.

I snapped out of it and shook my head, "No. It wasn't, and how could you tell anyway? You weren't paying me any mind."

He smirked, "Oh so you were watching me huh?"

I shook my head, "No. I wasn't."

I directed my attention back towards the show hearing a small chuckle escape him.

"You just can't be real to save your life."

I looked back in his direction, "What's that supposed to mean?"

"You frontin. I already know you're crushing on me," he said slyly.

My eyes widened with shock.

"Just like I know you're crushing on me too. I just don't want to put up with your bullshit," I replied as he furrowed his brows.

"What's my bullshit?"

"I watch the way you treat women Don. I'm not like those other girls. I'm not blind to the way you are. I've been through enough, so I refuse to tolerate any nonsense."

He stared intensely into my eyes causing my body to slightly shiver under his watch.

"You think I treat you like them? Me and you may bicker a little, but I don't treat you like them," he said softly.

Everything in me could feel that he didn't even want to admit that.

"What's so special about me then?" I questioned.

He was quiet for a moment seemingly reading into the depths of my soul.

"I don't know yet. That's what I keep trying to figure out. Your stubborn self won't give me a chance to," he said causing me let out a short laugh.

We were both quiet for a moment until he spoke up, "You hungry?"

I hesitated before I nodded my head, and he quickly stood up from the couch, "Let's go get some food then. I'm buying," he said walking out of the living room as I followed him with my eyes.

"So...like a date?" I snickered wondering what his response was going to be. I'm sure anything but that.

He grabbed his keys off the kitchen counter and smiled at me, "Like a date."

Donovan.

I snuck a peek at Bobbi and watched her look over the menu that was lying on the table; she stared into it intensely. She looked so pretty tonight. Her smooth brown skin seemed to glow underneath the reflection of light, and her straightened hair flowed effortlessly with each move she made. Her full lips curved to the side while wrinkling her small nose as if she was deciphering what she wanted. I couldn't help but just take it all in.

"So," she started while tucking a piece of hair behind her ear continuing to browse the selections, "You take all your hot dates to pizza joints?"

She looked up and flashed that beautiful smile of hers revealing her high cheekbones causing me to smile too.

"This is my favorite New York Style pizza place. They have the best pizza on earth I swear," I exaggerated as she chuckled.

The waiter came back to our table and took our orders. I ordered a slice of meat lovers and Bobbi got a slice of pineapple and ham.

I watched her take a sip of water while looking around the slightly packed diner before she looked back at me.

"Last time you've been on a date?" she questioned forcing me to think on the idea.

"Damn...I don't know. It's been some years though. Back in high school, chicks wouldn't let you get to third base without a date," I admitted honestly earning a giggle.

"You really haven't taken somebody out on a date since high school?"

I shook my head "no."

"Not even Stacy?"

I scrunched up my face, "Hell no. Her ass would just always end up at the same places as me. Stacy was never girlfriend material."

"Oh really? And what's girlfriend material?" she inquired as I shrugged.

"Couldn't tell you. Never had one. I just know who isn't," I responded flatly.

She nodded slow while smirking at me, "I think I'm starting to figure you out."

I tipped a brow, "What's there to figure out?"

"You're afraid to get close to people, women, I should say, because you feel like every woman you love will leave you, whether it is physically or emotionally." she said softly as hearing those words gave me goose bumps. It was a realization about myself I had chosen to ignore for a long time. Wasn't ready to get that deep with Bobbi yet, at least not about me.

"Yea. Anyway. Your last date?"

She chuckled and shook her head, "Ok. Changing the topic because that was too real for you."

I gave her a sly grin as she cleared her throat before speaking. "Mine was about a year ago."

My eyes shot open, "A year ago? For real? I would've thought you swore men off forever,." I teased as she rolled her eyes.

"Yeah, well this girl from school had set me up on a "blind date" with her cousin. Worst date of my life," she groaned.

I smiled with anticipation to know more, "Word? What happened?!"

She smacked her lips, "First off. Dude ain't even have a car, so I had to pick him up from this random ass I-Hop. He was ghetto as hell. Loud. Being rude to the waiter. Pretended that there was hair in his food and said he left his wallet at home, so I would have to pay for my own meal," she answered bitterly.

I was in tears from laughing so hard, "I can see your evil ass looking at him mad as hell!"

I laughed as she joined me.

"Man I was! I was so annoyed you don't even understand. Gone have the nerve to ask me on a second date. I was so angry after that," she growled, as I smiled at the cute annoyed expression she had on her face.

She looked up at me and smiled sweetly, "What made me so special that you invited me to accompany you to get food? We barely get along."

I stared into her deep brown eyes, "I don't know. You're different to me. Something about you keeps me coming back always wanting to make it right. That's not like me at all."

"I can tell," she bit her cheek a little before she spoke again, "I wanted to tell you that...I'm sorry for how I reacted to you that morning."

My eyes widened at her words pressing my fingers against the back of my right ear, "What was that? I didn't catch it."

She crossed her eyes, "I said I'm *sorry*. I ended up remembering later that day and felt dumb for how I treated you."

"I knew you remembered the day you came in the shop," I said smoothly; her brows sunk to the middle of her forehead.

"How?"

"You were responding to me better. More apologetic. Wasn't being the typical jerk that you normally are."

She nodded before revealing a small smile, "You're a good kisser." Her compliment made my heart skip a beat.

"You're a really good kisser yourself."

We stared shyly at each other for a few moments before our slices of pizza arrived. Hers smelled amazing.

She bowed her head for a few short moments before she picked up her pizza to take a bite. She laughed when she saw me staring at her closely.

"You want a bite? Damn! All up in me and my food's business!" She laughed as I did too. She held the pizza in my direction, "Have some. Open your mouth."

I did as I was told, and she placed the tip of the pizza in my mouth so I could take a bite. Her pizza was good as hell!

"Damn that's good! What made you pick that combo?" I asked chewing on the food as she smiled and began to eat.

"It's my mom's favorite. I like the sweet tang to it from the pineapples. My favorite fruit," she chimed with my mind quickly going south.

I got excited just thinking about her juices tasting like pineapples. I had to calm myself down.

After we finished eating, I watched Bobbi pout while looking down at her watch.

"What's wrong?" I asked as she poked her bottom lip out.

"It's still early. I'm not trynna go back home yet. I'm always in the house. Plus, I don't have to be at work until noon tomorrow," she said in a sad tone.

I thought of an idea.

"Well, we can get a redbox and go back to my house...if you want?" I suggested. I truly had innocent intentions. I just hope she could read them.

"...Okay."

****

I opened the door to my apartment with Bobbi following close behind. She looked around the space nodding her head in approval.

"Damn," she said in surprise as I looked at her questionably.

"What is it?"

"Nothing. It's just so...clean. Wasn't expecting that for a 23 year old man's house."

"Well yeah. I have OCD, so I'm peculiar about my shit." I chuckled motioning my head towards my room, "We can watch this in my room. The DVD player is built into the flat screen."

She nodded and took off her shoes at the door before following me down the hallway to the bedroom.

"Such a man's room," she chuckled as I smiled to myself and walked to the TV to put the movie in.

"You mind if I dim the lights...or no?" I asked after turning the movie on and walking by the light switch.

"You can turn them off if you want. The TV has enough light," she said sitting on the bed. I cut the light off and joined her.

We had argued over a movie to watch when trying to select one, so we both just settled on <u>The Avengers</u>. Neither one of us had seen it. I used the remote to hit play and got more comfortable as the movie began. Bobbi wasn't slick. She kept inching her way closer to me by pretending to stretch and get comfortable. I chuckled in my mind before pulling her close and wrapping her in my arms. I wasn't really the type to cuddle, but I did it simply because I could tell she wanted me to. She snuggled close to me resting her head on my chest as I held her closer and began to gently rub my hand up and down her arm. I felt like a sap, but it wasn't stopping me from showing my affection. Bobbi was turning into something more for me; someone I genuinely liked being around.

I was alert and awake during the entire movie. I loved action and adventure type of films, Bobbi on the other hand, was out cold. When the movie ended, I looked at the time then back at her trying to decide if I was going to wake her up to go home. She looked so peaceful and nothing in me wanted to, so I pulled the covers back and carefully placed her legs underneath them. She stirred a little in her sleep getting more comfortable against the pillow. I was preparing to walk out and sleep on the couch when I heard her voice vaguely call out.

"Don't leave," she whispered causing me to turn around to look at her.

Her eyes were still closed, but I knew she had heard me attempting to leave the room.

I sighed stripping out of my pants and hooded sweatshirt climbing into bed behind her. I couldn't believe I was doing this but none of it felt wrong. I wrapped my arms around her small frame pulling her close to me taking in her scent. Within moments, I was drifting off to sleep.

Bobbi.

I stretched a little before blinking my eyes open adjusting to where I was. I was slightly confused at first until I remembered my date with Donovan and felt his arms wrapped tightly around my waist. I hadn't slept with someone in years, and it was the best sleep I had had since then. Being engulfed in someone's warm embrace and to feel the care in it, was everything. I wanted to do something nice for him to show my gratitude. Back in the day, Jo would wake up to morning sex, but I didn't know Donovan like that, and he damn sure wasn't getting that from me, so breakfast would have to do.

I carefully removed Don's arms from around my waist and slid out of the bed before tip toeing out in the hallway. I quietly closed the door behind me and then made my way into the kitchen.

I opened his fridge looking for anything I could find to make a decent meal with. I decided to cook him steak and eggs with hash browns and freshly cut fruit on the side. I got to work preparing his meal and smiled to myself thinking about our night. Don was stubborn and stuck in his ways at times, but I enjoyed the small little soft spot he had for me. I was growing one for him too and couldn't explain my reasoning for allowing it.

While I was preparing to scramble the eggs, I felt my phone buzzing in my pocket and rolled my eyes when I saw it was Jay calling.

"What you want?" I answered placing the phone between my ear and shoulder so I could continue cooking.

"Where the hell you at? Why I wake up and you still gone?" he questioned my annoyance rising.

"I'm a grown woman Jay. Don't question me."

"You're a grown woman in a new city. You don't know how people are out here man."

"I'm at Donovan's. I'm cool," I replied flatly adding salt and pepper to the eggs.

"Donovan?! What?! Ya'll fucking now?!" he growled as I smacked my lips.

"Hell no! I just fell asleep over here. He slept on the couch," I lied. Jay was already too much in my business, and he was throwing me off.

"Man, wait till I see-"

I cut him off, "I gotta go Jay. I'll see you at the house later. Bye," I said quickly hanging up. Finding an apartment was going to be first on my list of things to do when I got off work. I apparently couldn't find my own way still living in the same house as my suddenly overprotective cousin.

I was carefully fixing Donovan's plate to look as appetizing as possible when I saw him walk into the hallway scratching his stomach and looking questionably at me before he smiled.

"Morning Gorgeous," he greeted causing the blush to settle underneath my cheeks.

I had never heard him compliment me before. It meant everything coming from him.

I tucked some hair behind my ear and smiled, "I uh...made you some breakfast," I said picking up the plate and walking towards the table. He looked at the plate and his eyes widened.

"Damn! You just cooked this?! Out of my kitchen?" he asked quickly sitting down in front of it.

I chuckled before I nodded, "Yeah, I wanted to thank you for allowing me to stay the night last night."

"Shit, you can stay every night if you gon make breakfast every morning. Didn't even have to lay it down," he joked.

I chuckled lightly before walking back into the kitchen to put some eggs and hash browns on my plate. I carried my items back over to the table and sat down next to him. He prayed over our food and we began to eat.

"I think I like going on dates now," he confessed before blushing at me.

"Oh really?" I asked while taking a sip of my apple juice. He quickly nodded.

"Going out with you was cool last night. It's not so bad. Good food and good company can never be a bad thing," he replied cutting into his steak. He took a bite and moaned a little, "This is cooked perfect!"

"Thanks. I'm pretty domestic," I chuckled as he looked over at me.

"You are. I'm not used to women like you. Your ex was dumb as hell. You're a man's dream."

He looked shocked at himself that he admitted that to me, and I just smiled. This was new and weird for him and I could tell. It was weird for me too.

"Um, what time do you have to be at work?" he asked changing the subject.

I looked at my watch, "Noon to eight today."

"You want me to give you a ride? I have to be at the shop around that time too. I'll just take you home to get ready and stuff," he offered as I shrugged.

"Sure. I'd like that."

Donovan.

I kept looking at Bobbi out of the corner of my eye while driving towards the shop after I had taken her home to change. The blue color of her scrubs brought out her brown complexion. She was pretty in whatever she wore.

"It's still kinda early, so you can park at the shop if you want. When it gets closer for me to go to work, I'll walk over there," she randomly said noticing we were getting closer to the street we worked on.

I smiled to myself because I knew she wasn't ready to leave me just yet. I didn't want her to go either. I parked in my usual parking spot, and we got out the car. I was doing my best not to act weird around her. This letting your guard down shit was still kind of new. As we walked towards the door, she turned to say something to me, "So about last night. I think we should-"

Shane swung the doors open and looked sternly at me, "You're late."

Bobbi and I both directed our attention towards him, and he smiled at her, "Hey Bobs. You look nice."

She chuckled shaking her head before heading into the shop, and I gave Shane a perturbed look. He fucked up our moment.

"What?" he asked as I continued to mug him.

"Bruh, you're blocking," I scolded.

He looked at me strangely, "Blocking what?! Ya'll ain't doing shit. You got a customer, Yasmin." He shrugged before he turned and walked into the shop.

I shook my head following close behind.

"Heyyy Donovan," a thick exotic woman cooed. I looked her up and down before looking around for Bobbi. She was skimming through a book of pictures.

"Uh, hey. You trynna get a tatt?" I asked the sexy stranger receiving a smirk followed by a nod from her.

"Yeah, I was referred by a friend. Heard you were the best," she said seductively biting her lip. Bobbi looked at the two of us, and all of a sudden, I felt uncomfortable. I didn't want her to see how I was with clients for some reason.

"I was thinking," the girl started pulling down the brim of her pants and rubbing her hand over her waist, "That you can do something sexy right here. I'm not sure what though." She knew what she was doing and my dick was slowly falling for the bait. I had to get out of this situation.

"Okay, pick out what you want and I'll be back to get you set up," I told her as she smirked.

"You wanna come with me to my office?" I asked Bobbi before receiving confirmation from her. I placed my hand on her waist guiding her back there feeling eyes being burned in the back of my head by my client.

Bobbi laughed when I closed the door behind her.

"What?"

She chuckled shaking her head at me, "You're funny," she said simply causing me to raise a brow.

"How so?"

"I'm not your girlfriend Donovan. You don't have to remove me from a situation that you think would be awkward for me. You're an attractive guy; I can understand why any girl would be open with her lust towards you," she replied while looking around my office. She stopped and picked up one of the few pictures I had up. It was of me and my mom.

"She's beautiful," she said admiring the picture before putting it down.

I felt that she was burning to inquire more about her, but she stopped herself, probably for the best.

"I felt uncomfortable," I admitted as she looked up at me. I wasn't letting what she said go.

"You shouldn't. We had a nice date, but I understand, you know?" she said looking up at me. I knew what she meant, but in reality she didn't understand. I barely even understood.

"Don't do that," I said shaking my thoughts and really analyzing her words.

"Do what?"

"Downplay my feelings like you know what they are. You don't know how I'm feeling. I'm okay with feeling uncomfortable with someone flirting with me in front of you," I explained.

She folded her arms over her chest in a protective manner. She really wasn't ready for what this could mean.

"But maybe I'm not. We don't know each other well enough, and this whole thing is still new. I don't want you to get caught up in the idea of me until you know the real me," she said as I chuckled in disbelief.

"Do you even know the real you?" I asked her.

She twisted her face at me, "Do you?"

I wanted so badly to confess that I only do this when I'm with her, but fuck it. I wasn't going to go the extra mile and continue to put myself out there if she was fearful of me to do so. Last night was one of the best nights I've had with a female in a long time, and she had no idea of how much it meant for me to let her stay, let alone, hold her the entire night without trying shit. She wasn't ready for that Donovan, and personally, I was starting not to want to even give her that.

I remained silent causing the awkwardness to flood the room. She sighed before looking at her phone.

"I should probably go," she said going for the door as I made no attempt to stop her; just followed her out. I can't chase someone who doesn't truly want to be chased. At least, that's what her actions were telling me— I knew her heart was speaking a different language.

We reached the door, and she turned to say "goodbye" before I pulled her into my arms, gently lifted her chin, and planted my lips on top of hers. I didn't care who was looking just needed her to realize what she was passing up, and if we didn't get it together, we were going to have problems.

I removed my lips from our intimate exchange and looked into her eyes, "Don't push me away before I even have a chance to get close," I said softly before turning around and leaving her there dumbfounded.

Bobbi was playing. I may need to give her space to get her mind together.

Shane and my client both looked at me strangely as I smirked at the two of them.

"You pick out what you wanted?" I asked her.

She gave me a soft nod, so I motioned for her to follow me into one of the back rooms. She handed me the picture, and I took it from her so I could scan it.

"Your girlfriend is pretty..." she said quietly probably out of embarrassment causing me to look in her direction.

"Thanks."

****

Shane and I were closing up the shop after a long busy day. I hadn't stopped doing tattoos and piercings since I walked in that morning.

"Yo, so what happened with Bobbi? Why ya'll arrive together?" he asked watching me wipe down all of the couches and chairs in the front room.

"I took her to get some food last night when we left Jays, and she uh...stayed over," I said casually receiving a strange look from Shane.

"She what? You let her stay at your crib bruh?!" he asked to confirm as I nodded.

"Seriously! So I'm sure you hit then right?" he questioned as I shook my head, "The hell? Who are you and what have you done with my best friend?"

I shrugged, "I'm not the same when it comes to her man. I try so hard to act like I don't give a fuck when really I do. Something about her is different," I said shaking my head as Shane did the same.

"She got you right where she want you," he assured me.

I nodded in agreement, "She's starting to. Which is why I'm finna fall back. Bobbi ain't ready for what all I was willing to give her. I need to know that she wants me too, so until she starts showing me that, I'm chilling."

"You get that fine bitch's number earlier? That Yasmin chick?" he asked me changing the subject as I shook my head.

"Nah."

"Why the hell not?! She was willing to fuck you outside!" he proclaimed.

I shrugged my shoulders, "Ain't want her. She was sexy, but her approach was too obvious." I told him as he gave me a straight face.

"Uh. We *like* obvious. Man, Bobbi got you slippin. You finna be out here with desert dick dealin wit her."

I smirked, "Nah, not for long. Bobbi a freak."

He scrunched up his face at me, "How you know?"

"I can tell she's the type of girl that likes to please her man in every way possible. She's already catered to me and cooked me breakfast. She definitely caters in the bedroom as well. I know what I'm holding out for. I won't be disappointed."

"So you really ain't gonna have sex until you hit Bobbi?!" he questioned as I gave him a crazy look.

"I ain't say all that! I just ain't gone try her until she ready for me. I still got my needs. Ion don't like to use my hands," I finished as my mind instantly went to Lynn. I knew I could always give her a call.

Bobbi.

"So....ya'll ain't have sex? I'm still trying to wrap my brain around this," Tierre asked for the fourth time as I chuckled and shook my head.

Her shift was over and she was at the nurses' station bothering me until Aaron came to pick her up.

"Nope. He held me all night like a gentleman."

Her eyes widened at that, "That just does not sound like Don in the *least*. For one, you stayed at his house. He ain't never even let *me* stay at his house, and for two, he didn't try shit. He likes you."

I sighed, "I know, and that scares me."

"Why?" she inquired as I let out another small sigh.

"Just don't want to get hurt. I thought I did everything right in my last relationship and still got cheated on. Plus, I really don't think I'm his type."

"He spooning with your ass, you're his type. Stop dismissing yourself. He kissed you before you came over here, and he doesn't kiss people. I know deep down, Don has the potential to be a good guy, and for whatever reason, he wants to be that with you. Take the opportunity."

I scrunched up my nose, "Don't know if I'm ready."

She smacked her lips, "Don't expect him to wait around for you to be. Don't be mad when you see another girl tuggin at his shirt. Just saying." She finished up as Aaron walked up smiling at the two of us.

He strolled over and gave me a warm kiss on the cheek before greeting Tierre.

"What ya'll over here yappin about?" he asked.

I kept my lips zipped. Tierre had other plans.

"Her and Donovan went out last night!" she blabbed as I shot her an evil look. "What?"

Aaron furrowed his brows before looking at me, "Donovan? Thought ya'll hated each other?" he asked earning a small shrug from me.

111

"He's not so bad..." I said in a small voice feeling his eyes on me. For some reason, I really didn't want him to know about Donovan and I.

"Hmm...guess we got a lot to catch up on then." He smirked.

I gave a nervous grin, "Guess so."

****

"So," Aaron started as I looked across at him at the table. He had invited me out to lunch on one of our off days, "What's all this I'm hearing about you and Don?"

I shrugged my shoulders before looking down at the menu, "It wasn't anything serious. We went out, and I haven't even heard from him since." I said flatly.

Truth was not hearing from him was bothering me, but I wasn't about to budge and hit him up first.

He chuckled, opening his menu, "That doesn't surprise me one bit. Don is like that."

I was intrigued to know more. Most of the people I had surrounded myself with were always praising Donovan. I wanted to know the truth about him.

"Really? Why doesn't it surprise you?"

He smirked at me before lightly shrugging his right shoulder, "He just is. That's how me and ol' girl happened back in the day. Donovan was always leading her on and then backing up when shit got real. She was fed up by the time he actually wanted to voice how he felt. To us, he would play it like they were just friends and eventually she started believing it. Didn't see any future in it, so she stopped messing with him and me and her just happened. We were talking one night, about him of course, and she came on to me. I'm a guy. I'm not going to say 'no'. And like I said, he would put it to us like she wasn't anything to him."

Hearing this information from Aaron, now that we had made a connection, made me feel some type of way, especially since I was starting to feel like he was doing the same thing to me.

If Donovan was already attempting to play games, I wasn't trying to involve myself.

"I don't know. I'm just not trying to get hurt in this situation," I admitted crumbling under Aaron's watch.

"Then the last person you need to be dating is Don. Don't get me wrong, you being Jay's cousin probably wouldn't make him 'dog you out', but right now I think all he sees you as is a chase; something new and different," he answered bluntly as I let out a deep breath.

Donovan not speaking to me after our date only confirmed what Aaron was telling me.

"Well, I guess I should let that fade to black huh?"

He hesitated before nodding, "I just don't want to see you get hurt that's all. I mean, I don't talk to Don, so I can't say I know 100 percent what's going on, but if it's anything like what happened with Ashley, which was the last girl I know he cared about, I wouldn't get my hopes up."

Donovan.

I walked through the nursing home doors with flowers in my hand and greeted the woman at the front desk.

"Hey Sophie," she looked up and smiled at me.

"Hey Donovan! I believe Dorothy is in her room right now. She'll be happy to see you," she greeted as I gave a half smirk before making my way down the hall to my Grandmother's room. It was my weekly Tuesday visit with her.

I knocked on the door softly before entering and she looked up with a meek smile present on her face.

"Hi MiMi," I said setting the flowers in her arms before kissing her cheek softly. She continued to look at me closely.

"Danielle's mini me," she said warmly which made my heart smile. She remembered who I was.

"I am. Look just like her," I agreed. She looked back at the television for a few moments and then turned to look at me. She furrowed her brows this time as if seeing me for the first time all over.

"You look like my Danielle. Did you know her?" she asked breaking my heart into pieces.

"Yes MiMi. I knew her..."

****

After leaving my visit with my Grandmother, I headed over to Jay's to help him draw out the new sleeve he wanted to put on his arm. He had been talking about it for months and finally had the balls to get it started. I was nervous about seeing Bobbi at first but then didn't care. After talking to her that day at the shop, she hadn't made any attempts to contact me or even see what was good. Tierre had told me her and Aaron had been kicking it lately anyway. Just happy I saw what she was on before I wasted my time catching feelings.

I pulled up to Jay's and went through the garage since it was open. He was sitting at the table with Lisa. He greeted me with a head nod as Lisa smiled.

114

"Hey baby," she greeted standing up on her toes to plant a kiss on my cheek, "How was your visit with Dorothy?"

She knew I always saw my MiMi on my off days.

"It was...hard," I said simply before sitting down. She nodded empathetically before placing a hand on Jay's shoulder.

"Well, I'm about to go upstairs and catch up on Scandal. If ya'll need anything come get me," she told us before disappearing up the steps.

Jay and I quickly got to work coming up with ideas and drawing some things out. After about thirty minutes he carefully looked at our surroundings before he spoke.

"Yo. Why Bobbi been hanging with Aaron tough lately? I thought ya'll was starting something?" he questioned as I looked at him.

"What you mean hanging tough?" I replied, playing dumb, wanting to get Jay's insight on the situation.

"You know...tough. Like I've seen this dude every day since ya'll went out. Something is coming off like he on some fuck shit. I think he's getting in her head about you or something."

I smacked my lips shaking my head, "It doesn't matter. Bobbi ain't checkin for me. I'm not going to chase someone that makes it clear they're not ready for what all of this could mean. I'm not ready either but I try with her. You know me. I normally don't care."

"Yeah, and I know my cousin. She likes you-"

I quickly cut him off, "I'm not going to kiss your cousin's ass bruh. She's cool, but she wants me to prove all this shit. When all she's proven to me is that she backs up when things get real. I can't deal with someone like that. You know why."

He nodded in understanding. It was quiet for a moment.

"Where is she?" I asked still wanting to see her. *Soft shit*.

"Upstairs in her room," he said looking back at the paper with his future tattoos on it. I quickly stood up and made my way upstairs knowing which one was hers. It was my old room.

I knocked on the door softly and heard some shuffling before she answered the door. Her robe was open revealing her matching lace bra and panty set. She looked surprised to see me; must've thought I was her aunt.

"Damn..." was all I could manage to say quickly running my tongue across my bottom lip.

She rolled her eyes attempting to close the door before I stopped her.

"Quit playing. Let me in," I said softly.

She crossed her eyes holding up her finger signaling for me to give her a moment. I waited, and she came back opening the door with her robe closed tight. She looked good as hell in that bra earlier.

"What are you doing up here?" she asked with attitude crossing her arms.

Here comes Ms. Rudeness.

"You never called me," I said simply stepping towards her a little.

She stayed put, "Phone works both ways."

I let out a sigh in frustration to her response, "Why are you doing this Bobbi? What's Aaron been telling you? Some ol dumb shit about me? To make you even more afraid to talk to me?"

Her face filled with confusion, "How you know I've been talking to Aaron?" she asked as I chuckled.

"People talk, and I'm not stupid. You rather be with him now or something?"

She looked at me crazy, "No! And who even said I wanted to be with you?" she snapped back.

"Who wouldn't?" I teased causing her to groan and looked away.

"You're so full of yourself," she said shaking her head, so I decided to mess with her some more.

"You like it."

"Uh...I don't actually."

I couldn't help but laugh in her face, "Why are you such an asshole to me Barbara? What I do to you?!" I chuckled while she let a small smile become present on her soft brown face, "Just quit

116

playing these games and admit you like the kid already." I said arrogantly as she turned her nose up at me.

"Look I don't know whose pussy you've been up in lately to have you thinkin you're the shit, but you're not."

I laughed, "You really think I've been in some pussy?"

"I know you have. I'm not stupid. I'm sure the girl at the shop got your number that day and the ride of her life," she said with confidence as I just smiled at her.

"Jealous ass."

She smacked her lips, "Far from jealous. Have all the hoes you want," she retorted fanning me off.

She tried to walk away, but I quickly turned her around, pulling her close to me then placed my hand firmly on her lower back. She looked up lightly biting her lip.

"She didn't get my number. I was too stuck on you that day," I said looking down into her eyes.

"Oh yeah? What about the next day?" she asked back with sarcasm.

I backed her up towards the bed, "Nope. No hoes the next day either."

The back of her legs were pressed against the edge of the bed, and I slyly pulled at the belt holding her robe together. It opened allowing me permission to examine her perfect shape and soft skin. I placed my hands on each side of her waist then leaned in to press my lips against hers. Ever since the first time we kissed, I couldn't get enough of how our souls danced every time we physically connected. I came up here to be rude, and here I was back weak.

She fell back onto the bed as her hands firmly gripped around the back of neck deepening the kiss and igniting the fire within us. My hands roamed her body making their way towards her center when a yell from downstairs took us both out of the trance.

"Aye yo Don! Come here!" Jay yelled forcing me to pull my lips unwillingly from hers.

She looked up at me with so much lust and desire in her eyes. I wanted to take things further, but at the same time, I didn't want to confuse her. We'd have our time where we would really rationalize this to see where it was going.

I slowly got up and she did too, tightening her robe back up. No words were exchanged. I just left.

Bobbi.

I sat at the nurse's station, with my left cheek in my palm, looking blankly into space as my mind went crazy with thoughts. I couldn't get the encounter with Donovan out of my head, and the fact that he wasn't answering my phone calls for the past week bothered me as well. Any time I thought we were moving forward, his actions towards me proved we weren't going anywhere at all.

"Hey," Tierre greeted causing me to jump a little, "Damn girl, you alright? You've been acting weird all week."

I sighed placing my hand over my heart trying to cause my heart rate to slow down. I thought she was my supervisor for a quick moment.

"It's Don."

At the mere mention of his name she let out a small groan.

"What his dumb ass do now to mess up something that could potentially be good?" she asked setting her purse down onto the counter. It was one of my midday shifts, so she was getting off at five while I was getting off at eight.

"He's sending me mixed signals. When we're around each other, I can tell he's interested, but when we're not, I don't hear from him. This week I even attempted to call and he hasn't answered or returned them. I just don't understand what he wants me to do or how he expects me to respond to this," I vented as she gave me a remorseful look.

"Don't respond. Move on. Honestly, you've been through one bad situation too many to waste your time liking him. He won't provide the stability you need after being in a bad relationship. If he loses out on you, fuck it. His loss."

I nodded slowly taking in her words. Yes, Aaron and I were getting closer, but it didn't compare to how I felt with and around Donovan. He provided me something that Aaron couldn't. I just hadn't placed my finger on what exactly it was yet.

"You're right. It's a risk. And I guess, if I start dating again...I should play it safe," I said, not even confident in my own response. It was just another thing I was going to force myself to believe until it became true.

We chatted a little more until we saw Aaron coming down the hallway to the station. Tierre didn't have a car, so when he got off work he would always come to pick her up on his way home. I was just waiting to save up enough money to get my car shipped out here so I would be able to take myself to work. Depending on the bus, Auntie, and Jay was getting tiring.

Aaron said something to Tierre in her ear before handing her the keys. She laughed a little and shook her head before looking at me.

"I'll see you Monday B," she said giving me a short wave as I did the same. I looked up at Aaron who was looking back shyly.

"What's with you?" I chuckled while raising a brow. I've never seen him look so nervous.

"Oh. Uh...just wanted to talk to you by myself for a second before we went home," he stumbled scratching the back of his head.

"Okay, well, what's up?"

"Do you...do you have plans tomorrow?" he questioned as I thought about it. I normally had to work Saturdays, but tomorrow I was off.

I shook my head, "Nope. I got the whole day off. Why?"

"Uh. There's this music festival happening in Santa Monica, and I wanted to know if you would like to accompany me to it?" He took a sigh of relief; I'm assuming happy that he got his question out.

"That sounds fun! Why were you so nervous about asking me though? We do stuff like that all the time."

His face remained serious, "Because. I'm not asking you as a friend type thing. I'm asking more so of a...date."

My eyes widened at the last word, "Date? But-"

He cut me off, "Look Bobbi. Over these past few weeks that we've been spending time together, I started to see you in a different light. You're a beautiful person, and I don't want to miss out on an attempt to even see where this could go. I find myself thinking about you constantly and picturing your smile. Just corny shit. I'm not saying you have to feel the same way back, but at least give me a chance."

I was speechless. What he said sounded so right, it was just coming from the wrong person. If Donovan wasn't willing to be the person that Aaron is trying to then I had to move forward; be serious with someone who wanted to be serious with me.

"What time do I have to be ready tomorrow?" I smirked.

Donovan.

"Ay Papi! Yes! Right there Daddy!" Bella moaned as I continued to thrust in and out of her vigorously from behind gripping her hips. She was a Cuban I had met in the shop earlier this week who invited me over to watch movies. That movie was on about two minutes before she began placing kisses on my neck.

I continued my pace until I felt my ejaculation reaching its peak. She had already busted about three times, but I wasn't stopping until I got mine.

"Aw shit," I hissed, before pulling myself out of her, and releasing into the condom.

She sighed collapsing on the bed as I stood up to dispose of the soiled latex in her restroom. While taking a step back from the toilet, I caught a glimpse of myself in the mirror. My eyes were tired and beads of sweat trickled down my wrinkled forehead. Disgust was the emotion present while staring at my reflection.

I took in a deep breath and closed my eyes before adjusting my pants then securing them around my waist. I stepped out of the bathroom and back into her room searching the floor for my shirt.

"Where are you going baby?" Bella asked standing up. She was still fully naked but even that couldn't snap me out of the mood I was in.

"I gotta run," I found my shirt and threw it over my head.

She wrapped her arms around me from behind running her fingers up and down my torso.

"What if I don't want you to go? Stay a little longer," she begged as I stepped from her embrace. I didn't like being held like that. Like a possession.

I found my sneakers and made my feet slide swiftly into them, "I can't."

She pouted, "Why can't you? You basically just got here."

I sighed before looking into her dark brown eyes, "Gotta see my mom."

****

The only sounds present were my shoes walking across the ground navigating their way through the dimly lit cemetery. I clutched the flowers I brought for her tightly in my sweaty palm while my heart rate increased with each step. It had been over a year since the last time I came to visit, and I was ashamed of that fact.

As I stepped closer to her tombstone, my stomach dropped at the sight of her name. I held back the emotion and leaned down to plant the dozen pink roses right in front of the cracking stone.

I stood up shoving my hands in the pockets of my jeans and paced back and forth keeping my eyes from looking at her grave.

"I'm sorry Ma," I choked pacing a little faster and looking towards the sky, "I'm sorry I waited until your birthday to come see you."

I stopped for a moment and put my head down in shame, "You just don't get it. You don't know what it feels like to not have you here. Everything has been bullshit since you left." I covered my mouth as if she was looking directly at me, "I'm sorry for cussing, it's just how I feel. MiMi doesn't even know who I am Momma. She has no idea. She only mentions your name every so often now. I just know pretty soon she's going to be next to leave me. Everything I love leaves me man. It's like some curse on my life. You remember that day Ma? I was four years old, and I think you and my dad had just got done arguing. You were in the kitchen crying a little, and Dad was in the living room with a bottle in his hand. I didn't understand what it was at the time, but I just wanted to make it right. I walked into the living room, and crawled into his lap. He wouldn't look at me, acknowledge me, nothing. I placed my head on his shoulder, and told him I loved him for the first time on my own. He never told me it back before that day. He just looked down at me, rubbed my head, and said he loved me too before he stood up, walked out the door, and we never saw that bastard again."

My fists were balled tightly at this point starting to pace again, "That was the first person Ma. First person I loved to leave me man. Why ain't that man want me huh? I understand ya'll had problems, but why ain't he want me? I ain't do sh-" I caught myself before cursing again, "I didn't do anything. I was four, and I looked up to him because he was my father. Wanted to be just like him, and he left; not a phone call, not a letter, nothing! We don't even know if he's alive or dead. A part of me just hopes he's dead. That's the only excuse I'll accept for him not being here."

I sighed brushing off that memory and continued with my rant. "Then you. You were my world. Everything in my life revolved around you. You were the sweetest person on earth Momma. Always smiled even through the pain and did everything you could for me. And you, of all people had to get breast cancer? You didn't deserve that! I could count tons of people who didn't deserve to walk this earth. You deserved it. You deserved the world placed right at your feet. You were my Queen, and God took you from me. I loved you, and you left. Just like I loved Ashley, and she left. I never told her though, and after all that happened, she didn't deserve to know how I felt."

My legs started to give out with how hard I paced, so I sat down in defeat placing my elbows over my knees.

"I keep disappointing you. I can feel it. The man I am today is not the man you raised me to be. I'm just cold Mom. I don't want to feel because it always hurts in the end. What good is having emotion if it's just going to hurt? I don't understand why these girls choose to care about me, when they see I don't even have the capacity to care about them back."

Bobbi's face instantly came to my mind.

"And the moment I feel something for someone I push them away. Something about Bobbi, Mom. She's so stubborn and hard headed and immune to my arrogance and harsh nature. Probably because she's just like me in so many ways. We hurt the same way, and I can feel that we're supposed to be each other's cure, but every time I think I'm ready, I realize I'm not. I don't want to hurt her. I don't want to cause any more pain in her world. I just want her in mine so bad though. What should I do?" I questioned finally fixing my eyes back on her stone: silence.

"Must still be mad..." I started before being interrupted by my phone vibrating. It was a text from Jay:

Yo. What you into tonight? Bobbi on a date wit Aaron n Im bored!

I read the message over to myself and felt a slight bit of anger rise within me.

"That's my sign huh Ma? History repeating itself. Guess I gotta get it together," I softly chuckled to myself before standing up. I placed a hand on the stone looking at it somberly.

"Thanks for always listening, and showing that you're not mad at me. I...I miss you. More than anyone realizes."

Bobbi.

The car ride back home with Aaron was calm and peaceful, letting the music from his stereo take over the conversation. The festival was fun, something new and different, and I was happy to have experienced that moment with him.

"So," Aaron began interrupting the silence between us, "How are you feeling about everything? Like, how I do?"

I chuckled slightly at his question, "You did good. I had a good time today."

"Did you have a good time like in a friend way, or..." He was so nervous waiting for my response. It was cute.

"I could see this being a common thing. Making new memories with you. Just not trying to rush anything, you know? I like what we've already established, and I want to keep building on that foundation," I answered honestly as he nodded with understanding.

He carefully slid his right hand over to grab my left continuing to drive, "I'm not going anywhere Bobbi. I'll prove to you."

It felt good to hear those words, especially coming from someone I was already starting to trust. Everything he said and did was honest and in good nature.

Moments later we pulled up in my driveway, and I yawned thinking about my bed. I sighed a little before unbuckling my seatbelt locking eyes with my handsome date.

"So. Can I see you again tomorrow?" he questioned bashfully as I smiled and nodded.

"Yeah, Auntie always cooks Sunday dinner. You can just come over for that."

His eyes widened, "What? I'm getting invited to family dinners? That's big."

I let out a small laugh, "I have to ask first, but I'm sure she won't mind. I'll let you know for sure tomorrow."

He chuckled as we both stared at each other mentally figuring out how we were going to say goodbye.

He licked his lips before slowly leaning to my side of the car. I wasn't prepared to kiss him, so when his lips met mine, I was a little thrown off. They were soft but I felt....nothing.

I carefully removed myself from the kiss and forced a smile while looking at the satisfaction on his face.

"See you tomorrow pretty girl," he said biting his lip like he wanted another kiss.

I laughed a little while opening my door, "Bye Aaron."

As usual, the moment I closed the passenger side door, he was already making his way down the driveway. He never waited until I got in the house, and for some reason that bothered me.

I brushed it off, unlocked the door, and stepped into the house walking towards the dining room. I instantly grew irritated seeing Jay and Donovan in the living room. Something about the look on Don's face seemed distant, but I ignored it. Why should I care about him, when he's proven over and over he could give a damn about me?

"How was your date lil' ugly?" Jay asked not taking his eyes off the TV.

I smirked, "Best day I've had since I've been here." I slightly exaggerated just to piss Don off. He seemed unmoved by my presence.

"You kiss him?" Jay snickered as I saw Donovan shift a little in his seat. That got him.

"...He kissed me," I shrugged seeing the two of them flash me a quick glance.

Jay's eyes remained on me though, "Yo, you for real?" he asked as I nodded.

"Yep. Even though who I kiss is none of your business. Now if you excuse me, I'll be in my room. I'm exhausted," I finished turning on my heels and heading up the stairs. I decided to stop in Aunt Lisa's room before I went to mine.

I knocked softly waiting for her permission. Once I got it, I opened the door to see her sitting in the bed with her glasses on reading a book. She smiled when she saw it was me and placed her book down on her night stand.

"Hey baby. How was your time with Aaron?" she asked as I plopped down on the foot of her bed.

"It was fun. Still debating on where I see this going."

She continued to smile at me, "He seems into you. I always knew he liked you since the first time he was over here. He's a very accomplished young man," she complimented as I shrugged a little.

"I'm built more on connection. I don't feel that yet with him."

"Not like how you feel with Don?" she teased as I crossed my eyes.

"Between you and Tierre..."

"We can't help that you guys are cute together," she giggled at the irritated expression resting upon my face.

"Yeah well, I would give up hope on that if I were you Auntie. Don doesn't want me," I sighed standing in an upright position before walking to her side of the bed and placing a kiss on her forehead, "I'll let you get back to your book. Goodnight, love you."

"Love you too baby," she replied nestling back in her bed and opening the book back up. I smiled softly at the sight one last time before heading to my room.

I closed the door behind me and looked around at everything neatly in place. I always made sure to keep my room neat and tidy. I never liked coming home to a dirty resting area.

My feet made their way to my dresser drawers looking for a towel to take with me into the bathroom to wash off today's events. Clutching the towel in my fingertips, I went to turn on the shower and set it to a hot temperature. While undressing, I caught a glimpse of myself in the mirror, and for the first time in a while, smiled at the reflection. The girl in the mirror was a girl I had known long ago. She was feeling content, yet there was still something missing. One piece of the puzzle wasn't complete yet, and there was a daily battle to figure out what it was. Something that was lost in the crossfire had to be restored.

I released those thoughts stepping into my shower to wash away everything else. I would stand in the shower for hours if I could; it was soothing to me. Tonight's shower wouldn't last nearly as long; I was too drained from today to stand on my feet a minute longer.

After scrubbing off the last of the soapy residue, I turned off the shower, wiped my eyes and opened the curtain to reach for my towel. While standing in the tub, I lightly dried my body and then my feet before stepping out. I hated leaving drips of water on the bathroom floor.

I opened the door releasing the steam from one room to the next and a small scream escaped my lips at the sight of Donovan looking at a few paintings hanging on my wall.

"The hell Don?! You couldn't knock or wait until I was dressed to come in here at least?!" I questioned still trying to catch my breath from the fright he gave me.

He laughed still not turning to look in my direction, "Hi to you too."

I smacked my lips staying in place, "Is there something you need? I don't have time for this tonight."

He finally turned to face me and his mouth fell slightly open while admiring me in my towel. I clutched it tightly around my chest looking away to avoid all eye contact.

"Quit trying to imagine what I look like underneath this towel," I groaned walking to my dresser to search for pajamas, "Actually, you can get out while you're at it. I seriously have nothing to say to you."

I grabbed a pair of panties and a tank before making my way back into the bathroom to change. I hoped by the time I was done, he would be gone.

"Come stay with me tonight," he blurted before I could step foot onto the tile floor. I turned and looked at him as if he had two heads.

"No," I shook my head in disbelief.

"Just pack some clothes to wear for tomorrow," he continued as if I hadn't already told him my answer.

"No. I'm not staying with you. I'm not doing shit with you," I said growing agitated, "You think you can just ignore me when I'm not around, but the second you see me everything is supposed to go back to normal? Like I haven't been trying to reach out to you. I work right across the street from you, and you still couldn't say shit. I'm not one to be played with."

"I'm not trying to play with you Bobbi. We don't have to do anything. Kiss, nothing. I just-"

He paused before looking at the floor. His eyes were sad today. There was an emotion behind them, not the usual cold stare I'm used to seeing.

"What happened?" I asked softly, finally lightening up. Even though I didn't feel like he deserved any kindness from me, I couldn't bring myself to continue being mean.

"Um..." He swallowed hard while looking towards to ceiling, anything to avoid my stare, "It's...it's her birthday today, ok? And I just want to be around somebody. Nobody knows what today is but you and Lisa, and I'm tired of always opening up to Lisa about this. I just...I don't wanna be around anyone else but you tonight. No bullshit," he confessed as I just looked at him. I couldn't believe he wanted to share this part of his life with me.

"Ok. I'll come over. Just strictly as friends, okay? I think we should focus on a friendship right now especially since I'm dating Aaron."

I knew it wasn't something he wanted to hear, but he had to know the boundary I was setting. He had his moment where we could've tested to see where things would lead, but he didn't take advantage of the opportunity and that was something I've grown to accept.

He clenched his jaw tight before nodding bitterly, "Coo. I'll be downstairs."

****

The ride to Donovan's apartment was silent. He wasn't playing any music, and he wasn't talking to me either. I didn't even attempt to make conversation with him. I was still back and forth about my decision to come considering the treatment I had been receiving from him lately. I just sat in the passenger seat and texted Aaron, not bothered by how he would feel about it.

He pulled up to the closest parking spot near his building and parked the car. I stepped out and went to the back door to grab my bag, but to my surprise, Donovan had already grabbed it and was making his way to the front door. I sighed a little before following him.

We stepped inside, and I looked around like I did every time I came here. His apartment was always clean with everything in place. To me, that wasn't common for a young bachelor pad.

"I'm gonna set this in the room, but we can chill out here," he told me in his usual raspy tone as I nodded in understanding.

I took a step down into his living room area and made myself comfortable on one of his plush couches. He had a black and red theme in the resting space. His couches were black, but his rugs and curtains had a black and red pattern and his end tables, coffee table, TV stand were all black and glass structured.

A few moments later he returned quickly grabbing the remote off the coffee table to turn the television on. I never allowed my eyes to leave him.

He finally caught my stare flashing a strange look, "What?"

"Why did you invite me over here if you weren't going to speak? You don't want to talk about how you're feeling?"

He shrugged, "I feel numb. Nothing else to say."

"There's a lot to say. She was your mom."

He bit his inner cheek and continued to focus his eyes on the television screen. He and I both knew he wasn't watching it.

"How old were you? When she died?" I asked softly as he cleared his throat.

"I was sixteen. She had been in the hospital for six months before she died. I spent my sixteenth birthday with her. She asked a nurse in the hospital to make me a cake and get me some balloons from downstairs. They all said 'Get Well' and shit like that, but it was the best birthday to me. She did everything she could to make it special, allowed me to skip school, and just sit in there with her all day and watch movies. Doctors weren't even expecting her to be alive for that day, so it was special for both of us."

"I couldn't imagine," I said lowly. The thought of losing my own mother gave me chills.

He shifted in his seat. "I didn't cry when she died. I felt like every bit of emotion that was in me, left when she did. My MiMi and Lisa were all concerned about me because I shut everyone out. I didn't talk and was barely in school. I just dealt with it all internally, I guess," he shrugged picking at his hangnails.

"Your mom and Lisa were really close? I hear her talk about her all the time."

"Yeah, they were the best of friends. Met through Jay's dad because he was trying to hook up my mom with my dad, so supposedly they met and instantly clicked. I lived with Lisa after my mom died until we all graduated. My MiMi got sick around the same time everything went down, so I couldn't live with her."

My eyes widened, "First time I ever heard you say anything about your dad."

"I don't like to mention that piece of shit. I don't know where he is."

I could sense the change of tone, so I left it alone. I know how sensitive that topic can be with men.

It was quiet for a moment as only the sounds of the TV filled the room. After a few more seconds passed, he finally spoke back up.

"What about you? What your parents do?"

I furrowed my brows a bit looking in his direction, "I'm sorry? I don't understand the question."

He laughed a little before lightly licking his lips, "Your break up wasn't devastating for no reason. There was something deeper behind it."

I rubbed my arm a little and shook my head, "Not really. Just that..." I rested my neck on the top of the couch looking over at him.

"Well, tell me about your dad," he suggested locking eyes with me.

"Um, my biological father, I don't really know too much about. I used to see him more when I was younger, kind of, but my younger brother and sisters and I were all raised by my stepfather. He was more of a father to me than my real dad was. That's my Daddy," I smiled thinking of who I claimed as my father.

"When's the last time you saw your real dad?"

"Well before my college graduation, I didn't see him for two years. The last time we saw each other wasn't pleasant," I lightly laughed to keep my spirits up. When I looked at Donovan he seemed to be really intrigued with where this was heading.

"Why? What happened?" he asked as I sighed.

"We just didn't see eye to eye. I hadn't talked to him before that day since he told me he wasn't going to my high school graduation because his son was graduating that same year, and he had to choose one. His wife persuaded him he should go to their child's graduation and not mine," I answered biting my bottom lip.

"Damn, so he had other kids he took care of?"

I nodded, "Yup. I guess him and my mom weren't supposed to be all that they turned out to be. He didn't really want to be with her and wanted to be with his girlfriend, who's his wife now, so their relationship was always shaky. Then she got pregnant with me...so..."

I shrugged to hide the pain that was revealing itself. I never really opened up to anyone about my biological father.

"So what? Did he come and like try to apologize or some shit?" he asked as I shook my head no.

"Nope. That's all I ever wanted from him you know? To own up to the mistakes he made with me as a father. You know what it's like to want somebody to want you so bad? And they just don't? That man had the nerve to tell me that I should grow up and quit being a baby about the situation. He told me the truth about him and my mom and said I wasn't meant to happen. Tried to tell me he loved me, but if he could take it back-" I sucked in a deep breath and quickly jabbed at the tear that tried to trickle its way down to my cheek.

"How do you tell your child, that if they could erase you, they would? I get he didn't love or want to be with my mom, but I did nothing wrong. I didn't ask to be here Don. I didn't ask for him to mess with her and get her pregnant. None of that. Up until that point, I thought I was worth it. I thought I deserved to be here on this earth. I had so much self-value, even with him not really being in my life. I had my Daddy: the man who raised me and treated me as his own. I didn't need him. The only thing I needed him for was to give me life and for him to say to my face that he didn't even want to give me that... It hurt like hell," I choked out containing all the emotion.

Don was quiet for a bit then said, "You found out all this right before you got cheated on, huh?"

I nodded slowly, "Yeah. Worst timing. If I felt complete anywhere, and safe, it was in that relationship. I had known Jo a good part of my life before we started dating and my best friend...I had known her my whole life."

He furrowed his brows, "Wait. So your best friend fucked your man?"

The way he said it made me chuckle. It was the first time anyone made me aware of the situation, and I could laugh about it.

"Yeah. I knew she had hoe like ways and tendencies, but that... that I was not expecting."

"You used to tell her about the sex huh?" Don questioned making a goofy face.

"Yeah I did but to be honest...it wasn't all that. I probably exaggerated it more than I enjoyed."

"Yeah, your home girl was just a slut. They have no morals. They don't care who they're with. What probably happened was, one night when they was kicking it without you, they started talking, and he was claiming how unhappy he was. Drinks were being taken and one thing led to another, and more than likely, they just kept messing around. They didn't deserve someone like you in their life especially since I'm sure both of them knew what happened with your pops. I already know your relationship probably started tanking because your trust for men, and trust in your worth started diminishing. He didn't know how to handle it and took the pussy way out instead of being the man your father should've been."

I looked at Donovan in his eyes now. Somehow his words brought a lot of comfort to my soul.

"This whole time I was blaming myself for being so withdrawn towards him."

He shot me a crazy look, "You shouldn't have ever blamed yourself baby. He wasn't capable of helping you through that situation. I know what it's like to not feel wanted by a parent. That shit changes you. Makes you cold in a sense. How someone that created you, their blood runs through you, not want shit to do with you? No one understands but people like us."

"I discover more and more how alike we are," I commented as he shrugged me off.

"Little bit."

I was burning to start grilling him about why he hasn't called. Why he's making me go through with this thing with Aaron. Why he wasn't willing to just try and see where it goes with us, but my lips remained sealed. Tonight wasn't the night.

"So uh," he started as he leaned back a little, "How'd Aaron treat you today? Cool?"

I couldn't help but giggle, "You know you don't care. Why are you asking?"

"Just figured I'd show some interest. I know that's who you were with today."

"Well for your information, he treated me with respect," I said rolling my eyes as he nodded with understanding.

"And...the kiss?"

He looked over at me hesitantly while I stared back blankly.

"What about it?"

"How was it?" He squinted his eyes slightly when asking almost like he was afraid to hear the answer.

"It was...unexpected and quick," I answered honestly. I was going to lie to hurt his feelings, but I couldn't tell if it was even going to affect him.

I saw a sly look of satisfaction appear on his face before he wiped it away as soon as it came. He could tell by the way I described it that it wasn't enjoyable.

"We'll see how it goes next time though," I added just to crush his ego.

"Yeah whatever," he blew me off picking up on my game.

"How many girls have you kissed, Don?" I questioned as he cleared his throat.

"What kind of person asks a question like that? I'm twenty three years old. The number could be endless," he bragged as I shook my head.

"It's a valid question, and I know it's not."

He cut his eyes at me, "How you know? I'm a bad kisser?" he flirted biting his biting lip.

"You don't have girlfriends, so I know you don't kiss. Kissing causes connections."

He smirked and looked back towards the TV.

"Two," he answered honestly as my eyes widened. I was expecting a low number but not that low.

"Seriously? Only two people in your whole life?"

He nodded.

"Who was the first?"

"Ashley. We were at a park, and she was telling me about this party she had went to where they were playing truth or dare, and someone dared her to make out with some guy. But she faked like she was sick, so she wouldn't go through with it. Truth was, she had never kissed anybody and didn't want to get embarrassed at the party. I confessed to her that I never kissed anyone either and that I would practice with her if she wanted. I knew we both kinda liked each other, and she would go with it. I regret kissing her though."

"Why?"

"I thought it was just a small crush or something like that. After we kissed, shit changed. She got attached and I did too. Of course, eventually we ended up having sex, and I took her virginity. So after that she wanted a relationship...and to know I was all hers. I was going to give it to her too, but, my mom died around the same time all that was going down, so I backed up."

My heart started rushing as the next question escaped my lips, "How'd you feel when you kissed me?"

My breathing was slow and steady awaiting his response. He smiled to himself before he looked softly at me.

"How'd you feel?" he asked in his low raspy tone with a hint of seduction. For whatever reason, it made my heart flutter.

"I asked first. I mean for me to be the second woman you've ever kissed, it had to be something right?"

"Ah, someone's a little cocky tonight," he chuckled standing up and stretching.

By his actions and avoidance of the question, I could tell I wasn't getting an answer, if I ever get one.

"What did you get your mom for her birthday?" I sighed changing the subject.

He looked down at me and smiled.

"Same thing I get her every year. You'll see tomorrow, 'cause you're going with me," he said ruffling the top of my straightened hair with his fingers. I giggled pushing his hands away before fixing what he messed up.

"Going with you where?" I asked patting down the top and getting my part back straight.

"To church."

Donovan.

I had been awake for fifteen minutes just watching Bobbi sleep. Her chest would heave in and out with each deep breath she took, and I noticed the small twitches her body made while she dreamt. Nothing in me could explain why I was doing this; I was just in awe of her entire being. She was beautiful; even more beautiful than she realized.

We weren't supposed to be sleeping together. My whole plan was to sleep on the couch last night, but even with how mad she pretended to be at me, she still didn't want to sleep alone.

I inched my hand out stroking her face gently with my fingertips just longing to touch her soft skin. She stirred a little making an annoyed face in her sleep then turned over. I chuckled softly to myself hopping up to walk to the closet to figure out what I wanted to wear to church. I hummed softly looking through the array of clothes.

"You can sing?" I heard a sleepy voice yawn behind me. I turned looking at her sit up and stretch before rubbing her eyes like a baby.

"Eh, a little bit. Used to be in the choir at church and in school. Don't really do it much anymore," I shrugged pulling out a light blue button down shirt and khaki pants.

"I wanna hear you."

I chuckled shaking my head, "Not gonna happen baby girl. I don't sing no more." I declined as she shrugged in defeat.

"I don't know if what I brought to wear is appropriate for church. It's just regular stuff, and you look like you're going to dress nice," she whined.

I turned giving her a look like I didn't believe her. Bobbi always dressed good. I searched the floor for her bag picking it up to place on the bed.

"Hey! What are you doing?" she giggled watching me unzip the bag and looking through its contents.

I picked up some very sexy laced panties admiring them before she quickly snatching them from my fingers.

"Um! Excuse you! Those are not for you to see!" she shrieked hiding the underwear behind her.

"Hell, you got some sexy ass draws in here for? What you think was going down last night?" I laughed as she instantly began to blush.

"They weren't for you asshole. All my panties look like this," I chuckled shaking my head and pulling out the summer floral dress she packed.

"This is nice. What's wrong with this?" I asked her as she shrugged a little.

"Just haven't been to church in a long time. I don't want them to judge me."

"My Momma's church is small, but they're good people. I haven't been to church in a while either, so I'll be right there with you. Every step of the way," I assured leaning down and kissing her forehead.

She took in a deep breath and nodded expressing she trusted my words.

****

I parked in the church parking lot looking over at Bobbi whose face showed one of panic and fear. I reached over grabbing her left hand and rubbing it softly to ease her nerves.

"This is a good thing girl. Can't be afraid of what God has to tell you. He loves us no matter what."

She looked up at me causing us to lock eyes, and I felt my heart race a little bit.

"All of this is just surprising coming from you," she admitted.

"I'm full of surprises baby," I winked as she smacked her lips and playfully rolled her eyes. I laughed releasing her hand to open my car door.

Once we both were out of the car, I locked the doors and waited for Bobbi to reach me before walking to the building. I extended my arm, and she openly linked hers with mine. I wanted to show her that I was here for support in every way possible.

We reached the top of the steps, and I released myself from our interlocked arms to open the door for her. She bit her cheek out of nervous habit walking in with me close behind. Everyone stood with their heads bowed as Pastor Miller finished up his prayer before starting his sermon. Bobbi and I slid in at the end of a pew in the back and quietly set our things down before joining the church in an "Amen". We gave each other a goofy look taking our seats with the rest of the congregation knowing we were late and missed the prayer completely.

As we got adjusted an usher walked past handing the both of us a bible and signaling that the sermon was about to begin.

"Today," Pastor Miller started in his booming voice.

He was a young Pastor, in his early forties, but the gray already started to show in his hair and facial features. He had taken over this church after his father, who now sat on the stage with First Lady Miller, watching his son proudly.

"Today, we're going to talk about the freedom in forgiveness. If you're taking notes, that's going to be the title of today's message, but as always, I'm going to preach the Lord's message whether it matches my notes or not. Amen?" He softly chuckled with some joining him.

I sat upright listening intensely as Bobbi did the same but neither one of us brought anything to take notes with.

"Please take out your bible if you will. There is a particular scripture I would like to start with this morning which describes the way God views forgiveness in a nutshell. All throughout the bible, forgiveness is a common theme because it is so important to the body of Christ and also to the human heart. Please turn with me to Mark, chapter eleven, twenty-fifth verse. When you have it, say, I got it Pastor," he said amused while turning in his bible to the chapter he referenced.

Bobbi and I both scrambled in our bibles to find the passage he discussed, and majority of the church used the phrase he suggested to show they had reached the destination in their books. I looked over at Bobbi's bible to make sure I was on the right page, and she snickered a little seeing my struggle. I smirked nudging her with my arm as I tuned back into the Pastor's words.

"I'm going to read from the amplified version. And it says, 'And whenever you stand praying, if you have anything against anyone, forgive him and let it drop (leave it, let it go), in order that your Father who is in heaven may also forgive you your [own] failings and shortcomings and let them drop.'"

He finished looking at his bible then looking up at his congregation, "How many of you are holding some type of strife in your hearts against someone that has hurt you ?" he asked us raising his hand high and looking in the audience.

No one raised a single hand.

"Now, I know there are more people than just me that have held some type of harboring feelings against someone. Most of ya'll in here have ill feelings towards someone or something in your past that hurt you, and you are refusing to accept the responsibility of the effect it has had on your life. Now, all ya'll need to ask for forgiveness for lying in the house of the Lord," he ended in a slightly joking manner yet remained stern at the same time., "If you can't be honest with me or your brothers and sisters in here, at least be honest with yourselves. What are you holding on to?" He paced a little across the stage leaving his bible at the podium, "You know un forgiveness is like a double edged sword? Your intention is to hurt the other person, when all the while, you are pointing the blade at your own heart. You are killing yourself, your spirit, and jeopardizing your relationship with the Father by not forgiving someone that has caused you pain. You're holding yourself prisoner to it, all the while, giving that person all the control over your emotions: over your *life*. They don't deserve that much power. Even God doesn't ask for that much power, yet you are giving it to a person who doesn't even deserve it," he placed his hands behind him walking back to stand in front of the pulpit, "Some of you may say, Well Pastor Miller...that person doesn't deserve my forgiveness. You don't know what they did to me," he mimicked in a mocking tone locking eyes with as many people as he could.

"And I'm here to say, did your Father in Heaven not forgive you? For the same mistakes? Over and over and over again? For the same sin? The same shortcoming that you were going to make the next day? Without you even asking for it most times? He loves you so much that when you simply ask for forgiveness he wipes your slate *clean*. The wrong you committed never happened in his mind. His love is never wavered, never shaken, and never broken for you. You all expect this type of treatment but aren't able to do the same for someone who has broken your heart? You must learn to accept an apology that never came. Why? Because it is only damaging *you* in the end! You're the only one up at night, crying! Shedding tear after tear! And the person you can't forgive is going on about their life! Not thinking twice about the harm they caused on you. Yet, you're drinking the poison and waiting for *them* to die! What sense does that make?" he questioned calming down from the emotion that was beginning to rise. I looked over at Bobbi who was fidgeting her fingers, not taking her eyes off of Pastor Miller.

"That's not how God intended you to live. That's not how I want you to live. I want you all to find freedom in forgiveness. The freedom to be whole again. The freedom to be released from the burden you have chosen to carry. Jesus said, before you pray, you must first forgive those who have done you wrong, just like your Father has forgiven you. We break God's heart every single day, yet he loves us the same. He wants to forgive you. He wants to clean your record. That's what *love* does! That's what freedom is! The freedom to love your enemies, and move on like nothing ever happened. I know it's not easy, but for the sake of your soul, the sake of your sanity. It *must* be done! You can't be right with God, if you hold such hatred in your heart. Stop waiting for them to say sorry, because honestly, sorry may never come. But life goes on. You must go on. You *must* let it go!" he shouted, as a few people shouted with him, all feeling the effects of the message he wanted to get across.

"Stop carrying the heaviness of a broken spirit if you don't have to. Stop giving the enemy so much control of your life, over your emotions. Don't you remember what it was like to be full of joy? Full of that wholeness that God provides? Don't you remember? Remember that freedom to be yourself, to live with *no* strife! This ain't about them. You have to always keep that in mind. You're not forgiving them for their sake; you're forgiving them for *yours*. I know it hurt what Mommy and Daddy did, but it's time to let it go! Baby, I know that man wasn't treating you right, but it's time to let him and that relationship go! Sir, I know you feel wronged and betrayed, but it's time to let it go! It's time to set your hearts free from this self inflicted pain. There is Freedom in Forgiveness!" he roared as people were standing out of their seats, shouting and showing support of his words.

A lot of it was hitting close to home realizing the un-forgiveness I had harbored in my heart for a long time. The main person I couldn't forgive was myself.

Pastor Miller quieted down while the band started to play a soft melody sensing the sensitivity in the room. He looked out at all of us, some standing, some sitting, most with tear threatening eyes, the music touching their spirits.

"There are people in here, who suffer from the imprisonment of un-forgiveness. It has held you captive for days, months, even years. But God wants you free today. He wants you to rest in the freedom of forgiveness. He wants you to cast all of your cares, all of your burdens, all of your worries of the mistakes of others, to Him. In this walk, we are not alone. God is here to carry us the rest of the way. He wants that for His children. He doesn't want to see any of you broken, confused and bound. That's not the life He created for you."

He paused a moment, "If that's you. I want you to join me at this altar. I just want to pray for you, and with you. I want to help you forgive those that have hurt you. Leave it all here at the altar, so your Father can carry the sins of others. He did it once, and He'll do it again. Walk with me. Join me up here." He called as a few people left their seats to join him. I looked over at Bobbi who had her head down. I lightly placed my finger under her chin to lift her head up and noticed her tear stained face. This message had hit a deep place.

"Go up there baby," I encouraged softly as she gently shook her head.

"I'm scared Don," she choked, "I don't want to go up there."

I sighed a little knowing she needed the prayer he was offering, "Will you go if I walk with you?" I asked.

She hesitated looking at the altar and then back at me, "Really?" She questioned with worry in her eyes.

"Of course. I need it too. We'll walk together," I said holding out my hand for her to grab. She reluctantly took it and squeezed tight both of us standing to our feet.

I led her down the aisle and stood beside her as we reached the altar with the rest of the broken souls. Many were praying silently to themselves, some were crying, and others just simply had their head down in shame, all waiting for Pastor Miller to walk up and pray with each individual.

I could sense Bobbi shaking standing next to me, so I wrapped my right arm around her shoulder to provide support. She rested her temple against my chest, crying softly. I never knew what to do when people were upset, but with her it came natural. I had brought her to this element and made a promise to be there for her through it. She trusted me, and I couldn't let her down.

Pastor Miller approached the two of us and smiled softly at me. We had a good relationship back when my mother was still alive. He was happy to see me any time I came to the church, understanding that he wasn't going to see me every Sunday or back in the choir. He respected my decision and always lent a helping hand if asked.

He then looked at Bobbi who had still refused to lock eyes with the Man of God. I rubbed her shoulder a little, signaling it was okay to look up. She finally did and the tears were flooding from her eyes as the Pastor smiled softly at her. He extended both of his hands and waited patiently for her to grab them. She did and watched on as Pastor Miller began to speak.

"Mm." He said firmly, squeezing her hands tight. "Wow. The devil tried to take you out. He tried to take you away from us at one point in time in your life. And I'm here to tell you, that he should've been successful. There was a strong possibility that you weren't going to be standing here right now, with us. But God saw this moment. He knew that was not the end for you. You're special. Did you know that? Your purpose here on this earth is too great for you to have been taken from us so soon. You deserve to be here young lady. You deserve it. You deserve to be loved and cherished. You are a gift. A precious gift that needs to be handled with care. When I say this prayer for you, I need you to forgive your past. Forgive the ones that hurt you, and forgive yourself for allowing this to carry on for so long. God is not mad at you, no one is mad at you. You just need to release it all, so you can be filled with love and joy again. Your freedom will be restored after we say this prayer. Do you believe me?" he asked softly as she stood still, tears heavy in her eyes.

She sniffed a little before nodding causing Pastor to smile wide, "Let's sct you free."

Bobbi.

I sat on the hood of the car at the park waiting for Donovan to finish peeing near the woods with an undeniable smile on my face. I had never felt more at peace in my life. Going to church today allowed me to begin to release so many demons that I held in for so long that were stunting my growth; from my suicide attempt to my father and to Jo. I couldn't stop thanking Donovan as we left. He has no idea what he did for me today.

"What you smiling at?" I heard his raspy tone ask as he walked back up to me zipping up his pants. I scrunched my nose at the sight.

"Make sure you don't touch me the rest of the day," I warned. He chuckled and wrapped me in a huge bear hug.

"Like this Bobs? You don't want me to touch you like this?!" Donovan asked in a playful voice causing me to laugh.

"Get off me!" I begged which only made him squeeze tighter. Once he released me, he made sure to touch me all over my arms.

"You're sick," I whined wiping off whatever residue he left on my body. He chuckled and went for my camera that was sitting next to me on the hood. He picked it up and scrolled through some of the pictures I had.

"All these pictures and not a single one of you," he commented looking through the lens and flashed a few photos of the scenery, "Why is that?"

"My job is to be behind the camera," I informed standing up and beginning to walk the trail that went all through the park. He followed closely behind me still messing with my camera.

"Yeah, but if you're a photographer you would think that you would take and edit a few pics of yourself. Who better to practice on, if not you?" he asked still behind me as I admired the high trees that engulfed both of us along this hidden path.

"Maybe I'll start," I shrugged hearing his footsteps near.

"You think you can print those pictures I just took? I might wanna use them for my art show in a couple of months," I shot him a look.

"Art show?" I asked out loud earning a quick nod with a grin from him.

"Yeah, it's my first one in a while. Before I became a tattoo artist, I used to want to own my own gallery. Art was my first passion. Really graffiti art. I used to tag different alley's and shit. Would make huge murals that the city would go crazy over. I got Shane into it too after a while. We almost got arrested a few times. I'm trying to get back to my roots. Display my art for the world again just legally this time," he chuckled as I admired him.

I wished I was bold enough to put my photos on display or even take photography seriously for that matter.

"Can I come?" I asked softly as he darted his eyes in my direction.

"Sure. I'll probably invite everyone then if you come. There will be various artists there showcasing their work as well. Should be some big names looking to pay major bucks for pieces."

"I want to be there," I mentioned again, "I want to support you."

"Cool," he replied with a half smirk, "Thank you, for coming with me today. I was really proud of you," he confessed as I smiled before interlocking my arm with his.

"I'm proud of me too. I can't stress enough how much I appreciate you inviting me," I said, secretly intertwining our fingers to see if he would notice. I know none of this was in his character, but I was willing to push the envelope with him. See how far he allowed me to go.

He didn't say a word, just admired the landscape, and I smiled to myself feeling accomplished.

"So, Auntie is cooking tonight. Do you want to stay for dinner?" I questioned not wanting to leave his company as of yet.

"I mean, I was going to be over there without your invite anyway so..." he joked.

I laughed and nudged him with my shoulder, "Good."

We continued to walk the trail, laughing at something silly, when I felt my phone vibrate. I reached in my pocket to pull it out and frowned a little when I noticed Aaron calling me. I let go of Don's hand so I could step aside to answer the call.

He looked at me strangely while watching me step to the other side of the trail. I flashed an apologetic look before answering.

"Hello?" I answered peeking looks at Don who had his hands shoved in his pockets.

"Hey pretty girl. Haven't heard from you all day. Was wondering if we were still on for dinner tonight? You never got back to me."

"Shoot, I forgot all about that Aaron," I sighed smacking my forehead lightly. I glanced over at Don. He wasn't paying me any mind at the moment.

"It's kind of short notice to make sure she made enough food...maybe we can hang out later or tomorrow possibly?" I asked biting my bottom lip. Lying to him didn't feel right with my spirit. I just didn't want Donovan to leave.

"Yeah, it's cool. I understand. Just call me afterwards. I'm not doing much today," he replied with a hint of disappointment. I'm sure he had planned his whole day around me.

"I'm sorry. I will definitely hit you up," I said sympathetically feeling bad for messing things up.

"Don't worry about it."

Donovan.

My skin was boiling with irritation. I was honestly thinking Bobbi was over that little spiel she gave yesterday about taking Aaron seriously and pushing me to the back. And here she was, pushing me to the back right in front of my face. She thought I didn't notice that Aaron was calling her, and the fact that she clearly had invited him to this dinner before just asking me. It just made me realize I was stupid for starting to catch feelings and soften after what we experienced today. I thought things were changing, and we were on the same page about where this should go. Now...now, I questioned everything.

While she was finishing her call, I scrolled through my phone to find an excuse to leave. I came across Lynn's name, and even though she was still pissed about the night I didn't come through, I knew she'd be down to hook up again. I swiftly sent her a text before Bobbi returned.

"Sorry about that," she said breathlessly, after skipping back next to my side. She attempted to interlock our arms together, but I removed my arms from hers, pretending to still be texting.

"You don't have to apologize, we're friends remember?" I reminded her, as she remained silent for a brief moment.

"Yeah but still, I don't want you thinking-"

I cut her off, "Bobbi, you don't have to explain shit to me. I don't go explaining myself to Shane, or anyone else. You made everything clear last night," I said, dismissing the entire conversation and putting my phone in my pocket.

"We should probably turn around; I have to get going soon," I informed as she quickly shot me a look.

"What? I thought you were staying for dinner? Without my invite? Remember that?" she asked, mocking me as I rolled my eyes.

"Yeah, well something just came up and I gotta go tend to it. You'll be allright without me. Tell Aaron he can come through now," I turned around, as she did too, keeping her pace with mine.

"Is that what this is about? I invited him before you and I were even talking again-"

"Here you go, explaining shit. This isn't about him, or any other dude you wanna talk to. That's your business Bobbi, not mine. Realize that."

She crossed her arms and sealed her lips tight. She knew there wasn't much she could say because I was just honoring what she requested.

As we got closer to the car, I felt the notification from my phone, informing me I had a new message:

Be here at six. Don't bullshit me.

I smirked looking at the text, before looking down at Bobbi who was still giving me the silent treatment. I shrugged to myself, not giving a damn how she was feeling. She was just somebody I had to start letting go, physically and emotionally.

****

"So what made you want to get this design covering your entire side?" I asked my usual client, Champagne, as she winced a little at the needle driving into her skin. It was our third session of this array of half a dozen roses that went from her back and up to the cusps of her left breast. She was getting the color completed finally. Throughout this whole time, I never asked her why she was getting it.

"Two roses are for my parents, two are for my siblings, one is for my son, and the last... each petal is for every guy that fed me bullshit. That rose is for me," she answered, taking in deep breaths as I was completing the color for the last rose.

I laughed a little, "Why you want a rose representing that?"

"To remind me that in the end, each of them helped in creating something beautiful. I've learned so much about myself through the pain. I will never look at it negatively. They all reminded me of what I do deserve and what will find me one day. True love from a good man," she said with confidence.

I nodded in admiration, "Respect. That's a dope way to view things."

She squinted her eyes, "You have to learn from that you know? You can't let the hurt eat you up inside and make you some ol' bitter ass person. I just wanted to be better. I needed to be for me and definitely my son. He can't see me hating men and life forever. That's not how it's supposed to be, ya know? We were created as people to be loved and to love others. Can't escape from it. With each person I said I loved, I knew it was a risk. You can't love without first taking a risk."

"Wise woman," I said, dipping my needle back in the red ink quickly wiping down the area of her skin I was working on.

"You ever been in love D?" she asked hearing the front door chime. I looked up to see who was walking past, and felt my heart drop when I saw Bobbi and Tierre. Shane must've asked them to bring food.

"Nah. I don't fuck with the L word Pagne." I smiled at her as she just frowned at me.

"Don't know what you're missing," she said, covering her face with her arm, trying to distract herself from the pain. I grinned, looking up and locking eyes with Bobbi who smirked at me and waved. I ignored her gesture and continued to work on my client.

"Almost finished."

I put the finishing touches on Champagne and sprayed her down with alcohol before rubbing ointment on her body.

"How many times I gotta tell you Don? You keep touching me like this, we'll have no choice but to go on a date," she flirted, as I laughed a little, continuing to rub the ointment in before grabbing some plastic to place over it. Champagne was cute, but not necessarily my type. Plus she was too much of a regular client to have sex with.

"Came out real nice," I said admiring my work, as she scoped it out in the mirror. She smiled spinning to each angle.

"Sexy as fuck. I love it." She grinned before following me out of the room and into our main area. Bobbi and Tierre were sitting down eating and Shane was behind the register. His eyes widened at Champagne.

"Damn Pagne Pagne! That looks good girl!" he emphasized causing her to laugh. He stepped from behind the counter and walked up to her, looking at all sides of the tattoo.

"These two hours you've been in here worth it huh? Can you feel anything?" he asked as I stepped behind the counter to ring her out. I could feel Bobbi watching me, but I continued to ignore her presence.

"I can't feel shit. My whole side numb," Champagne said jokingly, causing Shane and me to laugh. She dug in her purse and pulled out the money she owed for the color.

"Keep the change Don. You already know after this heals, I'll be back for something else. You got me addicted to the ink." I nodded, pocketing the change she gave me for a tip and put the standard rate for her color in the register.

I walked her to the door, and opened it as she limped carefully to her car. I pulled out all of the money I had already earned for the morning and counted it over before smiling to myself.

"If I ain't know you, I'd rob your ass for flashing your money," Tierre said as I laughed, fanning her off.

"I'll be back," I said out loud, heading to my office. I really meant I was going to come out when they left.

I closed the door behind me and sat down in my chair before pulling out my phone. I wanted to look at the video Lynn let me record of us last night. For whatever reason she was being freakier than she normally was. I was hardening just thinking about it.

As I hit play, I was startled by a knock on my door and quickly closed out of the video. "Uh, come in." I said sitting upright in my chair and trying to calm myself down. My eyes rolled when Bobbi came through the door.

"Don't start. I just came to bring your food, since I know you're just waiting for me to leave." She spat sitting the container of food down on my desk.

"Not true," I lied, receiving a blank look in return.

"Bullshit. What were you in here doing? About to masturbate?" I furrowed my brows. *How the hell she know?*

"No, I was about to make a phone call."

"You don't like talking on the phone Donovan. Is there a contest going on for how many lies you can tell in a minute?"

I smacked my lips looking up at her. "You delivered the food. Is there a reason why you're still here?"

She crossed her arms and leaned back against the door, chuckling. "Real cute that you bailed on me to go have sex with some girl. Real cute."

"It's cute that you're assuming."

"The hickie on your neck that wasn't there before you left tells that story. No assumption necessary," I started to get angry.

"Why you care Bobbi? Come in here questioning shit. You crossing this 'friendship' line that you created."

She let out a laugh of disbelief. "You make sure to throw that in my face every chance you get huh?"

"I'm just reminding you of what you said. I don't see anything wrong with that. You wanted me to respect you as a friend since you're dating other people so I'm doing that shit. Now respect me and stay out of my business. If I wanna leave you and have sex, then that's what Imma do. I'm single and don't have to answer to anyone. Never had to before you came into the picture and don't have to now."

"Man, why are you acting like..." she started before she stopped and shook her head.

"Acting like what? Say it," I urged as she threw her hands up.

"I'm not saying nothing else. You right, I'll stay out of your business. And out of your way since that's what you clearly want," she said looking at me with saddened eyes. I quickly turned my head, not wanting to look at them.

"Happy we're finally on the same page," I answered bitterly, before pulling my phone back out and clicking into a random application.

"Whatever," she said lowly, slamming the door on her way out causing one of my paintings to fall off the wall.

Bobbi.

"It's my birthday bitches!" Tierre screeched drinking straight out of the Patron bottle, before Aaron quickly grabbed it from her. Jay, his girlfriend Felicia, Aaron, a couple of Tierre's girlfriends and I were all standing in their apartment, drinking before we went out to Graystone Manor where she was celebrating her special night.

"Let's try not to die of alcohol poisoning on the night of our birthday okay?" Aaron asked with sarcasm, causing all of us to laugh.

She smiled hazily at him, "It's my birthday though! I'm trying to turn up tonight! 23," she giggled, wrapping her arm around her friend Charity, who was getting just as drunk as she was. Felicia, Aaron and Tierre's other friend Simone were the designated drivers of the night. Everyone else was pretty much feeling their liquor.

I looked down at the black patterned romper I was wearing, that accentuated every curve I possessed. It was cut out in the back and opened in the front revealing my cleavage and chest in a tasteful way. I was wearing black opened toed Jeffrey Campbell shoes, with a hint of gold and gold accessories. I took a sip of my drink while holding my clutch tightly, waiting for the moment we left. I wanted to get as intoxicated as I could, knowing I would be running into Donovan sometime this evening. There was no way he was going to miss Tierre's birthday.

"You okay babe?" Aaron asked in my ear walking up and holding me from behind. I put on a fake smile and nodded before he kissed my cheek.

"You sure? You seem a little out of it," he asked looking past my shoulder, trying to read my expression. I looked up at him and nodded again, before he pecked my lips. He was being rather affectionate tonight, and I was doing my best to do the same in return.

"Ok, we're about to head out in a minute. You riding with me?" he asked as I nodded again, still not speaking a word. He smiled, before sneaking one more kiss and walking towards their kitchen. I looked up and locked eyes with Jay who was smirking at me. He and Felicia both were. I liked Felicia for him; she was Puerto Rican and black and a lot of fun to be around. I had met her a few times before tonight.

"What?" I asked them chuckling as they both smiled and shook their heads.

I ignored them and continued to drink what was left in the cup, allowing the alcohol to consume me. I needed it to provide the slightest bit of comfort before the night continued.

****

"Ayyyeeee!" Tierre yelled, grabbing my hand tightly as our group entered the packed, dark and high energy level club. The DJ was yelling something over the microphone as the new Drake song blasted throughout the venue. A couple bottle girls had passed us with lit Ciroc bottles as we made our way to the VIP section we all chipped in to reserve for Tierre's night.

There were already a number of people they all knew waiting and drinking as we walked up. All of them yelled a greeting the minute they saw Tierre. She looked beautiful tonight. Her usual wild and thick natural hair was straightened, nearly reaching the brim of her butt, and she was wearing a form fitting cream dress that showed her toned frame, with peach colored heels. Her makeup was perfect and the accessories she sported really made her stand out.

"It's my birthday guys!" she yelled, getting hugged and greeted from every which way. There were already a tray of what seemed to be a hundred shots waiting for all of us.

"Hey TiTi we got you all of these shots! Cherry bombs! Cherry vodka and red bull!" Shane yelled to her over the music as my heart dropped at the sight of him. Wherever Shane was, I knew Donovan was close behind.

"Birthday shot! Everybody grab one!" Tierre ordered, her Harlem accent thick. We all started walking up to grab a shot.

I felt an arm snake around my waist, and looked up to see Aaron smiling softly at me. I smiled back before directing my attention to my cousin who was standing on a couch with a shot in one hand and bottle in the other.

"Aye yo listen up!" he yelled, as everyone quieted down and looked up at him. The music was still blaring in the club, so our silence didn't really say nor do much.

"I'd like to wish my muh fuggin best friend a happy birthday! She's been my rollie for 13 years and I wouldn't change not one moment of knowing her crazy ass. Happy Birthday Ti! I hope you don't remember none of dis shit when you wake up!" he slurred, as we all laughed and took our shots.

I looked around nervously afterwards, while Aaron walked up to Tierre, wondering why I hadn't yet seen Donovan. After twirling on my heel a little, I spotted him. Sitting right behind me on one of the couches in our section, with some girl I had never seen before smiling and giggling all in his face. I could tell by his expression that he was drunk, and that this girl was nothing but a hoe. Her breasts and ass were bulging out of her overly tight outfit, and he was eating up every word she was saying.

"What I want," I heard Tierre say, wrapping her arm around my shoulder for support, "Is for you two to hook up on my birthday." She said turning and looking at me as I shot her a crazy expression.

"You know I came here with Aaron, right? Your cousin?" I asked her.

She smirked and looked at me. "So. You don't like him. You love him," she said, looking back at Donovan who was now looking at both of us strangely before turning his attention back to the girl.

"Says who?" I challenged. She pointed to the spot where my heart rested.

"Says this," she placed a kiss on my cheek and laughed before walking away. I turned to follow her, until Aaron appeared in my sight. He looked really good tonight, wearing a dark denim button up and camel colored cargo pants. The dark of the denim made his deep chocolate skin glow, and his hair was freshly cut. I couldn't deny that I was attracted to him, just didn't see things going further than that.

"I'm not about to keep letting you sneak away from me," he grinned, as I smiled up at him. He began to lean down and my heart started to race, knowing we were in clear view of Donovan. I went back and forth in my mind the closer his lips got, if I was actually going to allow him to kiss me in such a public setting.

Before I had another second to think, Aaron's lips were pressed against mine, and after a few moments of allowing it to linger I pulled away. I could tell he wanted to deepen it, but I just couldn't allow it to go that far. Donovan can pretend that he's following through with this whole just friends card as long as he wants, but that didn't give me the right to disrespect his feelings even though he's repeatedly disrespected mine.

Moments later I felt a body brush past me and soon noticed it to be Donovan with the girl following closely behind. They were headed to the dance floor where most of our section had already disappeared to.

Aaron shook his head and laughed at the scene, "He's still immature I see."

I just watched as they reached the rest of our group and began to dance, a hint of jealousy creeping upon me.

"Yeah," I finally answered, "He is. Wanna dance?" I asked changing the subject completely as Aaron quickly smiled.

"Of course. But I gotta warn you now, I'm pretty hard to keep up with. I don't play when it comes to my moves," he joked, as I gave him a devilish smirk.

"I'm pretty sure I got this," I assured, grabbing his hand and leading him down the steps and through the sea of people until we finally caught up with everyone else. Tierre was dancing with an attractive guy I had noticed in the section earlier, possibly the new dude she was telling me about, and everyone else was coupled up and dancing with a partner. I noticed the thick chick Donovan was with grinding her huge ass into him, as he gripped her hips forcefully. This pissed me off on the inside and I quickly pressed my body against Aaron.

Do Your Dance by Tyga came on, and I instantly felt my wild drunken nature hit me as I bent over and gave Aaron everything I had. He had to grip my hips in order to keep up with me, feeling him getting harder with each move, my ass connecting with his groan on beat.

I looked up to see Donovan looking evilly in my direction, before he began grinding harder into his partner. I hated the fact that he knew how to dance so well. Nothing I was doing was throwing him off. I started popping even harder into Aaron, feeling the competition begin to heat up.

We went back and forth like this, probably for three songs straight until he finally got pissed enough to walk away. A part of me was ready to stop too, since I was getting hot and thirsty from all of the dancing I was doing.

"You need a drink babe?" Aaron asked, sweat dripping down his forehead. I giggled a little and nodded, as he left to head back to our section to fix me one.

"Girl you was getting it!" Tierre squealed as she and a few of her girlfriends walked up to me. I blushed and swayed a little to the current song that was playing.

"I was just dancing." She gave me a look like she didn't believe me.

"Just trying to make Don jealous!" she said loudly, as I laughed and covered her mouth. She laughed too before licking my palm, forcing me to remove my hand.

"Eww!" I chuckled, while turning up my nose and looking at my hand that was now sweaty with a hint of saliva.

"Come on, dance with us. Ya'll hoes don't need to be hugged up on no dudes tonight. It's my birfdaayy!" she yelled, grabbing my hand and leading me away from the spot I was in. I drunkenly followed, not worried about the drink Aaron was going to get me. Tierre ended up handing me hers anyway.

We danced and continued to make sure Tierre was having a great time. After about the fifteenth song, my feet were aching in my heels, and I convinced her to head back to her section so we could take some shots, just so I could sit down for a minute. We had been dancing for a good hour by this point and I needed a break.

Donovan, Shane, Jay and a few other guys were standing on the couch dancing and sipping straight out of an Ace of Spades bottle, when we walked up. I smiled a little at the sight, noticing how cute Don looked tonight, despite our little feud. He was happy and living in the moment with his group of friends.

He soon noticed me smiling directly at him, and for the first time tonight, smiled at me too. I felt butterflies rise in my chest, knowing I had finally captured his attention in a positive light. It let me know that this fallout wasn't going to last for too long.

I sat around with the girls, drinking and dancing a little on the side of couches that weren't being occupied by the boys standing on them, and looked at my watch. It was already 3AM because we hadn't even arrived there until 1. Tierre wanted to make sure we went to the club officially on her birthday. The club was closing soon, and I was ready to go with the first person offering a ride home. A body then plopped down next to me, and I grinned seeing it was Aaron.

"What I tell you earlier girl? Feel like I haven't saw you all night," he said, draping his arm over my shoulder.

"Just wanted to make sure Tierre was having a good birthday. She is gone!" I said, directing my attention towards her. She was standing on the couch next to Shane with her shoes off, rapping along with the song that was playing, drunk as hell.

"Yeah, I need to get her home soon. She's gonna be hella sick in the car. I can already tell." He chuckled, shaking his head as I laughed.

"You riding back with us? You can crash at our place," he offered, as I released a small sigh.

"I was actually just gonna ride back with one of the girls that doesn't live too far from us, since Jay is going to Felicia's. I'm just ready to get in my bed," I lied, as he somberly accepted my denial.

"We're probably about to leave soon, so I'm gonna use the bathroom before we do," I said, standing up with him doing the same.

"Ok, gimme a hug in case I don't see you when you get back. Tierre got one more time to stumble before I'm dragging her ass outta here," he joked, trying to lighten the mood, before hugging me tightly then kissing me on the cheek.

"I'll call you tomorrow if I don't see you," I assured him, before walking away and looking for the restroom. I didn't really have to go; I just wanted an excuse to walk away.

I reached the hallway, leading to the bathroom, near the club exit and paused before I thought of what I was going to do for a ride home. Sighing, I ran a hand through my straightened hair, and tried to think. As I was gearing up to just head towards the exit to prevent myself from looking lost, I felt an arm tug at my wrist and spin me around.

My eyes fell on Donovan before he pulled me into him by my waist. "You were going to really leave without saying shit to me?" he asked aggressively, yet sensual at the same time. His cologne was still present, even with all of the activity he had done tonight, and I was mesmerized by its scent.

"Didn't think it mattered, friend," I answered sarcastically; he flashed a sly grin.

"Let me take you home," he offered as I rolled my eyes and shook my head.

"Cab's got it, thanks though," I said, attempting to walk away before he spun me around again. His hand rested on my lower back before he leaned closer to my ear.

"Ok. How about, I'm going to take you home. With or without your permission," he said in a low, steady tone before planting some kisses on my ear, causing me to rest my hands on his shoulder for support from the weakness I felt in my knees. He found a spot I didn't even know I had.

"Okay."

****

I opened my front door as Donovan stepped into the house behind me. He wanted to make sure I was completely safe before taking off. He always got more protective of me when he drank.

I allowed him to look through the house, making my way up the steps. I walked into the room and placed my phone on my iPod deck so I could play soft music until I fell asleep. I could never sleep in silence.

I then removed my shoes from my aching feet and swiftly walked to the closet to place them in their designated box. After tucking them away, I walked into the bathroom to brush my teeth, ridding my tongue of the combined liquor taste. I finished and dabbed the corners of my mouth, checking myself in the mirror. I fixed a random stray hair before walking out of my bathroom, slightly startled to see Don fidgeting with my music. He switched the song to Musiq Soulchild, <u>Love</u>.

"Why you turn it to this? You don't know a thing about love," I questioned, stepping closer to him as he turned around. His eyes widened when they landed on me.

Love...so many things I've got to tell you...

"What?" I asked looking down at my appearance wondering if anything was out of place.

"Nothing. You just look even more gorgeous in the light," he admitted honestly; my cheeks flushing with fever.

"Don't run game on me. I'm not any of your groupies," I played off rolling my eyes. He stepped closer to me, placing a gentle hand on my waist.

"Nothing I ever tell you is game. I meant that. You're beautiful."

From then on I knew, that by you being in my life, things were destined to change..

"You drunk?" He questioned curiously, tipping a brow.

I shook my head, "Sobered up. You?

"Nah.."

He moved some of the hair that had fallen just short of my eye, and tucked it behind my ear, then cupped my jaw in his palms, not breaking eye contact the entire time.

"Don, what are you..." Before I could finish, his lips were pressed against mine

Love...those who have faith in you sometimes go astray...

I opened my mouth allowing him to deepen the kiss. As he did, I wrapped my arms around his neck and pulled him into me, wanting to ignite the connection that sparked each time our bodies touched. He felt it too, wrapping his arms tight around my body, drawing me even closer. This motion led a moan to escape from my mouth into his.

Many days I've longed for you, wanting you...hoping for the chance to get to know you...

He swiftly began guiding me towards my bed causing me to land backwards on to it. I lifted up and aggressively pulled him by the collar of his shirt on top of me, our lips finding their way back to each other. Donovan was on top of me, allowing his hands to roam freely, as we kissed each other passionately, our anticipation rising with each enticing moment.

I know that you're real...with no doubts, and no fears and no questions...

He then suddenly removed his lips from mine looking into my eyes, "I wanna taste you baby," he confessed as the mere sound of wanting in his tone caused a gush of wetness to release. I bit my lip looking down and then back up to him.

"Can I taste you?" he whispered guiding his hand between my thighs, and beginning to rub his fingers over my pearl against my sheer outfit. I couldn't stop my legs from squirming. I've never felt a touch this good.

I nodded slow, not able to resist the desire to feel his lips against my lower set. He bit his bottom lip before leaning in to kiss my neck, still rubbing me softly below.

At first you didn't mean that much to me, no. And now I know you're I need, ohh. The world looks so brand new to me...

"Ahh..." I moaned in his ear as he continued to nibble and suck on my skin. After a few moments of enticing my desire, he lifted himself up and eyed me up and down.

Every day I live for you, yeah. Everything, that I do, I do it for you...

"Can we take this off of you?" he asked tugging at my outfit. I eagerly nodded and sat up to remove my arms first. He carefully slid my arm out of each sleeve, revealing my lace bra, and then guided me to lie back down on my back.

"Damn..." he uttered before he started to slide the rest of my one piece off my body, leaving me vulnerable in my underwear. I covered my chest up by crossing my arms over my body, and he looked at me sternly before resting his hands on each arm.

"None of that. It's me baby, ok? I'm not gonna hurt you. I'm going to take care of you," he said softly, before leaning in and planting a sensual kiss on my lips. My body craved for more as he released his lips from mine and laid my arms next to my side.

He leaned in to kiss me again, this time more passionate than the last, squeezing my left breast with his hand.

After a while, he broke the kiss and stared into my eyes, "Relax okay? No running."

I nodded and watched as he went lower, kissing every part of my body on the way down. He reached the brim of my laced panties and tugged at it with his teeth. My body shivered and shook, just waiting to feel his touch again. He used his teeth to guide my panties down to my thighs and then came face to face with my center, simultaneously pulling my panties down to my ankles with his hand. He then looked up at me for reassurance; I nodded slowly signaling it was okay.

He blew softly against my lower set of lips, and I giggled a little at the ticklish feeling. Before I had a chance to recover, his lips were pressed against me, and he began to lick and suck as gently as possible, sending my body into a fit.

"Ahh, baby..." I panted as each suck became more intense than the last. I was grabbing anything I could to calm my body down from the amount of pleasure I was feeling, but nothing made it better. I wanted to scream. I did my best to back up, but it went to no avail as Donovan grabbed me firmly by the waist, pushing my pearl deeper into his face.

"No running," he warned again before going back to lick every drop that released itself. He wasn't allowing me to move at this point, and I had no choice but to cry out. It felt too good for words.

"You taste so good," he hissed, the vibration of his lips causing my body to jerk. I began to squeeze my breast just to have somewhere to divert my attention. This only increased my passion and desire to feel more.

"I want you baby. I want you inside of me," I whimpered as Donovan just began to lick even more causing me to yell out with his teasing. I didn't want to feel his tongue any longer; I wanted to feel him.

"Baby...please... I need you. Please," I whined, before gasping as he stuck two of his finger inside of me while continuing to suck on my treasure. He started to thrust his fingers in and out, nearing me to the verge of my peak.

"Cum for me girl..." he demanded continuing to stroke me with his fingers. I vigorously shook my head and squeezed my bottom set of lips tight, forcing myself to stop the release.

"Shit," he hissed feeling the tightness around his fingers before he removed them and smirked up at me. "Are you sure?"

I nodded quickly, not wanting to prolong it any further. He stood all the way up before digging in his back pocket removing a condom. He placed the wrapper between his teeth, before taking off his shirt, pants, then lastly his boxers. I admired his body from head to toe, and gawked at the size of his fully erect member.

He blushed a little removing the wrapper from his teeth, "Only girl to see me fully naked," he admitted bashfully. I smiled and got up on my knees, meeting him at the edge of the bed. I grabbed the back of his neck and gently began pecking his lips before he joined me on the bed as well. I positioned him in a way to where he was now laying on his back and I was straddling him, never breaking this kiss.

I sat upright, and tugged at the hook of my bra, releasing the girls fully. Donovan looked up at me, his eyes low and focused, and caressed each breast evenly. I placed my hands over top of his, allowing this ecstasy to overtake my being. After a few moments, I leaned in and kissed his lips again. He opened his mouth, sliding his tongue in and let his hands roam up and down my body. I saw the wrapper resting at his side, and removed myself from the kiss to open the condom. I grabbed his penis in my hand, and stroked it gently to make sure he was fully erect before sliding the condom on. Once it was on securely, he surprisingly lifted me up and placed me on my back as he positioned himself on top of me.

"You want me?" he asked rubbing the tip against my opening, causing my eyes to roll back slightly.

"Quit teasing me..." I cooed as he slid only the tip inside before removing it. My body couldn't take this anymore, I had to have him.

"Tell me you want me, and I'll give you exactly what you want," he grunted, sliding the tip a little more inside and removed it. "Damn girl, you so wet. Shit."

"Please..." I moaned desiring to feel all of him.

"Not till you tell me you want me, baby..." he instructed again. I threw my hands back in defeat.

"I want you-" Before the words could fully escape my lips, he rammed himself inside of me, causing me to scream in pleasure. He began to give me long strokes, entering deeper and deeper into my sweet spots. I couldn't contain the screams anymore.

"You feel so good baby," he groaned, picking up his pace, grabbing my hips and ramming my groin into his. I had never felt this type of pleasure in my life.

"Aahh, harder!" I barked as he did as he was told, pounding my insides to smithereens. I squeezed my lips tight around his shaft as he bit hard on his lip, containing himself.

"Shit!" he hissed digging his fingers into my hips. I wanted nothing more than to please him, so I grabbed his shoulders and flipped him on his back, straddling him like I was before. I began to grind my hips into him, starting off in a slow motion. His eyes rolled back while resting his hands on my waist, allowing me to take over. I then picked up my pace and began bouncing up and down, making my ass clap onto his thighs forcing him to release a moan for the first time.

"Damn girl, got me moaning," he grunted grabbing my hips and took over, forcing my body to jerk on top of him, fast and hard. I rested my hands on his chest, to steady myself allowing him to do as he pleased.

"Stop controlling," I said between pants. He ignored my order and continued to thrust, hitting my spot each time. I felt myself on the verge of another orgasm, and quickly shifted my body into the reverse cowgirl position, so that my forehead was now touching his ankles. I bounced in rhythm on his shaft, feeling his hands aggressively squeeze my cheeks.

"Smack my ass!" I demanded as he did so. I moaned at the sting still lingering on my right cheek, picking up my pace.

"Harder baby," I cried, as he did it again, this time with a grunt, while bouncing his body up and down with mine.

"Ahh..." I moaned, feeling my legs begin to get weak with how good he felt, connected with me. He then lifted me up on my hands and knees and adjusted himself behind me while grabbing my thighs and forcing me to back into him. He smacked me again, before he began thrusting in and out of me hard.

"I can't hold it anymore baby!" I shouted, as he rammed even harder into me, slapping my ass for the third time.

"Ahh, I love y-" Before I could get it out, he pulled out of me and flipped me onto my back, adjusting himself over top of me.

"I just wanna take my time with you girl," he said softly, slowly sliding back into me as I arched my back. He continued to stroke, slow and steady while looking into my eyes. He placed the back of his fingers against my cheek, as if he were admiring my features for the first time.

"You're so damn beautiful Bobbi," he whispered sending a shock of intensity to flow through my body at his words.

He leaned in and placed a soft kiss on my lips, turning into another, while never breaking his pace. I placed my hands on the back of his neck, allowing the passion to increase and our tongues to intertwine as a moan escaped his mouth and released into mine, picking up his pace.

"Damn girl," he hissed against my lips as our bodies moved in sync with each other, our climax intensifying. I crossed my arms behind his neck, kissing him again as both of our bodies continued to rock with the other, getting faster with each passing moment.

"Shit, I'm about to cum," he groaned as I felt myself reaching the height of my climax as well. With one last deep stroke, I felt myself release against Donovan, and let go of the breath I didn't know I was holding. We both gasped for air, letting the moment over take us, and calming down from the natural high.

"Damn..." he said in shock while looking down, realizing he was still inside of me, as I rubbed my hand against his cheek.

I wondered if he came to realization that I just did. We didn't just have sex...we made love.

Donovan.

I lay awake, cradling Bobbi in my arms as she slept peacefully on my chest. I had probably been awake for a while, watching the sun rise through her window blinds. I couldn't believe what actually happened just a few hours ago, and the way I felt in the midst of it. I caught Bobbi almost tell me she loved me. I couldn't let her do it. If she had, I would've been obligated to say it back. I would've been responsible for knowing her true feelings, meaning I had to act on them. For some reason, church last week kept replaying in my mind.

I looked down at her soft and happy expression, probably reminiscing our night in her dreams. I couldn't hurt this woman. She deserved better than me, and already I could feel myself wanting to pull away, needing to pull away so she wouldn't get hurt.

I kissed her forehead repeatedly, before removing her arms from around my torso. I made sure she adjusted herself comfortably in her sleep, before pulling the cover over her and tucking her in tight. I couldn't be here when she woke up, that would show too much.

I looked around for my clothes, and put on each piece until I was fully dressed in my outfit from last night. I went to her desk and grabbed a piece of paper from her printer and a pen, to write her a note to let her know I would be back. I needed to get home to shower and dress, and not leave any trace to Jay and Lisa that I stayed the night last night.

I quickly jotted down what I needed to tell her, and folded it in half so it could stand on her dresser. I walked back over to her and placed one last kiss on her cheek, before walking out of her room and heading out the door.

Bobbi.

I reached out next to me, feeling for Donovan, and sprung my eyes opened when I felt an empty space. I sat up and stretched before looking frantically around the room, wondering where he had gone. I felt the emotion rise to my chest as I saddened thinking he had just left me alone, without any warning.

My eyes soon fell on a note that sat on top of the desk, and I reached over with my sheet wrapped tightly around my body to grab it.

Good Morning Beautiful,

Don't think I just left you, trust me, nothing in me wanted to. I just didn't want to get caught by Lisa or Jay naked in your bed. I'll be back after I shower and take a nap.

I smiled a little at his note, feeling a little better, but not quite, since he wasn't the first face I saw waking up. I lied back on the bed and took in a deep sigh, as my recollection of last night came back to me. I don't know what it was that allowed things to be taken so far with Donovan last night, I just couldn't deny how I felt any longer, and honestly didn't want to. This passion that was burning in my chest caused me to feel so alive and free and I wanted to bask in it as long as I could. Nothing was going to stop me from telling Don the truth about how I felt, and where I think we should go from here. I was connected, deeper than I planned to be, and I didn't want to let go.

Donovan.

I stood in the kitchen, helping Lisa wash dishes from tonight's Sunday dinner as the entire day recapped in my mind. Bobbi and I had been extremely clingy to each other all day because of the moment we had last night. I practically rushed back over here, not wanting her to think any different of me.

All day however, Pastor Miller's words to her kept replaying in my heart. How precious she was, and how much care she needed. Doubt continuously flooded my brain, realizing I wasn't the man she needed right now. I wasn't in my right mind myself, and there was no way I was in a position to add burden to her newly freed soul. I cared about her too much as a person to put her through any of my bullshit. But now, after what we expressed, it was going to be harder to let her go.

"I got the rest of this baby. You can go back with the kids," Lisa insisted, as I looked and saw there were only a few dishes left. I kissed her softly on her temple before drying my hands and heading upstairs. I knocked softly on Bobbi's door, and waited for her to give me permission to enter. Once she did, I walked in to see her admiring some photos in her hand.

"You did nothing but take pictures of me," She let out a short laugh and turned one of the pictures to face me. It was a shot I had got of her walking and running her fingers through her long wavy hair. It was an elegant photo.

"Is that a problem?" I smirked walking all the way in and closing the door behind me.

She chuckled and shook her head, "I just don't see how any of these could be of use in an art show," she shrugged setting the pictures down on the bed.

"You'd be surprised," I said softly, making my way to her. I was viewing her more and more as the days passed in a different light. I couldn't explain this feeling, what it meant or what it could be. All I knew is that I had to dead it before it truly grew.

"I gotta tell you something." I spoke as she nodded and smiled.

"I have to tell you something too. Well I actually wanna talk to you about something," she said, biting her cheek and messing with her fingers.

"Maybe you should go first."

She took in a deep breath, facing me completely, "I don't think I'm gonna see Aaron anymore." My eyes widened.

"Wh- why not? It's not because of me is it?"

She contorted her expression searching for the words to say.

"It's because of everything Don. I don't feel the way I do with Aaron that I do with you. And after last night, I just know that's not where I need to be. You and I both know that," she said as I tried to speak up to stop her from going forward. She was making this harder, with each word.

"Bobbi, I don't-"

"Listen, I know this is different, and new for both of us. And I'm not trying to rush anything. Just because we had sex, doesn't mean we have to have a relationship. I just don't want this feeling to leave from me. It feels good. It feels-"

I cut her off mid-sentence, finally gaining the courage to say what needed to be said.

"I don't think you should stop seeing Aaron."

Her smile slowly faded as she looked at me with confusion. "What?"

"Aaron is good for you Bobbi. Just because last night happened doesn't mean you should jump ship. I agree with what you said before. About us being friends."

I could see her heart falling in her eyes. If she only knew that this is what's best. I would ruin this before it even had a chance to start. If I hadn't already.

"You don't mean that," she said, shaking her head in denial.

"I do. Pastor Miller was right, you deserve so much more than what I could give," I said, reaching for her trying to give any type of comfort but she quickly backed away.

"No. That's bullshit! And you know it! You don't even believe what you're telling me right now," she replied, her voice full of emotion.

"Bobbi, I'm no good for you. When will you realize that? I will never care how you want and need me to. I can't be that person. I can't be all vulnerable and shit. There was a time when I thought I could be that guy, and then realized I couldn't. You deserve more than that. You've been through enough. You gon get caught up with me and go through even more bullshit."

She pursed her lips together tight, searching for the right words to say. "You can't. You can't do something like you did and then say you don't care. You can't. You made love to me...You saved my *life* taking me to church, Donovan. You don't save someone's life and then just try to walk away the minute you feel something real. That's not fuckin fair!"

"I didn't know all that was going to play out like it did."

"But you wanted me there. You invited me to come. When you could've went by your damn self, because you knew I needed it. You knew Don. You knew! And then you come in here and say I deserve better?! No one has ever done what you did for me. Nobody! No one saw it, but you. And then last night...the way you touched me...the way you held me..."

The tears were trickling down her face now, and I instantly felt like shit. The last thing I wanted was for her to cry.

"Please don't cry."

"Fuck you Don! Don't try to pretend like you care now. Don't pretend any more aight?! All you've been doing since day one is pretending. And you tried to tell me that I can't be real for shit? *You* can't be real! You can't accept when someone actually cares about your dumb ass, and wants to be a part of your life just as bad as you want to be a part of theirs!" she said pushing me hard in my chest. I quickly grabbed her hands to retrain her from pushing me again.

"You don't get it..." I told her as she looked up at me with glossed over eyes.

"I do get it. We're just alike! You're not the only person that's been hurt and abandoned in this world Don! But that doesn't mean I'm going to do the same shit! You won't even give anyone an opportunity to show you different! You won't even give yourself a chance to even love! I'm scared too, but I don't wanna be scared with you." She sniffed still looking up at me as I looked down at her. I released my grip from her wrist and began to wipe away the tears that were still present with the pad of my thumbs. I cuffed her cheeks in my hands, and let them stay there for a moment before leaning in closer. I just wanted her pain to stop.

Our lips met, and I kissed her softly and sensually before she found the strength to break away.

"I don't want to do this anymore. I can't. I'm going to end up making a fool of myself just trying to love you if I haven't already," she sighed, walking over to the bed and grabbing the freshly printed photos. She walked back over to me and extended the hand with the photos in them.

"You don't want to be here, I'm not gonna make you. I'm not gonna make you do shit. Donovan is gonna do what and who Donovan wants to do right?" she rhetorically asked, as I took the pictures but tried to grab her hand with my free one. Her reflexes were too quick.

"Don't feel bad. You know what you're doing right? Saving me from you. So do it. Just leave me alone. For real this time. Don't pop up on me, don't come demanding my attention and time. Don't do shit! If you don't want to be here, then just stay gone. No in between!" she said brushing past me and walking to the door, opening it for my exit.

"Bobbi, listen-"

She raised her hand to stop me.

"Get out Donovan. Nothing else needs to be said. I'll see you when I see you." She avoided my eyes, waiting for me to walk out. Before I did, I softly kissed her forehead as she scoffed in disbelief.

Later, she was going to thank me for this.

Bobbi.

I sat quiet in the hospital's cafeteria picking at the food on my lunch tray. It had been a few weeks since my blow out with Donovan and I still didn't really have an appetite. Following that night, I had told Aaron I thought it would be best if we remained friends. I wasn't giving him a fair chance, and I didn't feel a connection like I should have with someone special. After being set free, there was no reason to lie to myself or others anymore. That was the main reason why I had put everything out in the open to Don, especially after what we shared. I wanted more with him, and he rejected me, knowing deep down he didn't want to.

I finished what I could of my lunch and stood up to throw the remainders away. As I did, I was accidently bumped by a tall white coat figure. I looked up to see the most attractive man I had seen in a while. He didn't seem much older than me, and was a light brown complexion with chiseled features. His hair was smoothly laid, skin was glowing and his lips were slightly thin but had a soft texture.

He looked startled by our collision, but showed a toothy grin once locking eyes with me.

"I'm s-sorry," I stuttered clutching my tray as he smiled and removed it from my grasp.

"Apology is all mine, sweetheart," he said, reaching over and dumping the contents of my tray in the trashcan and setting it with the others. He focused his attention back to me. "Maybe you can help me?"

His voice was so strong and defined. He sounded so educated just with the way he spoke and conducted himself. I was in awe of this man.

"Um, yeah sure. Anything," I replied, not trying to sound so eager. I was just excited for our interaction to last a little longer.

"I'm a new resident doctor here, and I'm supposed to be in General Medicine. I can't seem to find it. Do you know where it is?" He asked me, placing his hands behind his back and searching my eyes. I was frozen for a second.

175

"Um yeah. That's my department. You can walk with me up there if you want?" I suggested, as he smiled and accepted my offer. He waited for me to walk before he followed.

"I'm Julian by the way. Julian Michaels," he introduced, extending his hand for me to shake.

"Bobbi. Nice to meet you Dr. Michaels." I smiled as he chuckled and stuffed his hands in his pants pockets.

"Julian is fine," he corrected.

"Can't call you Julian on the floor. I'll get in trouble," I told him as he nodded in understanding. We reached the elevator and I pressed the button to head upstairs.

"You're a nurse?" he questioned.

"Yeah. I'm new here though, and still have yet to take my registry exam."

"What's the delay?" he asked looking down at me intently. I could get lost in his blue colored eyes.

"Just haven't found the focus. It's preventing me from being full time too," I sighed, stepping onto the open elevator with Julian close behind. His Burberry scent quickly filled my nose.

"You should go for it. I can help you study if you need me to. I'm always studying now during my residency. We're in the same spot," he winked, as I blushed a little.

We reached the floor of our office and he waited for me to step off first. Tierre looked up from the front desk and did a double take as she noticed who was walking closely behind me. She mouthed the words 'Oh My God', causing me to chuckle before turning to face Dr. Michaels.

"This our stop?" he questioned, smiling softly at me.

"Yeah. The residents normally meet in that conference room down the hall and wait for the attending physicians." I instructed as he looked to where I was pointing and back at me.

"Will you be here when I get back?"

I giggled and nodded.

"I'll be here the entire month you're at this office Dr. Michaels."

"Good," he flirted, before leaving me to go down the hall. The second he left I could hear Tierre whispering from behind the desk.

"Who is he?!" she asked as I walked up closer to her, still feeling butterflies from my encounter with him.

"Julian Michaels. New resident." Her eyes widened.

"I ain't never seen a resident that sexy before. Did you see how fitting his arms were under that white coat? Damn. He was checking you out too." I fanned her off.

"Oh stop. You think everybody checks me out."

"Hell, Donovan who? You need to see what Julian's about. And he's about to be a doctor in probably a couple years? That's husband material. Everything probably worked out the way it did, just for this moment. Right here," her superficial ass stated, as I laughed and shrugged.

"I don't see a doctor being interested in a part time nurse. Plus he's probably married or something. You see how perverted the residents are with the medical assistants. Half of them have wives and children at home."

"That man ain't got no damn body. A man that looks like him is single. Stop acting like you're not good enough. You're more than good enough, for anyone. Don is just dumb," she assured, as I smiled a little and looked out the window. You could see their shop across the street from the one window in the lobby area. I missed him, wasn't going to deny that. Just had to move on.

****

I was ordering prescription refills for patients, and notating files when I felt a presence approach the nurses' station. I looked up only to see the handsome face I had the pleasure of running into earlier.

"Hello again, beautiful," he greeted, as I attempted to hide my smile from the compliment. He made me feel so childlike each time we had a conversation.

"Hello Dr. Michaels. Bobbi is fine," I explained, jokingly rolling my eyes as he chuckled.

"Beautiful suits you better, in my opinion."

I cleared my throat and folded my arms before the keyboard.

"If I didn't know any better, I would think you were flirting with me doctor."

"I would think that you would be right. I could hardly concentrate during our class because I kept thinking about your smile, and the cute expression you make when blushing. I had to make sure I saw that face one more time before I left," he confessed, my mouth falling slightly agape.

"I made quite an impression off one small conversation."

He shook his head no.

"You had my attention before we even spoke. It's just...when I'm really determined about something, and feel strongly towards it, I don't waste time going after it. I want to get to know you Bobbi. I can't explain why, I just do. And seeing how we're both busy individuals here, maybe after work, or even when my month is over, we can do just that." He spoke with so much confidence and poise. This was how a man approached a woman. And he was proving every bit of how man enough he was.

"You have me intrigued," I told him, still holding a slight bit of resistance to his actions. We weren't about to just jump the gun and start going out together outside of work just because I was impressed with his approach. I needed to know him deeper than that.

He laughed a little, catching the hint. "Let's start with lunch? Our lunch is every day at noon. We can eat together some days, if you don't mind?"

I smiled, liking the slower approach. "I won't mind that at all."

Donovan.

I stood in the back of the shop painting vigorously as Shane and I both waited for any walk in clients. Our books were cleared and it had been a slow morning, so I decided to use this time to prepare for my art show.

"Tierre bringing us lunch. What you want?" Shane asked me walking up. I shrugged; hadn't really been eating lately.

He smacked his teeth before he put the phone back to his ear. "Bring whatever. He don't care. Aight." He shoved his phone back in his pocket and stared at me while I painted.

"What's up with you man? Why don't you just go get your girl back?" he asked, as I finally looked at him for the first time. He and everyone else knew Bobbi and I weren't on speaking terms and weren't ever going to be. I was doing my best to deal with it.

"I'm not doing that," I replied in a low tone, dipping my paint brush in the red mixture of colors.

"Why not? You realize the relationship is messed up because you're getting in your own way right?"

"What you know Shane? You ain't had a girl either," I snapped as he groaned.

"That don't mean I ain't never been in love Don. I'm coo with how that feels, I'm not afraid of it. You just need to quit being a crybaby about the whole situation and suck in your pride. Go apologize, tell her you ain't mean it and get her back. Why you making this hard?"

"Stay out of it." Shane huffed and started to walk back towards the front room.

"I ain't gon say shit else. You'll see what you've done sooner or later."

A part of me wondered what he meant by that statement, but as quickly as the thought came, it left. I placed my headphones back over my ears, and let the music overtake me as my brush collided with the canvas.

What seemed to be forty-five minutes later, I was interrupted by Tierre placing her arm on my shoulder. I removed my headphones and looked at the art that was laid out in front of us both.

"Dope," she said, giving an impressed nod. She turned, stood on her tippy toes and placed a friendly kiss on my cheek.

"How you?" she asked softly as I searched my mind for the right way to answer that question.

"Cool. Workin." I was short with my response and she looked into my eyes for the truth.

She smirked a little before walking away towards the center of the shop. There were pizza boxes sitting on our coffee table. "Hey when's your art show again? Bobbi wanted me to ask."

The sound of her name nearly caught me off guard. I was surprised she still even wanted to come.

"You lying," I said in disbelief, leaving the canvas to join Tierre on the couches. Shane walked from his office a few minutes later, rubbing his hands.

"Yes! Pizza. This smells so good TiTi," he said, kissing her on the cheek and plopping down right in front of the food. Neither one of us had even touched it.

"Why would I lie about that? She asked me about it today. I tried to get her to come over here with me and ask herself, but she goes to lunch with someone every day now," she said in a nonchalant tone, while reaching for a slice of pizza. I tipped a brow.

"Who she going to lunch with?"

She chuckled.

"Does it even matter? It ain't us."

I decided not to push the issue further. The crew was doing a good job of keeping us away from each other and knowing the other's business. Didn't stop me from wondering though.

"Show is the twenty-third," I finally answered, getting comfortable on the couch. I wasn't hungry, and now I couldn't stop wondering who Bobbi was going to lunch with.

"Is it okay if we bring dates?" Tierre asked, with her mouth full. Shane looked at me for an answer as well.

"I don't care. Tickets are ten dollars presale. I'll have some ya'll can buy next week." I looked at Tierre suspiciously. "What dude you bringin?"

"Got a little boo thing. Everyone is probably going to be coupled up, so I'm not gonna go solo."

Shane's eyes widened. "Everybody? Shit. Who I'm bringing then?" he wondered out loud.

"Joi. Who else? The baby momma you love to hate," Tierre teased, as we laughed at the annoyed expression resting on his face.

"I'm not bringing her ass. Next thing you know we're a couple in her mind. I'm good on that. I'm sure I'll find somebody to fall through," he smirked, rubbing his chin.

"Like who? Don't bring no random hoe to introduce us to. She's going to be around all of us. Remember that," Tierre reminded him, as he blew her off.

"That's stressful. Fuck it. Imma go dolo. Don gonna be dolo too."

"Aww you and Don can be each other's date!" she cooed, as we both shot her an evil stare.

"Don't need a date," I said calmly, reaching for a slice of pizza.

Shane smacked his lips. "You just banking on Bobbi coming by herself."

"If she knows what's good for her," I warned, sitting back and taking a bite of my food.

"Guess she doesn't know what's good for her then," Tierre said slyly, as I ignored her comment. Bobbi wouldn't disrespect me by bringing another man to my event. At least I hope she wouldn't.

****

Shane and I stepped out of his car and walked up to Jay's door. He was having a small kickback at his crib to celebrate his father finally getting a job stationed about an hour away from their house, so he was home for good. We were down to come through, because all of us loved and respected Vince. He was the father we all wished we had.

Shane rang the doorbell and we waited a few moments before Vince answered the door with a cigar in his mouth. He removed it and smiled widely at us opening his arms.

"My boys!" He yelled as we did too, shocked he was the one that greeted us first. He stepped onto the porch and pulled each of us into a strong embrace. He was a little shorter than me, with a bald head and dark complexion. His years in the navy gave him strong arms, and a stocky build.

"Sup pops!" Shane chuckled as Vince rubbed his hand through his hair. Shane was in a phase where he was growing his hair out to let it get a little curly. I guess he was getting girls or some shit.

"Come in ya'll. Grab a drink. Grab some food. We got a pretty full house tonight," he said, placing his cigar through his teeth and opening the door wider for us to come in. We could hear some old school NWA music playing in the background. I already knew it was going to mostly be an older crowd.

"Hey Don, I wanna talk witcha before you leave too. Got some shit to tell ya," he said, placing a firm hand on my shoulder as I shuttered a little. I had a feeling what it was going to be about.

"I got you Vince."

He smiled and patted me one more time before scooping his beautiful wife up in his arms. Lisa was the most attractive older woman I knew. She had flawless skin, a gorgeous smile and always kept her short cut in a nice style. She reminded me of a slightly older version of Nia Long. Just as beautiful and radiant.

The house was full with Vince's brothers and sisters, his closest friends, Lisa's friends and Jay's friends which included Shane, Tierre and his girlfriend Felicia. Everyone but the person I wanted to see most. I chose not to ask about her whereabouts.

"Have a drink bro. Pops wanted nothing but dark tonight." Jay laughed as he poured Shane and me a shot of Jameson's whisky.

"Got damn. Jameson though? You know how this make me act." I frowned clutching my stomach and looking down at Jay.

"We finna be tore off bro. Pops want it like this. He happy to be home." He grinned as we both shrugged.

We took three shots together, and I was already beginning to feel under some type of influence. I coughed and looked around the room for Tierre, hoping that she would lead me to Bobbi.

"Yo, where's booty?" I asked to no one in particular, looking around. Jay nodded his head in the direction towards the front of the door.

"She went to meet Bobbi and ol' boy at the door," Jay said nonchalant.

I screwed up my face. "Ya'll invited Aaron? For real?"

The attitude was clear in my tone.

He chuckled and shook his head. "Hell no. Julian."

Julian?

As if on cue, Bobbi appeared from the hallway and into the dining area where most of the guests were mingling. Vince saw her and instantly swept her into his arms and admired his niece. She looked amazing tonight. She was wearing high-waist jeans, that formed perfectly around her small frame, a cropped off the shoulder white shirt, and her long hair was up in a bun that sat on the top of her head. She looked radiant and happy. As I continued to admire her, I noticed that her hand was connected to someone else's; some pretty looking dude that seemed slightly older than us. I listened intently on her introducing this man to Vince.

"Uncle, this is Dr. Michaels. He was working with me at the hospital this past month." She smiled, looking up at him with so much adoration.

Dude showed an amused grin, extending his free hand to shake Vince's, "Call me Julian sir. And it's an honor to finally meet you. Chanel was telling me about how long you've been serving for this country. I truly appreciate everything you do to protect us each and every day." He said giving a short bow of respect as I felt my blood boil. Here he was calling Bobbi by her middle name, thinking he was hot shit. I wanted to punch him in his throat.

"The honor is mine. You're a doctor?" Vince questioned, placing the cigar back between his teeth.

"Yes I am. I'm currently in my residency, and had the pleasure of meeting your niece during my study at her office. Now that we technically no longer work together, she decided to finally step out with me in public." He laughed as Vince joined him. I mockingly laughed to myself, mimicking this corn ball of a dude and turning back to take another shot. All eyes were on me.

"What?" I growled, snatching the bottle from Jay's hands. He and Shane both laughed at me.

"You feeling some type of way bruh?" Shane asked, humorously. I drank straight out the bottle, as the burn of the liquid made its way down my throat and settled into my stomach. The sting of the taste didn't allow me to do that much longer.

I made a face looking around for any type of chaser. While doing so, I accidently locked eyes with Bobbi before she directed her attention back to her date. My eyes rolled, as I found a cup and poured orange juice inside. I took a sip, allowing the taste of orange to overpower the strong taste of liquor.

"This what you wanted right?" Jay smirked, taking a sip out of his cup as well. Felicia and Tierre soon joined us in the kitchen, in mid conversation.

"Girl," Felicia started, with her eyes still directed towards the dining room. "I remember you saying he was fine, but not that fine. Jesus." She fake fanned herself as Jay pinched her sides.

"Come on man. Really?" Jay asked, not at all amused by her comment. She laughed and nudged him a little.

"I'm sorry baby, but Bobbi's boo is cute. Like grown man cute." Jay's face remained blank and Felicia turned to face him. "Not as cute as you though!" she teased, as the rest of the group chuckled at their interaction.

She continued to apologize, as I noticed Tierre staring at me. I looked away, avoiding her stare, but my efforts were no good because she soon stood next to my side.

"Penny for your thoughts?" she asked softly as I looked down at her.

"I messed up."

Bobbi.

I was sitting on the couch with Julian, both of us with cups in our hand and slightly buzzed at Uncle Vince's party. I had invited him last minute, not wanting to face everyone alone, and he willingly agreed to come. Uncle Vince and Auntie loved him already. Every chance Vince got he was leaning on Julian's shoulder saying some drunken nonsense about how the medical field is a scam.

"Thank you for coming with me here, tonight," I smiled, resting my head against the back of the couch. His arm was rested over top of me and he scooted in closer so we could talk more intimately.

"Thanks for inviting me," he said before looking behind him, then looking back at me. "Hey, I noticed you haven't really been around your cousin and his friends tonight. There's a few people around him I never met..."

I shrugged a little, looking into his eyes that were showing a hint of gray tonight. "I see them all the time. I just wanna be around you. You make me feel...safe," I confessed, still avoiding the word happy. He grinned, before gently grabbing my hand and caressing it.

"I can make you feel like this all the time, if you give me the chance to. I would make you the happiest woman in the world, if you allowed me." He removed his hand from mine, and used it stroke my cheek as I bit my lip. The alcohol or this moment was making me too emotional for words.

"Um, I have to use the restroom," I said abruptly, halting our conversation. "Don't let my Uncle torture you while I'm gone." I giggled, standing to my feet.

"Hurry back love." I nodded and walked through the dining room towards the hall, avoiding eye contact from anyone.

Since locking eyes with Donovan, I was feeling so many emotions flood back like they never left. We hadn't seen each other or spoken since that night, and that was over a month and a half ago. I knew we were going to bump heads, sooner or later, and

I thought I was ready for it to be tonight. I wanted him to see me with a new man on my arm, a good man at that, thinking it would spark some type of fight in him. It didn't. Nothing sparked, nothing popped off. Nothing happened. He didn't care. Even seeing me moved on, he didn't care. And he never was going to. My denial of believing differently started reeling its ugly head. His words rang true. He didn't want to be with me.

I stepped into my room and covered my face with my hands to prevent the tears from falling. I was having trouble accepting Julian, because Donovan still sat comfortably in my heart. I started to regret every heart to heart, every moment, every single minute I spent with him. Just wish I would've stuck to when I hated the ground he walked on.

"What you doing here with him, huh?" I heard the familiar raspy voice ask as I spun around, coming face to face with him. He stood tall, his slender body covered in a black t-shirt, gold chain, black jeans, Ken Griffey shoes, and black leather hat resting backwards on his head. Typical Cali boy.

I cleared my dry throat before whispering, "Wh...what are you doing up here?"

"Look like you needed me. So I came up here to give you that," he stated, standing his ground at the entrance of the door.

I shook my head slowly, still in awe of this moment. "No. I don't need you. You can go now." I dismissed, waiting for him to leave. Instead he stepped in further closing the door behind him.

"What if I don't wanna go?" he asked, revealing his strong jaw line. I felt chills shoot up my spine with how sexy he looked to me.

"I want you to go. I don't need you doing this to me right now Don. I've moved on from you," I said lowly, as he began to walk closer to me, the energy rising between us with each passing step. My body was beginning to feel overwhelmed with desire the closer he got.

"No you haven't."

We were inches apart. I started to back into my desk, trying to escape his presence.

"I have Don. You don't mean shit you say. You just wanna keep playin with me like my heart is some toy," I choked, as his stare down continued.

"What you wanna hear from me huh?" He asked stepping closer cornering me against the desk.

"You wanna hear I miss you? You wanna hear I can't stop thinking about your ass?" He gritted lifting me up in one motion and placing me on the edge of my desk. He parted my legs and stood in between them as he aggressively pulled me close by cuffing my bottom cheeks. I let out a gasp in shock and pleasure.

"I know you miss me, and I know you can't stop thinking about me but..." I stuttered, as his face was inches away from mine, the heat intensifying.

"Do you know," he started in a low breathy voice, "Do you know, I've never wanted someone this bad in my life?" His hands started rubbing up and down my sides as he pressed his forehead against mine; both of us resisting the kiss that was threatening to happen.

I placed his cheeks in my palms and forced him to look at me, his eyes were low and lustful, chewing his bottom lip.

"What you wanna hear from me baby?" he asked again. I swallowed hard, trying to steady my breathing.

"That you love me." He looked deep into my eyes. Without another word, his lips were hungrily pressed against mine, forcing our tongues to dance with one another.

He placed his hand on the back of my head pushing me further into the kiss, sending a moan to escape in his mouth. My hands made their way under his shirt, while my fingers roamed up and down his torso. He then pressed his pelvis firmly against me, allowing a rush of wetness to release from my center.

"Ahh," I hissed against his lips, causing him to pick me up and wrap my legs around his waist for support.

"What you doin to me girl?" He breathed, sucking his lips and holding me close to him. My arms were around his neck, holding on for dear life, not wanting this moment to slip away.

"I want you so damn bad," he moaned, before he took a deep breath. "I just..." He sighed not allowing himself to release any more secrets. I just needed him to say it. Just needed him to tell me what my heart was yearning to hear.

I softly kissed his lips, and began reaching my legs to the floor, regaining my body from our previous position. The moment they touched solid ground, I began adjusting myself and calming down from the state I was just in.

Donovan kept his head down in disappointment as I nodded slowly accepting the reality of it all.

"I'm not going to make you say something you're not ready to say. Or feel something you're not ready to feel." I shook my head, pressing my fingers to my lips. "I just shouldn't have allowed it to go that far."

I began to head for the door, until his voice stopped me in my tracks

"Bobbi wait!"

I turned on my heels and crossed my arms facing his direction.

"I don't want to lose you." A laugh of disbelief released from my chest. Only way I could stop the tears.

"Yeah? Well you have yet to prove that," I responded, shaking my head, leaving him there and never looking back.

Donovan.

I strolled back into the dining room, drunk and confused about what just happened. All I had to tell her, was how I truly felt and still couldn't express it. She had been open with me, pretty much confessing that she was in love with me, and I left her there. Unable to catch her as she fell. I searched the room for her face. The second I spotted her I felt a strong arm grip my shoulder, halting me from continuing my path.

"Come with me to the back son," Vince instructed, nodding his head towards the patio door. I assumed we were going to talk about what he mentioned earlier.

I did as I was told, and walked with Vince through the living room towards the patio door. I looked at Bobbi sitting back on the couch with that guy; she wouldn't even return my stare. They were both wrapped up in a deep conversation. I sighed in defeat.

Vince waited for me to step onto the patio, before he slid the door closed. He took a couple paces, looking out at the night sky before he turned to face me.

"Now that I'm back, I really wanna talk to you about Marcus. Me and him have been writing lately..."

I tuned him out after hearing the sound of my father's name. I knew this shit was gonna be about him.

"Honestly Vince, I don't wanna hear nothing about that dude. He's been missing for the past 19 years. We don't have anything to talk about," I said, beginning to turn and head for the door until Vince spoke up.

"He's...he's in prison Donovan. He's been locked up for 10 of those years," Vince explained, stopping me in my tracks. I turned and looked at him with a brow raised.

"Prison? Where?"

He sighed. "Santa Monica. I looked him up a few years back and we've been writing back and forth since then. He didn't know anything Don. Didn't know Danielle passed, didn't know ya'll moved, nothing."

I stood firm, clenching my fist tight. "Why he in there?"

"He wants you to come visit him. He wants to tell you everything face to face, man to man."

I vigorously shook my head, "I'm not going to see him. That's still nine unexplained years Vince. How you just walk away from your child huh? Walk away and never look back? Like he don't even exist? You've been more of a father to me than he has."

Vince nodded, "He knows that. I always told him I was always gonna look after you. Since the day you were born. But son, I know you've wanted an explanation all this time. I know you've needed answers, and he's ready to provide that for you."

I was quiet looking through the patio doors at Bobbi and her date. She was able to receive her closure and peace when it came to her father. It's why she found herself happier now. Guess I needed mine.

"When's his next visitation day?"

****

My palms were sweaty pulling up to the Santa Monica penitentiary. I hadn't seen this man in years, and here he was, requesting for me to visit him. He's been locked up for ten years, and now of all times, he wants to talk to me. Vince's address hasn't changed. He had multiple ways to find me.

I took in a deep breath and said a small prayer in my mind, asking God to prevent me from trying to kill him. Stepping out of the car, I allowed the cool air to also calm my nerves with each passing wind. I walked slow and steady to the prison's door and went inside to be greeted by a female guard. She was heavy set, and smacked her gum loudly while typing profusely on her computer.

I stepped up to the table where she sat and cleared my throat catching her attention. She looked up at me over her wide framed glasses and scoffed at my presence.

"Visitation?" I nodded. "Inmate name please?" she asked, sliding the clipboard sitting in front of her in my direction so I could sign in. I began jotting my name down before answering.

"Donovan Marcus McCall," I told her, filling out my name on the piece of paper.

"You Donovan McCall too?" she asked looking at the screen; I'm assuming seeing all of his visitors for the day.

"Yes I am."

"Please hand me two forms of ID and remove anything metal that you have on your person. We have lockers behind you where you can store your belongings until your session is over." I dug in my pocket to pull out my driver's license and social security card. Once she took it to make a copy, I started to remove my watch and chain, along with my cell phone and wallet. I went to the lockers she suggested and paid fifty cents so I could rent one for the next couple hours. After placing everything inside, she called me back over to the desk.

"Just walk through those metal detectors there and the officer will lead you to the visitation area. Have a good one," she said dryly as I stuffed the forms of identification in my pocket. I walked through the metal detector and was patted down the minute I passed through. After a thorough search, the guard led me through two bolt locked doors and into the main area outside of the prison's walls.

"They'll be arriving shortly," he informed. I nodded and took a seat at an empty table. I looked around me to see the other family's waiting on their loved ones to arrive. Most of them were smiling and excited to see them, I on the other hand had a stone cold expression. My heart was filled with mixed emotions; what I was going to say, how I was going to react. I just needed closure, and that's what I intended on getting.

A few minutes later, I noticed several guards escorting inmates from inside the building. I searched all down the row until I saw him. A face that resembled my own. He looked much older than I remembered. His skin was darker, and his hair gray. His eyes were sad and sullen as he frantically looked around for my face. I stood up, so he would notice me, and before I knew it our eyes were locked. He smiled for the first time and made his way over to me, shoving his hands in his pockets.

My heartbeat quickened the closer he got. All the anger I had built up over the years was flooding away, and now more than anything, I just wanted him around. I wanted him to accept me. I wanted him to love me. I sniffed back the sentiment threatening to reveal itself.

"My son."

He smiled, only inches away from me. Before I could respond, he pulled me into a firm embrace. I didn't resist, just hugged the man back. He rested his palm on the back of my head, and I heard sniffling coming from his nose. He finally released me and held me by the shoulders, looking at me close with tears in his eyes.

"My son," he repeated once more, this time with a happy chuckle. I half smirked looking at the older version of myself, before he patted me, gesturing to have a seat.

He sniffed some more making himself comfortable on his side of the table and clasped his hands together, after wiping the tears from the ducts.

"I'm sorry, just never thought I was going to have the chance to do that again," he said, releasing the breath he was holding. His voice had a hint of the rasp that also existed in mine.

"Vince convinced me to come here. Not for you, but for me," I said sternly, not taking my eyes off of him. He nodded in understanding before he spoke.

"I know. It took a long time of pleading before he even agreed to tell you where I was. He was very protective and mindful of your feelings." He nervously rubbed the back of his neck, as I sighed small.

"Why now? Why you wanna see me now? And why are you here?" I asked, keeping my composure. Just because we hugged, didn't mean I was going to let up on this dude.

He blew out a breath before he spoke again. "It took a long time for me to realize the kind of person I was and to accept the mistakes I've made, not only as a father but as a man. I wasn't in my right mind when you were little Donovan. I had an addiction, to many things."

I shifted a little in my seat continuing to listen. "I was very abusive to your mother. Physically and verbally, because of the addiction I had to cocaine and alcohol. You may not remember, but I used to be gone for days, sometimes weeks at a time. And Danni would take me back, each and every time for you. Me and you though? We had a bond like no other. You were always my little buddy, and the one person that never saw any wrong in me. You would look to me with hopeful eyes, and watched every move I made. Your mother made sure I never came around you high. She didn't want you to see me like that."

He stopped and smiled to himself, ripping a piece of grass into tiny bits. I searched his eyes, trying to see if I recognized them.

"That night..." he finally started again, after a few more moments of silence. "I'll never forget the night I left. Danielle and I were arguing upstairs, and I threw her around a bit. Drunk. I went downstairs to drink some more and just sleep it off. And then you came and sat on my lap. Said the most precious thing you ever said." He paused, reflecting on the memory as I tensed up.

"You said, 'Daddy. You're not a bad daddy. You're the best daddy and I love you so much. Don't be sad, ok?'" He said mimicking my small voice.

"That ate me up son. I knew I had to leave to get help. I didn't want to let you down. I didn't want to treat Danielle the way I was treating her. And I wasn't gonna come back until I was the man you believed I was. So, when I left I had the intentions of checking into rehab, which I did. But as soon as I checked in, I checked out. It was a long broken road from there," he sighed, now beginning to pick at a leaf that had landed on our table.

"I wasn't worth it to you? To get clean?"

He looked into my eyes.

"Son, when you're strung out off a drug, nothing else seems worth it. That's the honest truth. You don't think about nothing but the next fix. I was doing anything to get high. It didn't matter that I didn't have a place to live. I just wanted to get high to forget about everything else that fell apart."

"How you end up here?"

"Got caught up in some mess with the Latin Kings. So they made me smuggle some drugs across the border. I got caught getting high off the drugs they gave. They found the rest. Gave me fifteen years because I wouldn't drop names. I would've, had I not forgot what they were." He chuckled small as I did too with a shake of my head.

He took in a deep breath, lifting his head up, "To be honest witcha Don, this was probably the best thing that could've ever happened to me. I got clean, got in church, took some classes. Just bettered myself you know? I ended up getting a letter from Vince about seven years ago, telling me about your mom and how you were living with them now. He sent me pictures of how big you had gotten. Told me when you started your business. Everything. Said you became a pretty good man without me. I knew I couldn't raise you to be no man son. I was a lost soul, and would have created such a bad environment for you and Danielle. I know looking back, my actions were selfish, and it wasn't right to just leave you, but I couldn't hurt you by staying either. You needed a man, and I wasn't man enough to be him. I pray every day that one day you'll forgive me. Forgive me for not being there, missing you grow up, not being able to give you advice on girls and teach you how to drive. I used to cry thinking about how much I missed. As your father, I'm letting you know, I screwed up bad. I left some scars, that don't heal quickly. But I promise you, I don't want to miss a second chance at watching you develop even more and getting to know who you are now. I'm not gonna let you down this time son, I can promise you."

I bit my lip hard, trying to stop the tears from dropping. "You know how long I've been waiting to hear that? Just an apology? An explanation? I came up here knowing I hated you, knowing I wasn't gonna forgive you, possibly thinking about punching you in the face..."

I laughed a little, reflecting on my previous thoughts.

"But now, all I want is to have peace with this situation. I lost my mom, and I'm losing my grandmother. I'm not trynna lose you too Marcus. If I have a chance to make things better with you, I'm gonna take this chance. The second you fuck up, then just be prepared not to see me again. I can promise you, that."

"I can respect it."

Bobbi.

I was sitting at the table, studying for my upcoming registry exam when my Uncle Vince walked through the garage door, carrying several grocery bags.

"You need help Unc?" I asked him, fixing to stand up, before he quickly shook his head, closing the door with his foot.

"Naw, baby I got it. Just picked up a few things for Lisa on the way home so she wouldn't have to," he winked before walking into the kitchen to set the bags down.

"How you? What you doing home so early?" he questioned, as I heard some tussling in the kitchen, signaling he was putting the groceries away.

"I'm still part-time. That's why I'm studying for this test so I can become a registered nurse, get more hours, and make more money," I informed him, flipping a page through my book.

"Sounds smart," he sounded impressed. "I've noticed that doctor guy coming around more."

I chuckled a little, knowing Vince was bad with names. "Yeah, we've been seeing each other a lot more."

"You like him?" he snickered, earning a giggle from me. He sounded just like Jay when he gets childish.

"I'm interested and I enjoy getting to know him," I said, trying to concentrate and answer his questions at the same time.

"Doesn't sound like you like 'em to me." I turned around in my chair so I could see him in the kitchen.

"And how is that?"

He shrugged, "You just sound bored when you speak of him. He sounds good, like a good catch. Doesn't mean he's good for you."

I stopped for a moment, debating mentally if I was going to ask him this question. "You ever been torn Unc? Between what you want and what you deserve?"

He stopped what he was doing and looked at me. "Yeah." Then he smirked, "Till I realized I should have both. And not settle for anything less than that."

"How can you do that if someone has to the potential to be both, but refuses?" I asked, really needing an answer.

"Timing is everything baby girl. Some people just need that time to grow and develop. That doesn't mean you have to wait, just don't settle in the meantime. Can't work solely off of potential. Potential may never manifest." he smiled, before he began to put the rest of the groceries up.

"Think Imma cook ya'll dinner tonight..." he pondered out loud, rubbing his chin, changing our conversation completely. That's what I loved about my uncle; he never pushed a topic just because you opened up to him about it. He was available to talk, whenever you were ready.

****

"So," Tierre asked while parting another row in my hair to straighten it. "How you think Donovan is going to react to you bringing Julian to his art show?"

We were upstairs in my room; I was sitting in a chair as she stood and flat ironed the natural mess that had become of it after washing.

I shrugged. "I don't care," I lied, as she let out a chuckle.

"You do. Because this is a big deal, you bringing him around Don, especially at something so personal and special for him. It sounds kind of spiteful if you ask me."

"This is what he wanted. He wanted me to move on and be with someone better than him. I don't get your friend, I really don't." I sighed in frustration while feeling the steam from the flat iron against my scalp.

"Did you tell him how you felt?"

"Yes, plenty of times. Put myself out there just to get rejected. I just can't make him fight for something he doesn't want."

"He wants you though."

"When I'm around. It's out of sight out of mind with him. I don't cross his mind when I'm gone. He acts like I never existed. Then when he sees me, it's a whole different story. All he wants to do is kiss me and be up under me, and get jealous when he sees someone else all over me."

She was quiet for a moment before speaking back up. "What happened with ya'll? Like... what made you guys be done with each other?" she questioned nervously, as I adjusted myself a bit in the chair.

I bit my lip. "You really want to know?"

"Yes fool."

I laughed at her irritated response, "You can't tell anyone Tierre. Nobody you know."

She smacked my shoulder a little, "I promise, what's up."

I took in a deep breath, "You know the night of your party? Well...Don took me home that night."

"I thought so, because when I looked around, both of you guys were gone. I kept hoping you two would speak before the night was over. I love my cousin and all, but everyone could tell that you liked Donovan more. Even him. Just didn't want to accept it."

I just nodded at her words before I continued, "Well. That night when we got to my house he came in to like make sure everything was cool. And then he came upstairs to my room, both of us still a little tipsy. Then, we kissed...and one thing led to another.."

Tierre gasped before dropping the flat iron on the floor and pushing me in my back. "Oh my God! You two fucked?!"

I scoffed at the term she used, "We didn't do that. We made love Ti. Like genuinely. It was passionate and intense...and I could just tell he loved me just by the way he took care of me and looked at me in the midst of it all. I almost told him I loved him, but he cut me off," I confessed, as she still looked at me with complete shock in her expression.

"That is insane. So what the hell happened to cause ya'll to fall out?!"

I shrugged, "He couldn't handle it. Couldn't handle the way he felt when it happened and the emotions he was starting to feel. He backed up before he even gave it a chance and it caused a big argument. I didn't talk to him until my Uncle's party. Even then, I tried to get him to admit and he wouldn't."

She shook her head before picking the flat iron back up, "That's deep. I can't believe ya'll had sex! Nobody even guessed that shit. We just thought it was another thing between the two of you. Wow."

"Don't tell a soul," I warned again, as she snickered, grabbing another piece of hair.

"Oh I'm not. But Don is gonna be livid when he see you walking in with Julian. Like pissed beyond belief now that I know what really went down and got him acting like a goth."

"I don't care anymore. I really tried what I could, and I'm just not gonna fight for it. I look crazy fighting for affection that doesn't want to be returned when Julian gives it to me freely."

"Julian is nice, and you guys get along great, but does he make you feel better than D does?" she questioned as I bit my cheek to think.

"Honestly? He doesn't. But what can I do? It's not like I'm settling for him, because he's a great man and makes me feel like a woman. Just the connection that I'm seeking and yearning for isn't there. It's just the classic tale of a good girl who wants the bad guy over the good guy. I've had my share of bad guys, so I'm giving the good guy a fair chance. Just need Don completely out of my system."

"So what happens when Don decides to fight? What happens then? You walk away from what you have for him?"

I stared blankly ahead of me, searching for the honest answer.

"No." I responded firmly. "I don't."

****

"Wow, you look beautiful baby!" Lisa beamed, watching me step out from the hallway and into the spot light. I was wearing an all black maxi dress, with a deep cut in the front that covered my chest, and a gold plate connecting the top and bottom. My hair was straightened, down my back, and I had long gold earrings in.

Tierre had done light make up for me, and I had on nude lipstick to bring it all together. I felt beautiful.

Vince walked up and placed a gentle kiss against my temple. "Gorgeous baby girl," he complimented. I looked at both Jay and Felicia who were smiling at me. We were all preparing to head to Donovan's art show once Julian arrived.

He arrived about five minutes later and couldn't stop gawking at how wonderful I looked. I smiled bashfully all the way to his 2014 all black BMW. He opened the door for me, and I promptly sat inside, strapping the seatbelt across my chest, waiting for him to appear in the driver's seat.

"Chanel, seriously. You are looking good." He lightly bit his lip causing me to chuckle. Whenever Julian made a sexual notion in my direction I never took him seriously. He didn't excite me in that way.

"Thank you, love." He leaned over and snuck a kiss on my cheek before starting the car up.

"So this is a friend of your cousin? Right?" he questioned taking off down the road, following closely behind Jay and Felicia.

I nodded, peering out the window. "Yeah, Donovan. He and their friend Shane own the tattoo parlor across the street from the hospital."

"Oh? In that plaza? I've been over that way a few times. No idea, two young guys owned it," he said, impressed.

"Yeah, Donovan is the more artistic one of the two. I'm actually very excited to see his work," I admitted, smirking to myself a little. Out of all this time, I never really had a chance to see his artwork and was intrigued to know how he expressed himself.

"I'm assuming this is his first art show?"

I beamed and nodded, ignoring the funny look he was giving me.

"It is."

The rest of the ride was silent before pulling up to the popular gallery in Hollywood. There were already plenty of people there, from the rich and famous to religious art lovers. This show was to showcase new and aspiring talent in the greater Los Angeles area and was a huge spectacle to be a part of. The fact that Donovan's artwork was good enough to be a part of this, said so much about his talent.

Julian pulled up to valet so we wouldn't have to stress over parking. After he paid, we waited by the entrance for Jay and Felicia who were being closely followed by Tierre and her date, and Shane and Shai's mother, Joi. As much as he complained, we all knew he was going to end up bringing her.

After a short greeting we made our way into the beautiful and brightened gallery. So much art was on display and different artist were standing in front of their work, talking to different buyers and onlookers about it. I looked all around trying to see if I could spot Donovan's face in the crowd, but came with nothing.

"When I texted Don earlier he said his display was more towards the back. We're gonna walk around though, see everyone's work," Shane explained, as we all nodded in agreement, each couple heading in a different direction.

Julian grabbed my hand gently moving towards the left side. I couldn't help but get shy, seeing certain celebrities walking casually around the venue.

"There are so many famous people here," I whispered to him, trying not to make eye contact with a popular singer.

Julian chuckled leaning his shoulder into mine, "Get used to it sweetheart. The type of places I want to take you, we'll come across celebrities all of the time. Hell, me and my father have played golf with Magic Johnson and his brother." I laughed a little too, knowing he wasn't coming from a bragging place. Julian's father was a very successful and rich businessman, so he had been introduced to the fortunate life at a very young age.

"You think I have what it takes to be among such a high class? Rich people can be snooty," I said, turning up my nose a bit. He snickered at my comment while placing his head down to hide his amusement.

"They can be. But the ones I surround myself with are very down to earth and humble about their upbringing. We all look at it as, our parents are rich, not us. We're making a living in our own unique way."

I looked around at the many paintings on the wall, "So are you interested in buying any of these?" I asked, walking idly, arm in arm with my gorgeous date.

His deep blue eyes squinted at some of the work, until they opened widely at one in particular. He stopped suddenly causing me to stop as well.

"This is one is just beautiful." I followed his eyes to the painting on the wall and my heart instantly dropped. Resting before us was a painting of...me.

You couldn't tell from looking at it dead on, but because I was the woman in the picture, I knew. It was one of me walking along the path, surrounded by trees and scenery. The path behind me was filled with color, and the path ahead of me was black and white. Each step I took, I added a little more light to my surroundings. My head was tilted down at an angle as I watched the steps I had already taken.

Julian looked around. "I wonder where the artist is for this piece? I think I want to talk numbers."

I quickly pulled at his arm, trying to lead him away, "No, we should look at some more before-"

"Hey Bobbi," Donovan greeted, approaching us with his hands stuffed in his pockets. He was wearing black slacks, a black button up, and a patterned blazer, with glasses to add effect. Even fully dressed, you could see the tattoos emerging on his neck. He looked amazing to me.

"You painted this?" Julian asked, looking suspiciously between the two of us.

Donovan smiled and nodded.

"Yes, I did."

"You must be Donovan," Julian extended his hand. "I'm-"

"Justin, I remember," Don smirked while firmly gripping Julian's hand. I crossed my eyes, knowing he did that on purpose.

Julian smirked, "Ah. It's Julian actually. This though, this is an amazing piece," he complimented, not at all fazed by Donovan's asshole remark.

He quickly glanced at me before looking back up at the artwork, "Yes. This one is my favorite. Much different than the others I have on display."

Julian and I both looked at the pieces surrounding it, all more street and graffiti art. The one of me obviously required a lot of time and patience.

"You're right about that. What's the story? What's it called?" Julian asked, wrapping his arm around my waist and gently pulling me closer to him. I saw Donovan bite down hard, before regaining focus.

"I call it, Her Peace. Each step she takes, she's gaining more confidence to conquer and paint the world she once saw colorless and lifeless. She's building it back with each step, gaining more and more peace as she walks. She's bold and not afraid of what seems bleak in front of her, yet focused on the beautiful life she has already created as it follows wherever she goes." He explained, as I felt myself get full of emotion.

I saw Julian preparing to ask more when the rest of the crew came and greeted Donovan excitedly.

"Yo, this is major, son!" Tierre squealed pulling Donovan into a warm hug with Felicia following suit. I quickly sniffed to gather myself, while he was being greeted by our friends. Jay looked on at the painting Donovan just finished explaining before looking over at me and then back at it. I could see in his expression that he had caught on.

"So where's your date?" Shane teased looking around the room, as there were a few short snickers, causing me to feel even more awkward.

He flashed a look at me before he rubbed his nose slightly, "She's around." Everyone's eyes widened. I furrowed my brows a little but quickly changed my expression. If I could bring a date, so could he.

"No shit? Where?" Tierre blatantly asked looking around the room.

"Nosy ass," he sneered before conversation started amongst the group. Julian was still looking at Donovan's painting.

I rested my chin on his shoulder peeking at Don's other work. He was an amazing artist. I couldn't believe he was hiding this for so long.

"Your friend is really good. I can tell you don't want me to buy that picture though," he smirked, looking down at me.

"I don't care if you buy it," I answered trying to show the confidence that didn't exist in my voice.

"It's alright. Let's go look at a few others, if you don't mind leaving this spot?" he asked softly, so only I would hear. I looked at the group, all laughing and smiling with each other and then peeked back up at him before nodding.

"That's fine."

He kissed my forehead and grabbed my hand leading me in an opposite direction. I snuck a glance behind me and instantly caught eyes of the man that my heart still screamed for. I drowned out the screams, however, and continued to be led by what I deserved.

****

Julian and I stood at my front door. He was holding my hand loosely not wanting to say goodbye just yet.

"Thank you for coming with me again tonight," I said after a short silence. He kissed my hand softly, before suddenly pulling me into him. His slight aggression caused me to be turned on for the first time by him.

"I'm sorry, I just don't want you to leave me yet," he whined softly, rubbing the back of his hand against my cheek. I was getting lost in his eyes.

"It's just for a little while. You'll see me again tomorrow," I whispered, studying his lips now. Within moments, they were pressed against mine causing a sensual kiss to take place between the two of us. It wasn't too much, or not enough, just perfect.

I parted my lips from his, and looked up, as he snuck one last peck upon them.

"Goodnight babe," he said beginning to back up slowly off the porch, waiting for me to enter the house.

"Goodnight Doctor." I flashed a sly grin while jamming the key into the lock and entering my home. I sighed happily to myself before taking off my shoes and making my way to my room.

I hesitated a little when I saw something large resting on my bed. I walked up to it, and nearly gasped at Donovan's painting resting there.

I slid my fingertips gently against the rigidness of the paint and studied it. It was even more beautiful up close.

"I bought my own painting, just so you could have it." I jumped at his voice before I turned and saw him standing in my doorway; daring not to enter completely. The jacket he wore before was now gone, and his shirt was unbuttoned at the top with his sleeves rolled up to his elbows. He looked more relaxed in this setting.

"How long have you been standing there? What are you doing here?" I asked, breathing deep.

"Jay's hosting a little get together for me in the basement. Everyone's down there eating and drinking. I heard the door open."

I tipped a brow, "From all the way downstairs?" Even I know he wouldn't have heard me come in.

He shook his head firmly, "The kitchen."

"You were waiting for me to get home..."

"Just wanted to make sure you got in safe," he added as I nodded slowly and then looked down at the painting.

"You never intended on selling this did you?" he paused before slowly shaking his head.

"Then what was the point of putting it on display?" I crossed my arms waiting for the answer.

"I wanted it to be seen. I took my time with this painting, put everything I had into it," he explained looking down at his own work.

"Why? Why this one? Why even create it?"

He sighed, and lightly scratched the back of his neck, "Couldn't get you out of my head. So I had to put you on the canvas."

I held back the tears threatening to fall, "To let me go?"

He bit the inside of his lip before he shrugged and looked down, "To express how I felt."

"So what is this supposed to say to me Don? That you love me? Is this the I love you I get? You paint me and think that's going to solve everything?" I asked, the frustration growing clear in my tone.

"I don't know who it's speaking to Bobbi or what its saying. I just know that I want you to have it. I didn't want anyone else to have it but you."

I looked back down at the picture. It was beautiful, and I did want it the moment I laid eyes on it. I just wanted him to admit what he felt even more.

"He a good dude?" he finally asked. I could see in his body language he was going to leave after I gave him an answer.

"He's not you," I confessed honestly, desiring some type of reaction.

He chuckled softly before he tapped my door post with the side of his fist, "Probably a good thing right?"

With that he left, and the tear finally felt free enough to run down my cheek.

Donovan.

"Ya know, I've been thinking," Shane said aloud after a weird mid-day rush of customers. I had four hundred dollars in my pocket already.

"Aw shit. Don't hurt yourself." I groaned as he threw the pillow from the couch at my head causing me to laugh. I tossed the pillow next to my side before deciding to take him seriously.

"I'm playin man. What's up?"

He took in a deep breath before clasping his hands together, "We need to expand. Hire some people to work this one, and expand. Like out in Miami, or Atlanta. Some place poppin."

I raised an eyebrow in his direction, "Business is good. Scratch that, great here. Why not open another shop in LA?"

"Because that's just going to cause all of our Cali clientele to just split up, and it's not even going to make us more money. Just make things less busy. I'm serious about this shit Don. Big names know about us, and a lot of them tell us they would be regulars if were actually in Miami, or New York or wherever else they be coming from. We have perfected this business out here. I really think we should stack up the next six months for a down payment on a spot, one of us head out to Miami and stay there to find us a place." His eyes were light and hopeful as I still felt skeptical about the idea.

"We don't got people out in Miami like that. How we know who we can trust?"

"We do! You know my sister out there, and she know hella real estate agents that could help you find a place while I run things here-"

I cut him short, "Whoa wait a minute. Why me? All this was your idea, why can't you do it?" I asked him.

He smacked his lips, "Because of Shai dumb ass. I can't leave my daughter just yet, till I get shit figured out with her mom. You don't have shit here, so you got nothing to lose." His statement made me feel some type of way. Made me realize, I didn't really have much of a family. I had a father that was locked up, and a grandmother who had no idea who I was.

"What got you on this so tough? Why now?" I asked him as he sighed a little.

"To keep it one hundred, it was your art show. You're building your legacy Don; you don't need this tattoo shit or this shop to be someone. All I have is this. All I'm dedicated to is this. And I want to leave my mark. Our mark. We're two 23 year old successful business owners, and we make a decent living. But it could be greater, and something bigger. We settle for one little shop in West Hollywood. We both can be more than that," he expressed, as I nodded my head. We became business partners because I trusted Shane to do this with me. I knew if he felt strongly about this, we should take the risk.

"If this blows up in our face, that's your ass," I said extending my hand. He smirked before shaking it.

The front door chimed shortly after our moment and both of our faces went blank once we realized who it was.

Julian walked in dressed as if he was going to a business meeting, with his hands shoved in his pockets and scoping the place out like he was only slightly impressed.

"Uh, how can we help you?" Shane finally asked, standing up as I did too, sizing this man up. It was already enough that every time I saw him he was hanging all over Bobbi, now here he is in my place of business.

He gave the place one more look over before finally landing his eyes on me.

"You got a minute?" he asked, as I looked at Shane strangely. He shrugged before grabbing his sketchbook and heading towards his office.

"Holla if you need me man," he said disappearing behind the door.

I stood firm in front of Julian, not about to be belittled. He thought he was the shit because he had a piece of paper calling him a doctor, and from what I heard he came from money. I wasn't intimidated by him in the least.

"What's up man? What you need from me?" I asked making sure my voice stayed firm.

"I need to ask a favor from you Donovan."

I looked at him strangely, "What kind of favor you need from me?"

He grinned a little as he stood straight, "I need you to stay away from Chanel."

My face screwed up, "Excuse me?"

He chuckled, "You heard me. Stay away from Chanel. I picked up on that little exchange in the gallery, and how she always makes sure to keep me from you. I don't care what the two of you had before I came along, but all that ends today. I'm making this request, man to man."

"Who you think you are bruh?" I asked feeling my fist ball up. The fact he had the nerve to come and tell me this was some bullshit.

"I'm someone that loves and cherishes something you didn't. You had your chance, and for whatever reason you blew it. I am going to give that woman everything she deserves and more. She is going to be my wife one day, and I don't need you staying around causing her to get confused and conflicted when it comes to how she feels. She backs up from me every time you're in reach, knowing I'm the man she needs. You don't deserve someone like her Donovan. So allow a real man to handle it."

I scoffed, "You think you a real man? Coming in here like a little bitch asking for me to stay away from your girl? A real man wouldn't have any insecurity."

"Oh, I'm the insecure one? Why every time I'm around, you act like you actually give a damn? I can already see that the only person you care about at the end of the day is yourself. And it's not fair to her heart. You keep coming in and out, and I'm the one that's going to be responsible to fix it. So I'm telling you, just stay out. If you're not willing to do what I do, then just stay out our way."

"What if I am? No matter what you say it's not gonna change the fact that she's in love with me and not you. You being around for a couple months didn't change that."

He smirked, "You're not ready for this war you're starting. I'm giving you the option to bow out, gracefully, before you're forced out."

I was sickened by this son of a bitch. How could Bobbi not see through this arrogant asshole? He wasn't any good for her, he just wanted to be in control and get what he wants.

"Fuck your request. I'm not going anywhere. Now get the hell out my shop," I spat, fanning him off. Shane had walked out of his office by this point, hearing the tone of my voice change.

"And by the way," I called out forcing Julian to stop and face me, "She hates being called Chanel."

He gave an amused grin, "You'll be gone soon. Whether you're ready to accept it or not." Julian made sure to say before he walked calmly out of the building. The anger rising inside of me was making my skin crawl.

"You gon tell her?" Shane asked both of us watching dude drive off.

"I'll try."

****

My palms were sweaty approaching Vince and Lisa's house, hoping Bobbi would at least listen to me about dude. Over the past few weeks, I tried texting and even calling her, but none of my efforts were returned. I understood, but it still made the process aggravating none the less.

I rang the doorbell and stepped back awaiting an answer while hearing someone running to the front door. It quickly swung open, and there she was, looking...different. Both of our faces fell at the sight of each other.

"What's up with your hair?" I asked her with my nose turned up as she rolled her eyes.

"It's just Donovan," she growled to the background in disappointment before walking away from the door. I stepped inside, continuing to study her from behind. Her hair was straightened, but it had no life to it; just flat and straight, without a part, and slicked to the back. It was a type of style some rich asshole would rock, not her.

I stepped out of the hallway into the center of the house to see Lisa and Vince both in the kitchen and Bobbi and Jay setting the dining room table. Lisa smiled at the sight of me.

"Oh hey baby! Sorry, we thought you were my sister and brother-in-law. They're driving Bobbi's car down here," she said, wiping her hands on her jeans and walking over to me for a hug. I bent down and hugged her while still looking around at the scene.

"Oh. Am I interrupting someth-"

"Yes," Bobbi interjected cutting me off. Lisa laughed before looking at me.

"Not at all! I'm sure Bobbi's parents would love to meet you." My eyes widened before looking over at Bobbi who had an irritated expression written across her face.

"Um, no Auntie. Julian is coming over to meet them remember?"

"Yeah, but he's not coming until way after dinner. Donovan can stay and eat," she insisted, rubbing my back and walking back into the kitchen. I gave a devilish smirk in Bobbi's direction before she smacked her lips and vigorously began setting the table.

"Got to love these moments," Jay smirked sarcastically, as he and I shared a laugh. I didn't care that she didn't want me to stay; we were going to talk whether she was willing to or not.

"Don. How you doing son? How's the shop coming along?" Vince's voice boomed from the kitchen, as I stepped towards it a little.

"It's coming along great actually. I'm saving up to move, so we can expand."

"Move? Where you moving to?"

I could feel Bobbi's eyes on me now along with Lisa and Jay.

"Miami. Will be gone in a few months. We think it's best for business," I answered, placing my hands firmly in my pockets.

"For how long baby? I can't picture you not living near us," Lisa pouted, crossing her arms while studying me closely.

"We're not sure how long yet. Just want to get the place up and running, find a good manager and employees. Who knows, if I like it, I might stay. Can't be a Cali boy forever. Plus, I'm not really leaving much behind," I said, before locking eyes with Bobbi, who quickly looked away. I didn't expect her to care too much about it.

"It sounds smart son. I'm happy for you, and you know I've always been proud of you. I pray it all works out in your favor," Vince said, walking over and reaching his hand out for me to shake. My hand firmly gripped his, before we heard the doorbell ring and Bobbi shoot past both of us to answer it.

"Mommy!" she screamed as it was soon followed by a counter scream and then yells from a man. Lisa quickly put down a rag she was using to wipe the counter down before moving swiftly past me to the front door. She too soon screamed shortly after.

The three remaining men in the kitchen just looked at each other and shook our heads at the screaming and crying in the other room.

"Those women are nuts!" a strong voice said, making his way down the hall and into the center area joining the rest of us. Jay and Vince both smiled at him, as I just watched. He was an older and darker man, with specks of gray in his hair and mustache, slightly taller than me with a slim physique. I assumed him to be Bobbi's step-dad.

"My brotha!" Vince called out pulling this man into a hug. After their embrace, Jay walked over to greet him.

"Sup Uncle Randy," Jay said as Randy put him in a headlock. Jay was the smallest out of us all, which made him an easy target for bullying.

"Sup nephew! Still a lightweight I see," Randy teased while Jay struggled to get free. I shared a laugh with everyone in the room as Randy let him go.

"Come on Unc. Embarassin me 'n shit." Jay said lowly so his mother wouldn't overhear. Vince didn't care if we cussed around him.

"Embarrasin you in front of who?!" Randy asked aloud before he turned and came face to face with me. I held an awkward expression while Vince stepped in to introduce us.

"Randy this is my God-son, Donovan." Vince smiled proudly looking at me as Randy raised a brow.

"Little Donovan? Big head boy that used to chase Bobbi around?"

My face contorted into one of confusion. *I've met her before?*

"That's the one," Randy looked at me surprised before extending his hand.

"You grew up to be taller than I thought. Nice to see you again man," He firmly shook my hand as I still looked confused. Before I had a chance to ask questions, Bobbi was walking in with a woman who she had a striking resemblance to. They were the same height, same chocolate complexion, and same beautiful smile. I could see where Bobbi gets her hair texture from, because her mom sported a big and puffy curly bun that sat on the top of her head.

"Hey family!" her mother greeted before hugging both Jay and Vince tightly. She smiled at her husband while taking off her jacket before her eyes landed on me.

"And who is this handsome young man?" she asked while giving Bobbi a sly look before pinching her sides. Bobbi gave a short laugh before frowning in my direction.

"Ma that's just Donovan. No one special," she said flatly as I gave a short sigh followed with an eye roll.

Her mom shot me a weird look before looking at Lisa and lowering her palm shortly below her waist. "Little Donovan?"

Lisa nodded, "That's him." Bobbi and I gave each other a weird look before her mom wrapped me into a warm hug.

"Oh my goodness! You have gotten so grown and handsome! Wow!" she said stepping back while gripping my shoulders and looking me up and down.

"Baby," she said turning towards Bobbi, "This is the little boy that used to be just in love with you when we came and stayed here for two weeks. You guys were about 4 or 5. Inseparable!" she exclaimed as Bobbi and I quickly glanced at each other.

"I was just saying that Leslie before you walked up in here. Danni used to bring him over every day because she said he used to beg to come see Bobbi. Ol' bucket head over here was jealous," Randy said thumbing his direction to Jay. The mention of my mother's name from her parents caused my heart to soften.

"Used to cry and say Bobbi took his brother," he added before all of the adults in the room laughed. Every one of us had a clueless expression on our face, not knowing we were childhood pals for a short period of time.

"He was the cutest little boy," Leslie commented handing Lisa her and Randy's jackets.

"Well you guys get comfortable. Have a seat. I'm going to bring the food to the table," she insisted as I sat down in my usual seat next to Jay, while Bobbi and her parents sat across from us, leaving an empty seat next to Jay and the head of the table where Vince sat.

"It feels so good to be back in LA. That drive in was crazy," Leslie sighed as Vince chuckled.

"Ya'll got her so spoiled. Driving her car all that way. Should've just shipped it."

"You know Leslie can't say no to this one. Always wanting to help her out," Randy added, as both Bobbi and her mother gave an appalled look. You could tell they were really close.

"Don't hate," her mom defended while unfolding a napkin and placing it in her lap. Her eyes soon fell on me before she smiled.

"It is so nice to see you Donovan. Bobbi didn't mention she saw you this whole time," Bobbi rolled her eyes.

I gave a small laugh, "I'm not surprised Ms. Leslie. Your daughter can be rude when it comes to me," I said, slightly pouting at Bobbi who cut her eyes in my direction.

"I don't see how? She talked about you for weeks, maybe months when we left. You two seriously did not want to be apart from each other," she explained, taking a sip of water before looking at Jay.

"James, you don't remember? Your little butt was so jealous," she giggled with the adults joining her. Lisa was setting the hen she roasted down on the table.

"He was so jealous. Would ask me every day when Bobbi was going home so he could have his brother back," she laughed as I smiled a little to myself.

"I think I still got some pictures of the two of you somewhere upstairs," she added before disappearing back in the kitchen.

"Uh, enough of our childhood okay? It's certainly not like that now." Bobbi finally spoke up, trying to end the conversation.

"Oh, this isn't the guy?" Randy asked openly pointing to me as I smirked, knowing this was making her mad.

"No. Julian couldn't join us for dinner. He'll be over later," she said putting on a smile that I knew was fake.

Both of her parents frowned at her response while looking down, as if they were disappointed I was not the one that Bobbi was so excited for them to meet. In my heart, I wanted nothing more than to be the one she boasted of.

I should've been him.

Bobbi.

I looked annoyingly at my Dad laughing and joking with Donovan in the living room. All of the men were watching a basketball game while my mom and I were helping Lisa clean the dishes. I could feel my mom staring at me out of the corner of my eye, before slightly nudging my shoulder with hers.

"Donovan's a real cutie. A nice young professional too," she complimented as I shrugged, breaking my eyes from the scene.

"Yeah," I said shortly while continuing to scrub at the fork in my hand.

"What happened with ya'll?" she pondered aloud earning a sigh from my end.

"I couldn't even tell you ma. Doesn't matter because I'm with Julian now. He's a good man, and I'm sure you'll like him," I told her passing the utensil so she could wash it off and set it in the drying rack.

"If you don't look at him the way you look at Little Don, I won't believe it," she replied in a nonchalant tone before there was silence.

"And baby, what is going on with that hair. You love wearing your hair with life," she questioned, reminding me of the same statement Donovan made when he saw me. He looked at me as if he was viewing a stranger.

"Julian likes my hair like this," I said in a low tone as I caught her turning up her nose.

"Hmm."

We continued washing dishes in silence. My eyes soon fell upon Donovan smiling and nodding at something my dad was telling him. I was in awe of the bond they shared already, and felt a gush of sentiment flood to me. What my parents didn't understand was that this situation was not like this because of me. My decision to move on was forced upon by his actions.

While my mom and I were finishing up, Donovan soon joined us in the kitchen.

He gave a respectable look to my mother before he spoke.

"Hey Ms. Leslie, you mind if I borrow Bobbi for a sec?" he asked, softly reaching out and grabbing my hand to pull in his direction.

"Sure honey, go ahead," she replied shooing me away. I gave her a pleading look before continuing to follow Donovan out to the front porch. I was okay with him bringing me here, because Julian would arrive soon and I wanted to keep an eye out for him.

"What?"

My arms were crossed trying to decipher the reasoning for us to be alone.

He looked me over and slowly ran his fingers through my hair, "You're changing."

I shrugged, "Change is good."

"Yeah, if you were happy with it," he said before adjusting his focus. "Look there's something you need to know about your boy-"

I sighed cutting him off, "Here you go with this jealousy shit."

"It's not about jealousy Bobbi. That dude is not good for you. He's slowly changing you and you don't even realize it. Got your hair all weird and wearing frumpy clothes. You don't even wear stuff like this," he said tugging at my top.

"What do you know? Huh? You barely even know me."

He furrowed his eyebrows, giving an offended look, "I don't know you now? Seriously?"

I shook my head.

"I know one thing. I know you were yourself around me. And I never asked or requested you to be anyone else. Hell I didn't want you to be anyone else! That's why I fell for you. You didn't compromise who you were for nobody," he expressed as I felt my heart soften a little. It was the first time I heard him admit that he fell for me.

"I don't want you to lose yourself in anybody. Especially not no sneaky ass dude like him. You lose yourself in him, and he does something to hurt you, your whole world has changed. I can't just sit and watch that happen." I was getting angry now, just looking at him and listening to his words.

"Why are you doing this? Why now? I get comfortable without you, and then you go and pull shit like this causing me to get confused and emotional. You not willing to take his place, yet you're telling me to drop him. What fuckin sense does that make Don?!" I asked, voice full of emotion that I no longer could hold in.

He stepped closer to me, gently grabbing my hand, "I want to take his place. I belong in this spot." His voice was low and soft, and I could finally see the truth behind the words in his eyes.

My phone vibrating in my pocket broke the trance, and I quickly backed away from Donovan to pull it out. I saw Julian's name, but before the call could be answered, he was already pulling up in the driveway. I looked awkwardly in Don's direction who hadn't taken his eyes off of Julian's car.

My boyfriend soon stepped out making his way to the front steps. He sized up Donovan quickly, before his eyes fell on me, and a smile formed across his face.

"Sorry I'm late baby," he breathed before leaning in and pecking me on the lips. He then turned and looked at Donovan with a satisfied smirk, "Sup man. Is there a particular reason why you're here?"

Don's facial expression remained stern and hard before he went towards the door avoiding Julian's question all together and disappearing into the house.

"You look beautiful tonight girl," Julian said averting our attention from the awkward scene. He kissed me on my temple, "Love your hair like this."

****

"So Julian," my daddy started getting comfortable in his seat. We were in the den with my parents, Vince and Lisa, while Donovan, Jay and now Shane were all in the basement. They all wanted to take the time to get to know Julian more, and watch us as a couple. My eyes kept inadvertently peeking at the basement door, just hoping to see Don appear.

"What are your intentions with our eldest baby girl here? Where do you honestly see this going?" He asked. Julian gripped my hand tighter while clearing his throat. I was interested to hear this answer.

"Honestly Randy, I have nothing but pure intentions for your daughter. We have both agreed to remain celibate during the time of our courtship, and keeping things that way have truly allowed me to see her inner beauty. She is a strong, self-sufficient, compassionate, mature and gorgeous woman. Having her in my life has ignited a passion and drive in me that I never knew existed, and I want nothing more than to spend the rest of my life expressing my gratitude, if she gives me that honor." He answered so confidently, that even my mother had an impressed look on her face. I never knew he felt so deeply about me, in such a short period of time.

"How do you think she feels about you?" Daddy asked as Julian looked at me and smiled before directing his attention back.

"I think she still has her reserves when it comes to me. Still trying to figure me out, and let go of some things, or people rather, that are holding her back from opening up to me completely. I know I am a good man for your daughter; I just want her to believe it as much as me." He looked back again and placed a soft kiss on my forehead while gently gripping my hand. I was starting to feel like shit for developing feelings for Donovan all over.

"Are you going to say something baby?" my mom asked softly as all eyes fell on me.

I took in a deep breath.

"I care more than you even know. And I'm grateful that someone like you entered into my life at the time you did," I said, forcing a smile. My speech wasn't as great as his, but it was the best I could do. Whether Julian realized it or not, it was going to take time for my love to grow for him. Yes I'm attracted, and there are feelings there, it's just someone else had open access to my heart, and I realized then I needed to shut them out before I ended up alone.

My mother and I locked eyes before she softly smiled, she wasn't buying it, but she would be supportive.

Moments later we heard loud stomping, followed by boyish laughter as my cousin and his friends erupted through the basement door. We all shot our eyes towards them, causing their laughter to quiet down.

"Aye Ma, we about to go shoot at the park for a little bit," Jay announced, as Donovan smiled at me lovingly. It instantly sent chills down my spine, so I broke eye contact.

Lisa looked at her watch before looking back at the boys, "At 10 o'clock at night?" They all nodded.

"Street lights on. Best time to play Ms. Lisa," Shane smirked before they all looked at each other goofily. It reminded me of high school the way they were acting, it was cute.

"Well alright, be careful," she said hesitantly watching them all prepare to leave.

Jay looked to Julian, "You trynna come Doc?" he asked innocently as Julian declined.

"No, I'm going to hang tight here. Thanks for asking though." Jay shrugged before disappearing down the hall and out of the door.

After talking with my parents for a little longer, we soon said our goodbyes as they left to get rest at their hotel for the night. They were only going to be in town for a few days so we made plans to get together the following morning. Soon after, my aunt and uncle retired to their room, leaving Julian and I at his driver side door, saying goodnight to one another before he prepared to leave.

He smiled at me while placing both of his hands on my hips and pulling me close. He gently kissed my lips repeatedly before looking into my eyes.

"You think you could ever love me Chanel?" he questioned from a sincere place as I stared into his deep blue eyes.

"I want to," I answered honestly barely above a whisper. I was ashamed in my response.

"But will you? Am I worth it to you? Every day I'm with you, I find more and more reasons why you're worth it to me. Are you happy with me?"

I remained silent. I couldn't answer those questions honestly right now.

"Chanel, baby. I want to make you the happiest woman in the world. I can't do that, if you don't allow me to, or if someone is getting in the way of that. After everything you've been through, you deserve to be happy and treated with respect. Your feelings and emotions are precious, and they don't need to be played with. I'm putting myself out there, because I know you need to see this from me. I just don't want to continue to be in this relationship alone. I know what I can offer you, and I know everything that I want to do for you. Just let me. Please?" he pleaded softly, as I felt the tears welling up. I knew what had to be done.

"I'm in this okay?" I assured, "I'm here."

He nodded before grabbing my cheeks and placing a kiss on my forehead, "Show me then."

We lingered a little before finally saying goodbye for the night. I watched him pull out and disappear down the street. I looked at my watch, realizing Jay hadn't come home yet and Shane and Donovan's car were still parked. Without hesitation, my feet began making their way to the neighborhood park.

As I got closer to my destination, I watched as all three guys, who were shirtless, play an aggressive game of basketball. Donovan grinned when he made a shot over Shane and Jay before chasing after Shane who now had the ball.

I reached the court and stood against the post, watching them at the other end. Shane and Jay kept missing shots, and I laughed at all the shit Don was talking to the both of them. It looked like they were playing two against one.

His smile faded slightly when he retrieved the ball and saw me at the other end, making a timeout symbol with his hands.

"Ya'll weak asses need a minute to rest anyway," he teased as they smacked their lips and went towards their water bottles. A sweaty Donovan jogged up to me, and I admired his tattoo covered chest and arms, while flashbacks of his fully naked body flooded my brain.

"Sup beautiful," he greeted placing a messy kiss on my cheek. I frowned and wiped it off.

"Don't be wiping away Daddy's kisses girl," he joked as I crossed my eyes hiding my laughter behind a small grin.

"We have to talk Donovan."

"What's up?" he asked still catching his breath.

"I'm not going to stop talking to Julian. He cares about me deeply and wants to treat me right. He's not afraid to open up about how he feels or fight for what he wants-"

He scoffed before cutting me off, "And what? You think I am?"

"I don't think. I know. You and I both know we care more about each other than either one of us is willing to fully admit. I have someone here, that's not afraid to be with me...not afraid of what this could be..."

"It was never you that I was afraid of," he admitted as I shook my head.

"It doesn't matter."

"You don't even wanna be with him like that Bobbi. Every fuckin body can see that, including him. That fool came into my-"

"I'm going to try dammit. I'm gonna really give him a full effort and I can't do that until I let you go."

He quickly screwed up his face before stepping closer to me, "Are you serious? You gonna let me go? You can't do that."

"I can. And I will. I think it would be best if we didn't talk anymore at all," I said sternly.

In one quick motion he wrapped his arm around my waist and aggressively pulled me into him. Feeling my body connect with his sent an electrifying intensity throughout my entire being. My body had been longing for his touch.

"Stop..." I said weakly attempting to push him off of me.

"I'm not letting you let me go. Nobody in my life compares to you. Don't you get that? I know I've been fucking up, but that's just cause I don't know what to do. I never felt like this before. I can't even get out of my mind how you feel when I'm inside you. Nobody feels the way you do..." He hissed, sexually biting his bottom lip as I felt my knees getting weaker. I could just imagine the looks Jay and Shane were giving us on the other side of the court.

"I'm in a relationship now Donovan. I have to honor that," I said digging deep for the courage and strength the step away. As bad as I wanted to give in, I knew I couldn't. It wouldn't challenge him to change.

"Aight," he said nodding and stepping back, "Tell ol' boy he got the war he said he was looking for." He finished before picking up the basketball and smacking it hard with his palm.

I wondered what he meant by that.

****

"Ah," my mother cooed taking a sip of her wine, "This is the life."

We were at the Four Seasons in the hot tub next to the pool. We had spent a day in the hotel's spa, getting massages, manicures, pedicures and facials. It was nice to have a mother and daughter day while my dad was hanging out with Jay and Vince.

"That it is," I happily smiled sipping on my wine before placing the glass back down. It was the most relaxed I had felt in months.

"So now that it's just us, you can be honest about everything. Don't have to cover up in front of your aunt and uncle. How do you like LA? Really," she questioned, as I looked over to meet her stare. My mother was my best friend, and I was happy to have this time to talk with just her and face to face.

"The people I've met here have made this experience better than I expected. I came very reserved, timid and angry, and now I find myself having more good days than bad. It's just nice to be surrounded by genuine people, who only want to see you grow and happy." My mom was smiling proudly at me.

"It warms my heart to hear you say that Bobbi. You just don't even know. Seeing you consumed by your depression was one of the hardest things for me to ever witness as a mother. To see your baby, hurt and in pain at the hands of someone else's devalue of her, was heartbreaking."

I sunk a little in the tub, allowing the bubbles to overtake the top of my shoulders, "I never wanted you to take my decision and what I was going through so personal."

"It's hard not to. You're my heart baby. Everything I've ever done in this world is for you and your brother and sister. You've saved my life in ways you'll never understand, so to know that you wanted to take your own at one point...and there was nothing I could physically do to take the pain away. It was hard Bobbi. I'm not going to sugar coat that."

I nodded softly taking in her words, "I'm not that girl anymore momma. I can promise you that. There's nothing I want to do more than to live and experience life. Everyone around me appreciates life and lives it happily. I want that same thing. It took me going to church to realize that I had to let my past go."

She raised a brow at my last statement, "Church? Who took you to church?"

Swallowing hard, I found the strength to answer her, "Donovan. The Pastor said a special prayer for me so I could be freed from the burden and weight of un-forgiveness. I've been a much happier and honest person since then."

She smiled warmly before taking another sip out of her glass, "Julian go to church?"

I shook my head, "He doesn't believe in church per se. Religion in some ways, but not church. He doesn't claim a specific religion. He believes since there are so many, how can you only pick one to be right? He just believes in a higher power."

She turned her nose up a bit at my answer, "Interesting. Do you agree?"

I shook my head, "Not in the least bit. I just choose to let it be. He likes to debate about things like that; religion, politics, conspiracy theories. I don't really care about those topics, so I just let him rant."

A soft chuckle escaped her lips, "You know the two of you are nothing alike?"

"I know. Opposites attract though right?"

"No. Don't believe that for a second. In some cases it can work, but it will be forced. Me and your biological father were like that. Two totally different people. Didn't share the same interests, or anything, we just bonded off of physical attraction alone. We always fought, never got along, but I just didn't want to let him go, and didn't allow him to let me go. Then I got pregnant, and all Hell broke loose."

"Did you use me to keep him around?" I questioned for the first time in my life. I never really heard her side of things, and she was actually admitting her mistakes.

"Foolishly, yes. I lied and told him I was on birth control. I was a young and wild girl, chasing after a man that made it clear what all he wanted from me. It was stupid and selfish, but at the time I felt I was right. It took a few years of caring for you majority alone, and meeting your Daddy when I realized the type of girl I was at the time. Randy helped me become a woman. He loved me through the faults, and we shared everything together. My perfect match," she said thinking about her husband.

"I admitted all of that to say this. Don't force anything when it comes to love. What comes natural is right. Not what comes hard. You have no connection to Julian and he knows it. He's forcing it more and I don't want that for you baby. He may be good on the outside, and put together, but he can be that for someone else who will desire that from him."

I bit the inside of my cheek before responding, "So you think I should be with Donovan too?"

"I'm not pushing you into Donovan's arms either. There's a reason why you're choosing Julian over him, and until that reason becomes null and void, leave him alone. He'll chase you. He did when he was little." She giggled, as I looked at her strange.

"What happened?"

She ceased her laughter so she could recite the story, "The first day the two of you met, you guys hated each other's guts. I don't know why, but you were rude and mean to each other. And we were all in the backyard, while the three of you guys were out playing, next thing I know, ya'll are rolling around on the ground fighting. You were scratching and biting and he was kicking. It was a mess."

My eyes widened at the information she was sharing, "Seriously? I don't remember any of that."

She nodded, "Yep. You had a few cuts and he did too. But the next day Danielle brought him over because he had requested to come and see you. He wanted to apologize. He drew a picture of you guys holding hands under a rainbow and sun. And after that, we couldn't separate you."

I smiled trying to dig deep into my memory, but couldn't find it, "He just recently did that actually..."

"I wouldn't be surprised. Danielle said she never saw him do anything like that for anyone before. Said he cried because he felt bad about hurting you and wanted to fix it. She didn't even have to whoop him because he came to the realization on his own."

I grinned a little which was soon followed by a short sigh, "I really care about him a lot Mom. I really do."

"You always have."

Donovan.

I walked somberly into the nursing home where my grandmother was staying, and was greeted by Sophie who quickly frowned when she saw me.

"Dr. Phillips called you?"

I slowly nodded.

"She's been staying in the medical ward since last week. I'm so sorry," she apologized, before stepping from behind the desk to guide me to her room.

"Dorothy is really a remarkable patient. She was always so sweet and kind to all of the staff." she said, as we reached her room door. I peeked in to see my MiMi with oxygen running through her nose and pictures spread out all across the bed.

"She'll be happy to see you Donovan," Sophie touched my shoulder softly as I reached for the doorknob to open it. I got the call last week telling me she had come down with a serious case of pneumonia. Last night, they called to tell me that the sickness mixed with her disease was causing a lot of her organs to shut down, and she didn't have much time here left. They advised me to spend as much time as I could, while she was still able to move and talk on her own. Pretty soon, that luxury wouldn't be available.

She coughed slightly before looking up at me; the warmness was in her eyes again. She almost seemed like herself.

"Come sit with me baby," she urged before pulling her mask up to cover her nose and mouth so I wouldn't catch her sickness. It didn't matter if I got pneumonia or not, I just wanted this time with her.

She patted on the empty space next to her advising me to sit. I smiled to myself before happily climbing onto the bed and sitting next to her looking at all the pictures she had across her legs.

"Danni said she misses you and loves you very much. I saw her. In my dream," she said softly, but loud enough for me to hear her clearly. She handed me a picture of me and my mom. My MiMi had these rare moments where she functioned properly and

228

spoke clearly, as if she was her old self. This was one of those moments that I assumed her medication was working properly.

She coughed again, "I'm sick baby. The good Lord is about to take me on home," she told me looking at the same three pictures over and over. One was of her and my Grandpa, another was of the three of us, and the last was a picture of her in her younger days.

"I don't want you to go MiMi," I said looking at her as she avoided my stare and shook her head.

"You done kept me here long enough baby. It's time to let me go. I'm here because I love you, and you needed me. I'm ready to go," she mumbled, while still rotating the pictures, viewing each one like it was the first time she saw it.

"You see me baby? I was sharp!"

She smiled showing me the picture of her when she was younger. I looked her in her eye, trying to prevent the tear from falling.

"Oh come on now. Don't you do it. I'm always with you. You hear me? Everywhere you go. I'll be there," she scolded, looking at me close, knowing I was on the verge of crying. I wasn't ready to lose someone else. It had been almost eight years since I lost my mom.

"It's just hard MiMi. I don't get close with people. I don't want to love people because when I do they leave." I choked, as she frowned.

"That's foolishness Donny. I'm old, and I'm tired. That's why I'm leaving. I'm ready to be with the Lord and your Grandfather. I'm ready to be free again. I'm hooked up to all these machines. This ain't living baby. This ain't it. I never wanted to be here if I was gon be sick. I remained as strong as I could for you when everyone left me, but it's my time now. Can you accept that?" she asked, looking at me close as I sniffed a little and nodded.

"All I want is you to lay here with me. I just want to spend my last days here with you. Can you give me that? All smiles?" She looked at me close and I smiled before nodding again. She smiled too and went back to her pictures as I gathered a few more to add in her rotation.

I got more comfortable and rested my head on her shoulder looking at the pictures with her.

"I love you MiMi."

"I love you back."

****

"Strawberry Daiquiri please," Tierre ordered sitting next to me at the bar. I asked her to meet me at a small pub, not too far from our job after work. I needed an opinion, and she was the only female friend I had.

She patted me on my shoulder a little, as I took a sip of my Hennessey on ice, before turning to face her. She softly smiled, moving a few curls out of her face.

"Hey Booty," I greeted. Before she could respond, the bartender came back with the drink.

She handed him her card, "Leave the tab open. Might be a long night," she joked in a serious tone, her accent showing itself. I chuckled a little before taking another sip.

"What's up? I know it's something serious if you calling me for advice," she said getting comfortable as I sat up on the stool a little, circling my finger around the brim of the glass.

"What vibe you get off Julian?" I asked her directly.

Her eyes widened a bit before she shrugged her right shoulder slightly, "He's very attractive, but I don't know. He seems to say all the right things in front of all of us," she commented, before furrowing her brow at me.

"Why? You jealous?"

"Not so much jealous, more concerned. Fool came up in my shop telling me to back off a little after my art show," she gave a surprised expression.

"Bold as hell," Tierre chuckled with me shaking my head.

"You don't think something's different?" I asked her honestly looking into her brown eyes as her lips zipped tight.

230

Tierre saw and talked to Bobbi every single day; I know she would know more than anyone if something was off.

She nodded slightly, "She's different. She's just reminding me of a doctor's wife. They're like that. Pleasers, yes women, go with what he likes. They don't really have voices."

"See. And that's the thing. Bobbi is always expressive, whether it's rude or whatever. She always speaks her mind. And she was starting to get more comfortable with doing so until that dude came around. And after our little run in, I'm starting to think he's controlling her," I expressed with frustration clear in my voice, taking another big gulp of my drink.

"Either way, you really can't say shit Don. We all know she could've been better off, but right now she's playing happy until she really is. You wasn't doing nothing to ensure this wasn't gonna happen, so don't think anything you say or do will change it now."

"I can't get her out of my mind. Any female I come across, I'm comparing to her. I don't even like having sex with other bitches now. Nobody can measure up. It's like everything I do now; I do as if she's watching me. Hoping she's proud, hoping she's inspired, hoping she still cares. It's eating me up," I confessed, as Tierre just stared at me.

"What are you saying Donovan? You like her?" she asked annoyed.

I swallowed hard before meeting Tierre's stare, "I love her." It came out barely above a whisper. The first time I expressed it out loud, and even came to terms with how I truly felt. The three words I knew Bobbi was yearning to hear, just came out to her best friend.

"Loved her ever since we were little."

Tierre's mouth dropped, she never heard me say that before, about anyone.

"Yo. You serious?"

I slowly nodded before finishing the rest of my drink, "Now what?"

"One thing to say it, another to show it."

"All I've been doing is showing it. She can't end up with that dude Ti. He's no good. I know Bobbi, and I know she's just doing this to get over me."

Tierre laughed at my last comment, "You still think everything is about you Don. That's the problem. If you not fighting for her for the betterment of her, and just over some competition bullshit, drop it now. Bow out. Don't do this for your ego." She took long drags of her frozen drink through her straw as I sat quiet.

"I can't be that selfish."

"But you are. You was letting shit ride out until Julian stepped up to you. Challenged you as a man. He knows what he wants and has since the minute he met her. You on the other hand..." She frowned at me.

"He may have challenged me, but I always wanted her. I just wasn't confident. I've been trying to prevent all this feelings shit ever since I realized I liked the girl. Didn't wanna hurt her. And what I do?" I sighed playing with my now empty glass.

"You didn't hurt her Don. You confused the hell out of her, but she wasn't hurt. She understands you and she understands your reasoning for everything. She just didn't understand why she wasn't worth the risk. And why you didn't realize that she was afraid too. What ya'll had, and still have is pure, genuine and passionate. For an artist as yourself to know and appreciate beauty, you sure as hell are afraid of it."

I nodded taking in her words, "That's what I gotta do huh? Gotta show her that I'm not scared of the beauty within us anymore?" I looked at her as she gave an unsure expression in return.

"I assume. I don't know how you gonna pull off that shit. She's really doing everything in her power to let go of you."

I groaned a little out of frustration, "This is why people love? To be conflicted as hell and all over the place with their emotions?"

She gave a happy sigh, "Wonderful isn't it?"

Bobbi.

I looked down at the dress I was wearing and frowned before looking over at Julian in the driver's seat. We were going to a dinner party hosted by his parents at their mansion. He was more nervous than I was.

"You look beautiful tonight baby; I meant to tell you that," he said anxiously, grabbing my hand and starting to take an exit off the expressway.

"I hate this dress." He chuckled and kissed my hand softly.

"I know you do, but it's the way my mother dresses and I really want her to like you."

"So you're saying she won't like the real me?" I asked him softly as he quickly glanced at me before focusing back on the road.

"Of course she will! What kind of question is that?"

I sighed.

"You're dressing me the part. We've been rehearsing how to respond to her questions. You're not confident that how I normally act will genuinely impress her. You're turning me into the woman she's impressed by."

He released a breath before reaching a red light, and looking at me, "Chanel, I know I've been on you tough this week but that's just because my mom is a different breed. She's very observant and critical about the women I bring around. She knows if I'm introducing them to her, they mean a lot to me and I don't want her to scare you away." I nodded taking in his explanation and accepting for what it was going to be. I said nothing more and rested my head against the seat, looking out the window, and bracing myself to be around a high class bitch.

We pulled up to the luxurious mansion, and my mouth dropped at the sight. I had never been to a house so big in my entire life. I had no idea Julian came from *this* kind of money.

"This is where you grew up? Are you kidding me?" I asked looking over at him as he shrugged.

"Nothing to brag about. It's not my money," he answered nonchalantly while pulling up to the gate and entering the security numbers. A voice quickly came to the intercom.

"Welcome home Mr. Michaels," a strong male voice greeted as I looked at Julian wide eyed.

"Security," he told me before I even had a chance to ask the question. I zipped my lips and sat back straightening out the ridges of my dress.

There were cars lined up all the way to the garages of their home. This was a very exclusive dinner party by the looks of it.

"So why does your mom host this?"

"She likes to invite my father's partners and their families just to show how passionate and family oriented we are. She does it twice a year. This is her Fall Party." He pressed a button in his car that opened a garage door, and swiftly pulled in to park. He looked nervously at me while simultaneously removing his seat belt.

"I really think she's going to love you," he said kissing my cheek softly.

"As long as I stick to the script right?" I replied sarcastically as he gave me an apologetic look.

"Stick this out for one hour, and we're gone. I swear I'll make it up to you, and never make you wear that dress again," he promised as I giggled softly.

"Buy me a sexy dress and you have yourself a deal," He kissed my nose before gently kissing my lips and looking into my eyes.

"Done."

Julian stepped out the car and walked over to my side to open my door and assist me out. I sighed, wishing I had taken Tierre's advice to drink before coming to this. She was advising me not to even come, but I knew it would be more disrespectful to Julian and his family if I chose not to come when they all knew I was invited.

I held his hand tightly as he led me through the garage door and down a hallway where I heard soft music and numerous conversations being held at the end of it. We emerged from the hall into a full blown ball, it looked like. There were people scattered everywhere in the center room of the house. It was gorgeous. Everyone seemed to be in the midst of expensive conversations, and there were only a few people even remotely close to Julian and I's age.

"Julian! Nice to see you sir," an older white gentlemen greeted, stretching one hand to Julian and keeping the other wrapped gently around his wife's waist. Or who I assumed to be. He wore a wedding ring, she did not.

"Nice to see you Mr. Richards. This is my girlfriend Chanel. Chanel, this is one of my father's partners Conroy Richards," he introduced, as Conroy became the first of many I was introduced to. They all looked at me with lustful eyes. These rich men sure did love them a curvy black woman, and I didn't even possess many curves, and if I did, you surely couldn't see them in this tacky dress I was wearing.

"Where are your parents?" I whispered to Julian exhausted from holding a fake smile.

"Right here," he whispered back as we made our way to an interracial couple. Julian's mom was white and his father was black. He had told me they met because his maternal grandfather was the dean at Harvard who had high hopes for Julian's father.

"Julian, baby!" his mother called quickly scooping her son in her arms as if she hadn't seen him in years. She was a beautiful older white woman, with long blond hair and the same blue eyes that Julian also possessed. His father was a spitting image of him, same tanned complexion, and jaw line. He was a handsome older man. Money can ensure that you age well apparently.

"Hey mom," he smirked removing himself from the embrace and then extending a hand to his father.

"Hey Dad." His father smiled proudly.

"Hey son, good to see you could make it. Your mother has been dying to see you," he said, lightly tapping Julian's shoulder with his fist. I stood shyly behind him, not wanting to intrude on their family moment.

"Of course I would come. There's someone I want you two to meet." I cursed to myself as he gently reached for my hand behind him, revealing me to his parents. His father awed at the sight of me, and his mom frowned.

"This is Chanel. Chanel this is my mom and dad," I smiled and extended my hand to the both of them.

"Such a pleasure to meet you both. Julian speaks so highly of you, and I must say your home is very beautiful. This entire party is just exquisite." I made sure to be well spoken and look them in their eye with each word. It was so much pressure to not embarrass myself.

"Wow, you're beautiful," his father gawked as I saw the small nudge Mrs. Michaels gave him. I blushed a little before looking up at Julian who was smiling down at me.

"Thank you, Chantelle," she said purposely mistaking my name. I felt it was karma for what I had done to Donovan when we had first became acquainted.

"And what is it exactly that you do?" she asked me taking a sip of her wine as I cleared my throat, thrown off by the question.

"I-I'm a nurse," I answered self-consciously while being picked apart by her eyes.

"Well Julian tells me that you haven't exactly taken your registry, so what you have is a nursing degree, right?" she smirked attempting to belittle me. I avoided Julian's eyes, keeping mine on his mother.

"I'm employed as a nurse. And even though, I haven't taken my registry exam yet, I would still consider myself one."

She didn't look impressed, "Mm, what seems to be the delay?"

Mr. Michaels nudged his wife, "We're not here to find out about the girl's business ventures dear. We're here to find out more about her and why our son has fallen in love." He winked as I looked at Julian with question. The love word had not been introduced.

She smiled, "You're right. My apologies. So what do your parents do?" I gave a funny look before his father decided to interject again.

"Would the two of you like some wine?" he asked as Julian's mother and I continued to stare at each other. What was her problem? We had only been standing here not even five minutes, and already she only cared about how much money I made and came from.

"We'd love some Dad, thanks," Julian said tugging at his collar. I could tell he was more nervous about this awkward encounter than any of us. His mother's eyes finally left me and fell back on her son, as his father went to hunt down a waiter.

"So Julian, have you seen Jade? She's around here somewhere. She would be delighted to see you."

His father returned and handed us two glasses of wine. I kindly accepted mine before looking up at my date. "Who's Jade?" I asked while placing the glass to my lips.

Before he could answer his mother spoke up. "Julian's fiancée." I nearly choked on my beverage.

"Ex fiancée Mother. Why are you doing that?" he asked with an annoyed tone.

"I didn't know you were engaged to be married before," I said softly looking up at him. His mom placed herself in our conversation again.

"Oh yes. He and Jade were childhood sweethearts. They were engaged for two years and all of a sudden Julian called off the wedding. Very sad day for both of our families and Jade was devastated. It was just a year ago; I'm surprised he hadn't mentioned anything to you about it." She flashed a devilish smirk as I felt myself get hot with anger and confusion.

"Um, where's your restroom?" I asked looking around as no one rushed to answer to me. I slightly rolled my eyes and turned on my heels, "I'll find it."

I walked through the crowd aimlessly looking for somewhere to hide myself. Everything was so open with this stupid mansion; I couldn't see anywhere that would provide comfort.

As I was still searching, I accidently shoulder bumped an awkward built brunette. She was taller than me and had a very distinct look. Far from pretty.

"Oh I'm sorry," she apologized before looking at me closely then smiling. "You arrived with Julian?"

I painfully looked past her to see him and his father in a deep discussion; you could tell he was very upset.

I nodded. "Yes."

Her smile got even wider as she extended her hand, "I thought so. I'm Jade."

My eyes narrowed in while returning her gesture. How could someone as handsome as Julian, almost marry someone so distasteful at first glance.

"Oh, nice to finally meet you. You're all Mrs. Michaels raves about," I said flatly sipping my wine as she chuckled.

"She and I were very close. She was always like a second mother to me," she answered, before turning to look at Julian and his parents. "He's a great guy. You're very lucky to have someone like him. Have a good night," she ended, patting me on the shoulder before walking away. She seemed okay, just no one to brag about.

I continued on my path to seclusion and nearly gave up, preparing to round a corner until I heard familiar voices near me. It sounded like Julian and his mom, so I leaned closer to the edge to listen.

"You seriously did not have to talk to her like that mom. And then bring up Jade of all people?"

"You're still in love with Jade. This girl you're parading around is a mere replacement," she scoffed earning a growl from Julian.

"I never wanted to marry Jade. You wanted me to marry Jade, her parents wanted me to marry her, she and I did not want to be married. We didn't even want to be together. You forced it on us since we were young."

"She is a prestigious and well educated woman. More of a match, than a girl with an assistant degree. She could never be more than your assistant, not your partner. She doesn't match your qualities, and you need someone to. I see you want to chase around a hot little number but Jade-"

He cut her off, "If you mention Jade one more time... This conversation consists of relevance, and she simply isn't."

"I'm not approving of this Julian Andrew. And I never will. She is not someone I want carrying my last name or even my grandchildren one day. I can read her like a book. You're being foolish with all of this and careless of our legacy. You can dress her in gowns you know I would adore, but it will not change how I feel."

My heart was nearly in the soles of my feet at this point, and I couldn't take another minute of listening to this conversation. I stepped from around the corner as both of their eyes landed on me.

"I'm not asking to have your last name, and I'm not asking to carry any of your grandchildren. I came here, in this tasteless dress, and was nice to his tasteless ex, to impress you and the rest of the people here because of how much I care about your son. I don't want his money, I don't want this mansion, and I surely don't want to associate myself with people who believe they are better. I genuinely just wanted a friend. But I will not disrespect you or this function any longer. I'm leaving."

Julian stepped towards me, "Chanel..."

"And for the record, I hate my middle name. That's why I'm fine with everyone calling me Bobbi. Don't worry about taking me home Julian. Stay here with your mother; she wants to be your wife more than I do." By the look I gave him, he knew not to follow me. Space was what I needed at this point. From him and the woman he was trying to turn me into.

I rushed out of the front doors taking my heels off along the way; they were killing my feet. I looked up and down the street, while calling everyone in my phone. No one was picking up, and I didn't have any money to call a cab. I sighed, going to the name of the one person I was in no rush to call.

Donovan.

I pulled up to the address Bobbi had texted me to find her sitting outside of the gate with her knees tucked under her chin, and her shoes lying next to her. I frowned before putting the car in park and getting out. I walked slowly up to her before having a seat. She didn't move and didn't look up; she was ashamed that I had to come out here to pick her up.

"Want me to go in there and beat his ass?" I asked breaking the silence hearing a soft chuckle on her end. I looked over, trying to find her face, but she kept it hidden between her knees. I used my index finger to reach below and lift her chin.

"Chin up baby, you're stronger than this," I told her as she looked over at me with red and saddened eyes. I hated to see her so hurt.

"Will I ever be good enough?" she managed to choke out barely above a whisper.

"You're more than good enough. Fuck what his mom had to say. If ya'll rock with each other tough, it shouldn't matter. He was sticking up for you Bobs, you can't look past that." She gave me a puzzled look.

"You're on his side now?"

I smirked, "I'm on the side that makes you the happiest. There's something about him that you're into and I support it. I'm here picking you up as a friend. I know I wasn't the first person you hit up to come save you, and I respect that," I explained, hoping the front I was putting on was believable. I was happy as hell on the inside finding out what Julian's weak spot was, but if I truly loved her, I couldn't be selfish with her anymore. She had to know and see that from me.

She nodded looking at me close searching my eyes to see if I was telling the truth. She smiled small before sitting back. Guess she found what she was looking for.

"So we both gonna sit in front of this palace looking pathetic? Or we gonna dip?" I asked looking behind me, "I mean this house is big as shit!"

She laughed while turning her head to look back at the house with me; I was more than glad to be the reason for her smile.

"Yeah we can go," she said dusting off her knees. I stood to my feet and reached down to help her up before studying her.

"Um...what are you wearing?" I asked looking her up and down as she huffed.

"Stupid ass dress. I told her to her face it was ugly, and our dresses were almost identical."

I chuckled while walking to the passenger side of my car to open her door. "Word? What she say?"

"She ain't say shit just turned her nose up like she was offended. Snooty bitch," I closed her door shut and walked to the driver's seat. I got in, buckled up my seat belt and put the car in drive.

"Serves her right. Messin' with my Bobbi," I said in a goofy tone causing her to giggle some more.

"But hey, since I did a favor for you, I need you to do a favor for me," I started, changing the topic completely as we took off down the road.

"What is it?" she asked hearing the seriousness in my tone.

"I need you to ride to the beach with me. I gotta lay my grandmother to rest," Her mouth fell open.

"Why didn't you tell me Don? I would've been there for you! You should've called and told me she passed away." She had so much compassion and care in her voice. She knew how hard this was for me.

"I didn't tell anyone. I had my moment with her and that was all I needed. I'm at peace with it you know? She can get her life back. Join my grandfather and my mom up there. Now I have three angels looking after me. Every time I would go see her, more of her soul was gone from her eyes. She was lost here. Couldn't find herself, couldn't understand anything. Had no idea who she was or her purpose. I couldn't watch somebody suffer like that again. She's free now."

She nodded taking in my words, "I'm so sorry Donovan. All of this isn't a reflection of you or the people you love; I want you to know that." She softly grabbed my hand, and interlocked our fingers. I missed the comfort that holding her hand brought.

"I'm here for you. I know I tell you I want you to leave me alone all the time, but that's not what I want. I don't ever-"

I cut her off, "How we are is not your fault. I never blamed you. You don't have to explain anything to me. You and I is on me to fix," I spoke up, silencing her. I didn't want her feeling guilty and feeling like she was someone else that abandoned me. I knew deep down, she never would.

She gripped my hand tighter and rested her head on my shoulder, as I turned music on and let it take over the rest of the ride. I was grateful to have someone like her in my corner. I meant what I said about making us right, just had to show and prove.

We pulled up to the dimly lit beach, and I turned the music down before placing the car in park. I sighed before looking over at Bobbi who returned a worried glance in my direction.

"You sure you ready to do this? Let her go?" she asked rubbing my arm as I shrugged.

"I held on to her long enough for my own reasons. She needs this," I looked behind me at the erne her ashes rested in then reached back for them. Bobbi glanced at me one more time before opening her car door and I soon followed suit.

We walked quietly down the boardwalk towards the beach. Once we reached the end, we both took off our shoes and went barefoot against the cool sand. It was a peaceful night.

"What made you pick this place?" she finally asked me walking along the shore.

"Her and my grandpa had a house built about a block away. This was her favorite place in the world, and this is where she released my grandfather's ashes when he passed. After that, she wanted to move, but always told me that when she dies she wanted the same thing for her." I explained looking out at the moon hanging low over the ocean.

"She ever bring you here?"

I smiled, "All the time. Me and my mom stayed with them for years after my dad left. We always came here. Had picnics and all that shit."

I picked a spot to sit down, not ready to release the ashes into the water just yet. Bobbi wiped the back of her dress before she sat down next to me. I noticed her shiver slightly with the gust of wind, so I removed my jacket and placed it over her shoulders.

"You're not going to be cold?" she asked before accepting it completely.

I shook my head, "I'm good. You need to cover that outfit anyway,"

She laughed wrapping the jacket around her.

"When you gonna answer your phone and let him know you're good?" I asked hearing her phone vibrate for the fifth time tonight. She shrugged.

"Soon. I just need time to think."

"About? If you don't mind me asking," I set the container down next to me, then looked back over at her, awaiting a response.

"Just everything. Julian and I come from different places. And I'm just tired of feeling like I have to get adjusted to his lifestyle. He should be trying to fit in with me."

I chuckled, "No. You guys should be trying to find what works for the both of you."

She gave me a puzzled look, "How are you able to talk to me about this? You don't feel some kind of way?"

"I've just come to terms with things. I want to respect you Bobbi. You want to take him serious, so I'm trying to take ya'll serious."

"That's not you though."

"People change," I replied looking at her as she frowned at my response.

"I like you just how you are. Always be true to yourself and how you feel, no matter what."

"Who you telling that to? Me or you?" I asked seriously as she was quiet for a moment.

"Both of us," she said softly before we both looked out into the horizon.

"I heard you tell Uncle Vince and Aunt Lisa you were going to move. Is that true?" she finally questioned, breaking the peaceful silence.

I nodded, "Yeah, very soon. Me and Shane are trying to expand, and since he has his daughter to raise out here, I'm the one for the job."

"You plan on staying permanently?"

"Maybe. Been looking for a place, and the times I've went out there been cool." She was silent while taking in my words.

"I don't want you to leave," she admitted as my eyes widened.

"Seriously? Why not?"

"I just don't..." She shied away from answering truthfully and I let it stay that way.

"Do you ever," she started, stumbling over her words, "Do you ever think about that night? After Tierre's party?"

"Every day."

"Have you been with someone else since then?" I could tell she was nervous of the answer.

"Yes," I told her truthfully; I could sense the sadness in her body language.

"Have you been with someone else?" She slowly shook her head.

"I won't let Julian touch me in that way."

"Why not?"

"I just can't," she answered small while making lines in the sand with her fingers, avoiding my stare.

"Me being with someone else since you doesn't mean that's how I wanted it to be. It was the worst sex I've had in my life honestly." I chuckled, reflecting back on the random hook-ups I've had where the girls were in a rush for *me* to leave.

"It's your life Don. You don't have to patronize me."

I leaned up and lifted her chin with my finger, forcing her to look at me, "No woman compares to you. In no way. Not just physically. You mean more to me than just that. That's what made that night so special," I explained, avoiding the words *I love you*.

"You realized that too late huh?"

I sighed removing my touch. I could sense the disappointment in her voice.

"I did," I said nodding slowly, "But I refuse to lose you despite my mistake."

"How do you know you haven't already lost me?"

I smirked a little.

"You're here with me, when you could've stayed with him. When you realized no one was picking up, you could've taken a breather, called ya boy, and he would've left that party no questions asked. But you didn't. You called me."

"So?"

"So, I know you. You don't do anything you don't want to do. If you ain't want me to pick you up, my number would've never been dialed, and our paths would've never crossed. You miss me, just as much as I miss you."

She chuckled, "You're taking it too far with the *I miss you* shit."

"I'm not wrong though," I said slyly before turning to pick up my grandmother's ashes, "She would've loved you."

I looked at Bobbi who had a soft smile on her face before resting her head on my shoulder, "What was she like?"

"She was a beautiful person, inside and out. Did everything she could for all of us. Always kept God in her life and made sure to teach us about Him too. I always admired her for her faith and strength. I just think she started losing hope after my grandfather and my mom died a year after the other. I just remember her memory getting bad around the time when my mom got really sick."

She took in a deep breath as we both looked out into the ocean, "How do you cope with loss Donovan? Without it taking over your whole being?"

I paused for a moment, "I'm still trying to answer that question the right way. Been so disconnected to prevent it, but I now realize that it prevents you from having so much more."

Bobbi.

As Donovan pulled up to my house, my heart dropped seeing Julian sitting on the front porch with his head in his hands. I had been avoiding his calls this entire time, and for him to see me pull up with another man already had me nervous for his reaction.

He looked up eyeing the two of us in the car closely as I let a small sigh escape.

"Never returned that call huh?" Donovan smirked at me taking off his seatbelt. I didn't know what he was up to by getting out of the car with me, but I didn't want to make things seem any more suspicious than they already were.

Julian quickly rose to his feet the minute I stepped foot out of the car, "Baby you had me so worried," he said through his teeth, before pulling me into a tight embrace. He grabbed the back of my head softly, before placing a gentle kiss on the crown of it.

He backed up and studied me closely before realizing Donovan's jacket was still around my shoulders. He narrowed his eyebrows before removing it and staring in his direction.

"Thank you man, for getting her home safe," Julian forced while handing Don his jacket. He grinned before accepting it.

"No problem man. Just wanted to make sure she was alright before I took off. I'll talk to you later Bobs," he said nodding his head as I gave a small wave. For some reason having him around made this less awkward, and now that he was gone I didn't know what to expect.

"I would've taken you home, why didn't you call me?" Julian finally said, after Donovan's car disappeared down the street.

"I needed my space from it all. I didn't fit in there, and your mom made it clear that already she didn't like me. She barely even got to know me."

"My mother was out of line. And she knows," he chuckled a little, "After you left she actually said she respected you for standing up for yourself. No one has ever talked to her that way."

I wasn't amused, "I just don't see myself dealing with her and that lifestyle. And I don't think it's fair to you to have to force me into it."

He looked at me with concern "Cha-Bobbi. My whole life I've felt like I don't fit into that world. I wanted to grow up to be someone more meaningful and to have a job more passionate. My father wanted me to be the vice president of his company the minute I graduated college, but I turned him down. I always wanted to be a doctor for as long as I could remember. My passion is to help people in spite of their limitations. Not to always take their money."

"I want you to understand that you fit into my world and the world I want to build for us. I won't drag you to anything else that you're not comfortable with. Hell, I don't even want to go to those damn things myself, and I don't most of the time. I just wanted to show off the most beautiful woman in the world to me, and pray that everyone has the chance to see what I witness every day."

I blushed a little before pushing him, "You're so damn corny." He grinned before sneaking a kiss on my cheek and then going for my lips. I pecked his first, signaling that we were cool.

"There's something I'm not comfortable with though," he said with concerning eyes as I narrowed mine.

"What is it?"

He took in a deep breath choosing his words carefully, "Donovan. There's not room for both of us in your heart."

"It's not even like that-" I started before he quickly cut me off.

"I know you Bobbi. As much as you think I don't, I do. I've known since the first time you and I have both been around him. There's history there, deeper than what you try to let on. Now I've been avoiding saying something to you about it, because I wanted to leave room for you to make your own choices, but watching you pull up with him..." I watched him ball his fist before he calmed himself down internally.

"It just made me feel a certain way. I've been calling you nonstop this whole night, and here you are, calling him to be your hero. I want to be that guy for you. I want to be the man that makes everything right, when everything else seems to be falling apart. Whether I'm the problem or not. How would you feel if I always ran to another woman, before my own?" he asked sincerely, as I just looked down. I knew it wasn't right what I was putting him through with this situation; I just cared about Don too much.

"Donovan and I are just friends. He's one of the first people I connected with when I moved here," I said, trying to give some type of logical excuse.

He shook his head, "Your words and your heart are speaking two different things. I'm not buyin that. I'm really not." He turned away from me and stuffed his hands in his pockets.

"I love you Bobbi. You can't watch the person you love, be in love with someone else." My heart skipped a beat. He had no problem expressing his feelings for me. It was effortless, fearless, and courageous even.

"You-you love me?" I stuttered watching him slowly nod before turning to face me.

"I've loved you for a while just can't keep it inside anymore. I just want a chance more than anything. A chance for you to even try to feel the same way back."

"I don't want you settling for me Julian."

He stepped closer to me.

"Love is patient. I know you care, and I know it's going to take time. I never feel like I'm settling."

I feel like I am, were the words I wanted to say, but I didn't allow them to escape.

****

A few weeks had gone after the dinner party fiasco, I found myself sluggishly walking into the house, exhausted after taking my registry exam. I would find out in a few days if I passed it or not.

I dragged my feet down the hall and nearly jumped at the sight of Donovan, Jay and Shane all sitting at the dining room table. Don was drawing, while Jay and Shane were playing a card game. They all looked up at me and smiled.

"Sup girl," Shane greeted while shuffling the cards.

"Hey guys," I sighed taking a seat at the table with them. Donovan was avoiding my stare. I wondered what he was drawing on the large sheet of paper.

"What's up with you? How your test go?" Jay asked me while accepting the cards Shane was sliding in his direction.

I shrugged, "Eh, it was okay. I feel like I passed but, I don't know." Jay looked at me close.

"Doesn't sound like you care either way," he observed as I shrugged again before reaching for the bag of chips that were on the table.

"I don't," I replied in a flat tone while reaching in the bag. Don was still silent, concentrated on his current piece of art.

"Why you take it then?" Shane asked the question I knew was coming.

"Just seemed like that was what I was supposed to do next," I said staring intently at the drawing, trying to figure out what it was going to become.

I envied Shane and Donovan sometimes. Just for the fact that they were able to live their dreams. Ever since moving out here, I wanted to make photography a profession more and more. Dreams felt like they should be reality, not the security of a nine to five. Nursing was okay, but I wanted to do more with my passion. Take pictures for magazines, books, galleries, even families and senior photos.

I looked around for my camera, remembering I had left it in the living room. I stood up from the table wiping my grimy fingers on my pants before going to grab the device.

"Where you headin off to?" Jay asked watching me place the camera around my neck.

"Just about to go for a walk, take some photos. I'll see ya'll later."

I stepped onto the porch and noticed two small neighborhood girls playing across the street. I adjusted my lens and took candid photos of the girls happily playing with each other making a note to myself to give their parents the finished photos. They were beautiful.

I happily took off down the street capturing all of the stillness of nature in awe of how perfect everything came together. My phone vibrated in the midst of my natural high.

My lips curved into a small smile seeing Julian's face appear on the screen.

"Hey Love."

"Hey baby, whatcha doin? How did the test go?" he asked with anticipation clear in his tone.

"Uh, it went ok," I said feeling my smile slowly leave. The last thing I wanted to talk to him about was the test.

"Just ok? You don't think you passed?" he questioned with concern as I shrugged like he could see me.

"I don't know Ju. I'll know for sure in a few days though." There was a small pause and I spoke again to prevent from hearing the disappointment.

"Can I talk to you about something?" I asked nervously.

"Of course, anything."

"I've been thinking about trying to get my portfolio together and submitting it to a few studios around here," I bit my lip waiting for his response.

"For what? Your photography?"

I nodded clutching the phone tight, "Yes. Like making this a real profession."

I heard a small chuckle on his end, "Chanel, I thought photography was just a mere hobby of yours? Something you did for fun? There's no stability in it."

"That's how I felt at first, but it's becoming something more real for me. It provides an escape and I can just get lost in it. I can't keep ignoring this feeling."

"You do know that feelings change? I mean, I support your photography as something to do to pass time but nursing is a career. It's promising and in a never ending field."

"Julian-"

He cut me off, "My dream for us is to be able to open our own practice one day. You and me working side by side. Doing what we love. Medicine is what originally connected us and it's something that we can be truly invested in and profit from."

I sighed a little before placing my head down, "That's your dream. What about mine?"

"I always thought that was something we both wanted. And it's something we can obtain. Taking pictures for a living is not something to obtain baby, you can always do that."

I felt the tears begin to well up in my eyes, preventing myself from saying something I knew he couldn't handle. Why were my dreams not as important as his?

"I guess you're right," I lied quickly wiping away the tear that managed to fall.

"I'll talk to you later," I said hanging up the phone not waiting for a response. I took in several deep breaths before turning to head back down the street.

I saw Donovan shutting his back door looking like he had just placed something in it. I smiled at the sight of him. He waited patiently for me to reach the house.

"You done already? You're normally out here for hours," he said tugging at a loose curl in my hair. He frowned slightly after studying my eyes. I wondered if there was any hint of me crying left in them.

"I uh, lost motivation."

"If anything this should be the motivation. Lose yourself in what makes you the happiest."

"Is that why you've been drawing so much?" I smirked as he did too taking the attention off me.

"Good save. I'll press further later. Gotta go," he said kissing my forehead before pulling me into a hug.

"Where ya going?" I asked not ready for him to leave just yet.

"Work lil' girl. Appointments starting at one."

"When can I get a tattoo?" His face contorted to one of confusion before he laughed a little.

"I'll make one for you. Later." He disappeared in the driver's seat and immediately started the car. I was amused to see what he would come up with for me.

I looked down at my camera when he pulled off, inspired to take pictures again.

****

I walked down the halls in the hospital building, softly smiling to myself while gripping my purse tightly. I moved several strands of hair out of my face, happy that Tierre came over to do it last night. Today was a special day.

"My girl is too bad on her birthday!" Tierre softly squealed in my ear, after sneaking up behind me and hugging me close. I giggled before turning to face her as she handed me a card.

"You look beautiful. Never seen a chick so bad in scrubs before." I blushed while accepting the card. I always made sure to take extra time with my appearance on my birthday, seeing as how it was the one day of the year I was expected to get the most attention.

"Thank you for the card. I'm going to open everything tonight."

"Yes, before we get crazy at the club. I'm too excited." She smiled while taking my hand and walking with me towards the break room. Our shift didn't start for another five minutes.

"So what did the doctor get you? Something over the top and fancy I'm sure." She playfully rolled her eyes before looking at me, awaiting an answer.

"Um nothing yet. I haven't heard from him today." She scrunched her nose up.

"I was almost positive the two of you were going to be together last night since you said he wasn't coming to the party."

254

I put my things away in my locker before turning back to face her. "I never invited him to the party."

She nearly choked on her coffee.

"Why the hell not?"

"He works crazy hours at his new rotation and I knew if I would've asked him to come out and get drunk with all of my friends he would've found a reason not to come. It's cool. I'm sure he'll surprise me at lunch or something," I shrugged, before forcing a smile.

Truthfully, Julian and I weren't on the best of terms ever since he had belittled my dream. Because of him, it was something I was putting to the side and trying not to think about.

"If you say so."

****

The day passed on and I was getting numerous notifications from text messages to social media, all wishing me a happy birthday. Not one word from my boyfriend.

As I was preparing to leave for lunch I was startled by a bouquet of flowers appearing in front of my eyes. The smile resting behind them warmed my entire being.

"Happy Birthday beautiful," Donovan greeted with a toothy grin.

I was lost for words while carefully taking the flowers.

"I remember you saying lilac was your favorite color, so I thought a dozen of those versus roses would be a better fit." He slightly shrugged as I couldn't get the smile to disappear from my face. I was overjoyed that he remembered my day and actually went out of his way to do something special.

"These are perfect Don, thank you," I finally said, sniffing my flowers.

"You about to head to lunch? Your gift is in my office."

I furrowed my brow, "Gift? The flowers aren't the gift?"

He scoffed before fanning me off.

"Of course not. That's just to have something nice to look at while you're sitting here doing paper work. Your present is better than any flowers," he said with confidence, piquing my interest.

"Give me a minute to clock out."

****

The door chimed as Donovan held it open for me to their shop and I was instantly greeted by Shane yelling at the first sign of me.

"Happy birthday Bobs!" he yelped, before pulling me into a large embrace.

"We popping bottles on me tonight," he told me, while patting his chest causing me to chuckle at his actions.

"Thank you Shane, I'm excited for the little get together."

"Oh, it's gonna be popping. I'm gonna have everyone buying you whatever you want tonight. Don't even worry about it." He pulled me into a hug again as I laughed and fixed my hair back. I looked up to see Don waiting patiently by his office door for me.

"If I don't see you before I leave, I'll see you tonight," I said, beginning to walk away.

He nodded before greeting a potential customer that entered through the door.

I stepped into the office as Donovan closed the door behind us before placing himself behind his desk. His cheeks were slightly red, signaling he was nervous.

"What's up with you? I've never seen you red before." He gave a nervous laugh.

"I just want you to like my gift." I smirked.

"I'm sure I'll like whatever you give me Don. You didn't have to get me anything."

"Nah, I wanted to. I've been thinking about your gift for months honestly." He reached down and pulled out a birthday decorated bag and softly handed it to me. I was going to wait to open it, but this seemed like something personal, not just a simple card with money inside.

I carefully removed the comic strip paper he used to stuff it with and laughed to myself that he remembered how much I read the comics. I saw a leather black book resting inside and looked at him questionably.

"Open it up," he urged, with the cutest grin on his face. I did as I was told, placing the book in both of my hands and noticed my full name engraved in the bottom right hand corner.

I opened and nearly gasped at what lied in the pages. They were pictures. My pictures. Donovan had created my own portfolio filled with some of my best pieces.

"I uh," he stumbled, scratching the back of his head. "I just see the passion you have for photography. It's your art, your release, your escape from reality. I know how much it means to you, how much you reverted to it when you were going through your tough time. I mean to answer your question with how I cope, it's through my art. I didn't realize how much I loved it until after my mom died. And I see that your art is through the lens. How you see the world. And you portray beautiful pictures. I just...wanted to give you a boost to go for that. Do what makes you the happiest, regardless of how anyone else feels about it... I don't know." He giggled at the end, nervous that what he was saying was wrong. I couldn't stop the tears from flowing before finally looking up.

"This...this is the best gift I've ever gotten. I just...how'd you know?"

He wiped a few of my tears with the pad of his thumb before resting his hand on the back of my neck, "How'd I know what?"

"That I was feeling this way? About wanting to pursue photography more?"

He shrugged. "Something I could feel I guess. The way you rave about us having the shop, and my art show. You always got your camera. Always working hard on your pictures. Just the way you look when you're doing that, then seeing the way you look when you drag yourself into that hospital. Life is too short not to enjoy what you do. I just wanted to help you see that it was possible. For you especially."

I smiled softly while flipping through the pages. "How did you get these pictures?"

"You didn't realize your laptop was missing for a few weeks?" he asked, as I chuckled.

"So you had it when Vince said he was getting it fixed," I said, remembering the day when Vince lied, telling me that he screwed up my laptop and took it to get looked at.

"Yep. Hacked in all your shit," he joked, sharing a small laugh with me.

"Thank you. This is...amazing. I really can't believe that you did this without me saying a word to you about it."

"Guess you can say I pay attention more than you think I do." He tucked a piece of hair behind my ear.

"You're just...one of the best friends I've ever had." I breathed as he looked intently into my eyes.

I wanted so bad to just tell him how much I loved him, and needed him in my life. All the time. Every minute of every day.

Before I could say anything, a soft gentle kiss was placed on my lips. We both allowed it to linger before pulling away.

"Bobbi listen-" he began before we were both interrupted by knocking. I looked at him questionably, wondering if he was going to continue. He decided against it and went to open the door.

"Yo, you got a client," Shane informed him, as Donovan nodded, looking at his watch.

"Tell em give me a minute," he said, giving Shane permission to leave. He then looked to me with apologetic eyes.

"It's cool, we'll talk about it later," I told him, still feeling my lips tingle from the kiss we shared.

He sighed a little before placing his palm on the back of my neck and slowly kissing my forehead.

"Happy Birthday Bobbi."

****

"So tell me what happened again when he called you?" Tierre asked, while she turned onto the express way.

She was taking me to some elaborate restaurant for a birthday dinner before we met up with everyone else at the club. I was sporting a tight black dress with sheer sides and red open toe shoes, while Tierre was wearing a sexy all black dress as well, revealing more of her cleavage than anything and her hair was slicked back into an elegant ponytail.

I frowned thinking about my conversation with Julian.

"He didn't say anything. Just was talking about work and how late he was gonna have to stay tonight. I asked him what today was, and he simply just said the date like it didn't mean anything to him."

"Damn, he really forgot your birthday? Have ya'll talked about it recently?"

"No. I don't really force my birthday on people. The reason why this party is happening is because of Jay."

She nodded in understanding before she smirked.

"Donovan's gift to you was so sweet. Didn't know he had it in him."

"Me either. It really left me speechless. It was the perfect gift at the right time," I said looking back at all the gifts I had collected from everyone throughout the day. I had kept them in Tierre's car so I could open them while we were at dinner.

"Don't you think it's about time you made a decision about the two of them? I really don't think either of them can co-exist in your life."

I shrugged a little while looking at my manicured nails. "Yeah I know. It's just not the easiest decision to make. After today though, my mind is really all over the place with Julian."

"Well let's just get too drunk to care about it all. Tonight is your night, and we're going to celebrate you until we pass out."

I chuckled and nodded in agreement. I didn't want to think about my relationship woes; I just wanted to have a good night.

About twenty minutes later, Tierre pulled up to the valet of the restaurant and we both exited the car. I grabbed my things from the back and followed her inside.

As we reached the hostess stand, I was quickly greeted by a group of familiar faces.

"Surprise!" The group consisting of my aunt and uncle, my cousin and his girlfriend, Shane, Donovan, a few of the girls I had connected with from Tierre's party and last but not least...

"Julian?" I asked, his face the only one mattering at the moment. He grinned widely and stepped up to me holding a small wrapped box.

"I could never forget your birthday baby. Just wanted to surprise you with everyone else," he said, kissing me softly on the cheek as I looked back at Tierre who had a questionable look on her face. I don't think she knew he was going to be invited.

"Wow, thank you everyone," I finally said, making sure to go around and greet them all with a hug, before Tierre grabbed my hand.

"Come on boo, the table is ready." I followed her before looking back and locking eyes with Donovan. He looked extremely uncomfortable to be here, but I was glad he was. His face was the one I was most excited to see.

There was a large table reserved for us in a quiet, dimly lit area in the back of the restaurant. We all got comfortable and began browsing the menu after ordering our drinks. I was looking over the appetizers when I felt a hand gently grab mine.

"I'm really sorry I didn't show you much attention today," Julian apologized again, as I softly smiled over at him.

"It's okay, just make up for it the rest of the night," I assured him, still looking over the menu, planning not to order anything heavy because I planned on drinking. I was surprised he had even ordered an alcoholic drink to have with his food. It wasn't like him to drink much at all.

"I am. I didn't even know they were throwing a party for you until Lisa and Jay told me. Why didn't you say anything?"

I lightly shrugged, feeling a little bad about it.

"I just didn't want to put you in an uncomfortable position. I know that's not really your scene."

"But it's your birthday babe. Anything you're a part of, I want to be there to celebrate with you."

I nodded taking in his words as he leaned over and placed a gentle kiss on my forehead and then my cheek. I locked eyes with Donovan just as the waitress returned with my drink. Perfect timing.

Donovan.

"Dog, I'm too excited for the new parlor. Rachel was sending me pictures of a few spots today," Shane said, continuing to take bites of his food.

I was tuning him in and out. I kept sneaking looks at Bobbi and Julian being more affectionate than usual. He was showering her with attention and buying the two of them back to back drinks.

"Yeah, I'm excited too," I said flatly, while taking a sip of cranberry juice mixed with Grey Goose.

Shane kissed his teeth before looking over at me.

"You're not even paying attention and you leave in a month. You sure you can run business out there solo? If I gotta come, I will." He scolded as I fanned him off, and chugged the rest of my drink.

I coughed as the liquor burned down my throat and settled abruptly in my stomach.

"I'm good man, just not trynna talk about all dat right now." I needed alcohol to be able to deal with the rest of this night.

He looked at me, unconvinced, before glancing up at Bobbi and her date.

"That's what it is. You jealous." He spoke so only I could hear. Most of the table was lost in their own conversation.

"I just don't know what else to do to win her over. I thought the present was gonna be it," I sighed, my voice filled with disappointment.

"Ok, but did you tell her how you felt?"

I shook my head.

"Well that's why. You ain't say shit."

"How am I supposed to?" I seriously questioned, realizing the liquor was causing me to be emotional.

"You man up and tell her D, I don't know. You make this harder than it has to be. It's not that hard bruh." Shane shook his head, taking another bite of his food.

"What if she leaves? What if she doesn't feel the same and just leaves? Wit ol' boy? What I do then?"

He shrugged. "You take it as a loss and move the hell on. I mean, that's just the risk. You ain't gon know until you say something."

I looked up and caught Bobbi's eye for what seemed like the 100th time tonight. It was almost like she was apologizing for being affectionate with her boyfriend in front of me. I smiled at her and she did the same. Julian looked back and turned his nose at me before moving more in front of Bobbi forcing me to disappear from her view. I laughed, enjoying the fact that I made him insecure.

"I'm gon say something, tonight." Shane's eyes widened at me.

"Tonight of all nights?! I don't know if that's a good idea," he warned, as I blew it off.

"I can't keep this in no more. I just gotta know. Especially before I leave."

"So you can't wait till tomorrow? Like when she's not being hawked by her dude?! You asking for trouble man." He shook his head.

I looked back over at Bobbi and Julian smiling sweetly at each other. I felt my skin get hot.

"I don't care."

****

I was blasting music, while riding with Jay and Shane to the club where we had a section reserved for everyone invited to Bobbi's gathering. Jay's girl decided to ride with Tierre just so all of us could have our time before being around the group.

"Man, Jay, tell your bro he playing with fire by trying to talk to Bobbi about his feelings tonight," Shane said, leaning up from the back seat.

Jay busted out in drunken laughter before placing his hand on my shoulder from the passenger seat.

"I knew it! I kneewwww it," he slurred, while laughing and wagging his finger at me.

"Man ya'll chill out. This...this real life!" I stuttered, feeling the effects of all the drinks I had at dinner. I can't believe they trusted me to drive.

"You done got soft Don. Never thought I'd see the day. For my crazy ass cousin at that." I dropped my shoulder so his hand would move, taking offense.

"Aww, you done hurt his feelings," Shane cooed, while grabbing my cheeks, causing me to swerve slightly.

"Quit playing man! I'm too drunk," I snapped, only fueling them to laugh harder. I gained my concentration back on the road.

"Which is exactly why you shouldn't say anything to her about it tonight. She's not going to take you serious," Jay said, shaking his head.

"I'm not drinking at the club. I'm going to sober up some more, so that I sound sincere. I just gotta do it while I have the confidence to."

"You sure about this? I don't want you going all crazy if she turns you down," Shane empathized, finally sounding concerned.

"She's not going to turn me down."

The rest of the ride was a haze before we pulled up to the packed club. I stepped out, along with my friends, and handed the valet the keys to my car before stepping onto the curb. Several eyes from attractive women were looking in our direction, but I only had mine set for one woman, hoping she would hear me out.

We walked in, greeted by smoke, music, and loud talking before walking towards the back where most of the VIP sections were. The ladies and Julian were already posted, awaiting our arrival. Their faces lit up when they noticed us approaching.

"Finally, ya'll made it!" Felicia yelled excitedly, before placing a gentle kiss on Jay's lips.

Tierre walked up with a tray of shots and instructed all of us to get two.

"Gotta take some shots for the birthday girl!" she squealed in her Harlem accent, while her long thick pony tail bounced as she moved around the circle.

I chuckled while grabbing two tiny cups of liquor before quickly combining the two into one. This would be the only bit I would have tonight before requesting a glass of water from the bar. I wanted to be fully aware of every action I made.

I looked up and caught Julian and Bobbi laughing together while spilling their shots. They were both highly inebriated and making me even more envious with every smile. I wanted to be the reason for her happiness. I wanted to be her reason for everything.

"Okay listen up errybody!" Tierre yelled, standing on top of the couch, shoes already off. I shook my head slightly at the sight.

"I just wanted to say, that this past year that I've spent getting to know this girl has been crazy, yet enjoyable! I've watched her grow from a broken soul, to someone so beautiful and a true joy to be around. I'm proud of you and look forward to spending another crazy and fun filled year with you! Love you girl!"

Bobbi blushed after the speech and we all raised our shot glasses in the air.

"Happy Birthdaayyy!" Jay yelled randomly, as we touched cups causing us to laugh before gulping the liquor.

My body shook while it made its way down my throat, and I coughed from the strong taste.

Swiftly, I left the section to head to the bar and request a cup of water. While walking, a gentle hand grabbed a hold of my forearm, and I smiled noticing the nails belonged to the woman of the hour.

"I've been trying to talk to you all night," Bobbi cooed happily to me, while interlocking our arms, keeping her pace with mine.

"I can't tell," I said flatly, my voice revealing my jealousy.

"I'm sorry about that..." she apologized softly, before regaining her smile again. "I'm really happy you came out tonight. It means everything that you're here."

We approached the bar and I looked down, simply captivated with her beauty. Bobbi was naturally and effortlessly beautiful. Her soft brown skin always glowed, with or without make up, her lips were delicate and full, and her almond brown eyes always showed their true color with light.

She chuckled a little after our intense staring contest. "What?"

I smirked and shook my head. "You're gorgeous."

She bashfully turned her head, avoiding my stare any longer.

"Shut up," she finally uttered, as I laughed a little before catching the bartender's attention to order my water. Her eyes widened at my choice, but she kept her lips sealed tight.

"Your boyfriend not mad you over here with me?" I asked, while waiting for the drink to appear.

She shrugged. "Is it his birthday?"

"I'm just saying. He's been keeping you from me all night," I commented, handing the bartender a dollar for bringing me my drink. I took a sip and leaned my back against the bar, standing arms reach in front of her.

She started playing with the ends of her hair, searching for the right words.

"Yeah, I noticed that. Listen-"

Before another word could escape, we were joined by an ominous presence.

Julian.

"Baby, all your friends are looking for you," He announced placing his hand around her waist, marking his territory.

"I'm sure, but I'm talking to Donovan right now," She objected, slowly removing his hand while looking up at him.

He finally looked my way, meekly acknowledging my existence before giving her a pouty look.

"Well the two of you can come be around the rest of us huh? How about we go dance." He flashed a smile, joining their hands as she gave me a subtle look of somberness.

"Okay," she sighed, giving in to the pressure of having to make a decision between the two of us.

I rolled my eyes watching them walk away. Feeling my initial confidence diminish, and the effects of alcohol still present, I hung my head in defeat.

"Head up, cutie," I heard a voice say, causing me to look up.

It belonged to a woman who wasn't necessarily my type, but cute enough to hold my attention for the duration of this night.

"You okay? You look sad." She frowned, watching me close.

"Nah, just drunk," I admitted, causing her to chuckle in my response. She had a nice smile.

"You should come and kick it with me and my friends over there," she suggested, turning behind her and pointing towards a group of girls on the dance floor.

Her friends were attractive and I noticed Shane coming in my direction. He reached us, just as she was turning back around looking for an answer.

"Can my homeboy roll too?" I asked, placing my arm around Shane's shoulder as he looked between the two of us.

She gave a flirtatious grin before nodding.

"Yeah, come on." She led the way with Shane and me following closely.

He tapped my chest with the back of his hand before looking up at me, "Yo, what's this about?" He said so only I could hear.

"Her friends wanna party."

He furrowed his brows.

"Thought we was partying with Bobbi and her friends?" I rolled my eyes at the thought.

"Nah, her dude wanna be the only person in that party."

"So what? You over it?"

I looked over at the section, catching a glimpse of Julian kissing on Bobbi's neck, making my heart sink down into my stomach.

"For now."

We stepped onto the dance floor, and the girl that brought us introduced us to everyone like we had known each other for years, even though I had no idea what her name was. Shane and I just got behind the cutest ones and began to dance. That's what I appreciated about going out with Shane or Jay. We weren't shy to dance at a club.

We were soon joined by Jay and the rest of the crew and I was finally feeling myself begin to have fun. My no drinking rule left when Tierre handed me a drink she brought for me, realizing I was distancing myself from the party.

I sipped on the drink and rocked with the girl I was currently dancing with. Feeling eyes burning into my skull, I looked over and caught Bobbi staring at me as Julian awkwardly danced behind her. I nodded my head to be a smart ass only causing her to roll her eyes. I didn't understand why she was tripping, she had someone. I didn't.

Feeling annoyed from our interaction, I began dancing with the girl harder. She felt me get more aggressive, so she got more aggressive as the song picked up its pace. I nearly spilled my drink on myself, so I quickly gulped it down, and handed the empty glass to Tierre. She looked at me crazy before accepting it.

"The hell I look like?" she asked, as I gave a drunken laugh, losing focus of the girl I was dancing with.

Still trying to mess with Tierre, I suddenly felt two hands wrap around my neck. The girl was now facing me, grinding from the front. I shot Tierre a confused look while she stared on with her mouth dropped. We both knew I didn't like to be touched like that in public.

"Hey uh..." I started, trying to remove her hands from my neck.

Before I could, she jumped up and wrapped her legs around my waist, thrusting with all of her might. I was in awe of the whole situation.

"Yo, chill!" Tierre yelled, pushing the girl off me as her friends caught her.

They and the girls we were with began getting into a small verbal battle. I started looking around for Bobbi, not wanting her to think I was trying to do that on purpose. I searched and saw her walking towards the restrooms, and quickly fled the scene to catch up with her, while Julian was attempting to settle the girls with Jay.

I was nearly knocking people over, trying to catch her before she disappeared in the crowded women's restroom. I tugged at her arm, and she quickly swung around, disappointment written on her face when she saw me.

"What?" she growled with much attitude.

I pulled her to the side away from everybody else attempting to release their buildup of drinks.

"What's with the attitude?"

She gave a look of bewilderment.

"What are you worried about my attitude for? Ol' girl was keeping you busy enough," she spat, crossing her arms and looking away.

I couldn't help but chuckle, "You jealous or some shit? You been hugged up all night and wanna get mad at me for dancing wit someone?"

She crossed her eyes and attempted to walk away, but I grabbed her before she could.

"What Donovan? What did you even follow me out here for?" she asked with irritation, while snatching away from me.

"I wanted to finally talk to you. For real. I didn't get to say everything I wanted to say at the shop earlier," I said calmly, expressing the severity of the situation.

She relaxed her body and looked up at me.

"You said a lot. I thought you said everything," She shrugged as I sighed, trying to work up the courage.

"I didn't. I didn't get to say how much of an ass I was for letting you walk away so many times. I didn't get to apologize for pushing you to open up, and then not knowing how to handle it once you did. I didn't get to tell you how much it hurts to see another man doing everything I should be doing, because I know, given the chance, I could do more, and make you happier than you ever been. I didn't get to thank you for pushing me to be a better man in ways you don't even know..."

I was pacing at this point, trying to get everything I needed to out. Her eyes were planted on my every move, taking in each word I had to say.

I stopped myself and took in a deep breath before stepping closer to her, our hips inches apart. I placed my hand softly around her waist and let it rest on her lower back.

"Most importantly, I didn't tell you, how I think about you every single day. I draw images of your smile, the way you look at me, how you study me. How infatuated I am with your beauty. How proud I am of your growth."

I was leaning in closer with each passing word.

"And also..." I breathed, delicately lifting her chin with my knuckle. "How deeply, I've fallen in love with you."

Her brows quickly furrowed as she looked into my eyes. Before she could speak, we were forcefully yanked apart.

"What the hell you doin' touching my woman like that?!" Julian roared, nearly knocking Bobbi onto her feet with how hard he pulled us.

That sent me into a rage.

"Aye man don't be touching her like dat!" I yelled back, pushing him hard into the brick wall, causing his back to collide heavily into it.

Several people dispersed from the scene, not wanting to be mistakenly in the middle of the confrontation.

I quickly was at Bobbi's aid, helping her to catch her balance as she looked with confusion between the two of us, "You ok baby?" I asked, inspecting her.

Her eyes widened looking behind me and I turned around just as Julian's fist connected with my jaw. He was fixing to hit me again with his left, but before he could, I gave him a blow to his face with my right and then two hard punches in the abdomen with my left. While he doubled over in pain, I was preparing to knee him right in his face but he locked his arms around my waist and tackled me to the ground.

"Julian stop!" I heard Bobbi scream, as a crowd formed more around us; both wrestling for domination in this battle for one woman's heart.

She attempted to tear us apart, but Julian pushed her away. I got pissed and pushed him off of me, trying to get up and check on her, but he quickly got a hold of my neck before I could move another inch.

"I told you to stay your ass away from her!" he growled, attempting to put me in some awkward choke hold move, while I clawed at his hands to release me.

"You fight like a lil' bitch!" I taunted, elbowing him hard in his gut, forcing him to free my neck. He shot back up and began coming for me again, before three large men with *Security* written over their shirts broke through the crowd.

"Aye ya'll break this up!" a strong 250 pound voice said, before he picked me up and began pushing me towards the exit of the club.

"Man I ain't do shit!" I yelled back, trying to break free, but his hold was too strong.

He was carrying me past our section, and everyone looked at me in shock, while I got carried out of the club. Shane was quickly by my side, panic written all over his face, trying to make sense of the situation without words.

Bobbi and Julian were nowhere in sight.

Bobbi.

"Can you believe the nerve of that ignorant bastard?!" Julian ranted, speeding off from the club.

The security guard forced me to follow in Julian's direction instead of Donovan's. I was frozen in the passenger seat, replaying everything that happened in my mind. Only one part in particular mattered the most.

Donovan told me he loved me. Not just that, but he was in love with me.

"I don't want you anywhere near him Chanel! You hear me?! He is toxic! No got damn good. Not for what we got going for us. He own a petty tattoo parlor and think that's doing something. I have a doctorate degree. I can't fight with scum inside of a club of all places! I shouldn't even have been seen inside a club!"

I shut my eyes closed and rested my temple against my fingers. He was giving me a headache.

"Oh and that gift he gave you. We're throwing it away," he said firmly looking over at me.

I felt my blood boil. I was at my breaking point.

"I'm not throwing away shit."

He swerved the car looking over at me. He was still angry from the fight. He's lucky the security guard came, because Donovan was ready to get in his ass.

"What did you say?" he gritted, while I held my composure.

"I'm not throwing away shit! That's my gift. You have no right to tell me what I will do with it. And you have no business telling me who I can and cannot associate with. If I didn't want to talk to Donovan anymore, I wouldn't. Simple as that!"

"What? You defending him or something?! He doesn't give a damn about you! Why can't you see that!"

I shook my head at his response.

"He does give a damn about me! More than you! You didn't realize how aggressive you were being with me! Pushing me and tossing me like some damn rag doll! Each time you did, that's when Donovan got in your ass! You couldn't even see it!"

He gripped the steering wheel as if he was refraining from wanting to hit me. I didn't care. I wasn't saying anything reckless.

"Just take me home Julian."

"I'm not taking you home. You need to be with me tonight."

I scoffed at his comment.

"I need to be at home! Away from you! I can't do this man," I sighed, not being able to hold it in any longer.

The pressure of forcing myself to feel something I didn't was too much.

"Do what?!" His voice was getting loud again, and I nearly jumped at the sound of it. I was on edge around this man now.

"Do this! This relationship! Ever since we've been together you've been subliminally trying to control my life! Pushing me to take this exam, when really I don't even want to be a nurse anymore! Talking about marriage and opening practices and all this other bull shit! That's not my life! I'm young! I like to go out and have fun with my friends. I like to take pictures of shit. I take *good* pictures of shit. I like being open and obnoxious at times. I like being me! Not the me that you're trying to turn me into. I'm not that person. I'm not the one you're looking for, and you're trying so hard to make me her."

He was quiet as he steadied his driving; actually taking the exit that goes towards my house.

"I only pushed you, because I thought you wanted those things too." he said softly, shame apparent in his tone.

"I wanted those things to make you happy, and because it's a decent plan. Just not my plan. I used to be like that with my ex. Always conforming to make him happy, and I lost myself in it. I lost myself so much, that when he left I didn't know what to do. Felt like I didn't have a purpose and it drove me to be someone I wasn't. I can't do that to myself again. I can't settle to be anything less than happy in any situation. I'd rather be alone, than unhappy."

Tears were present on my face as the car grew silent.

"I'm sorry... I'm sorry I couldn't be her, Julian." I said placing my head down, watching a tear collide with my thigh.

"I'm sorry that I couldn't be him," he said bitterly after a few moments of silence. I threw my head against the head rest, internally praying for this ride to be over with as soon as possible.

He barely waited for me to step out of the car before he quickly backed out of the driveway and sped down the street. I looked at my phone seeing all the missed messages from Jay and Tierre, wondering what happened to get us kicked out and where we were. I looked up at the house, not ready to face them yet and then looked at my car parked on the other side of the driveway. There was one important stop I had to make before I called it a night.

****

My heartbeat was racing the closer I got to his front door. It wasn't like me to pop up on someone, so I had no idea what to expect. What if another woman was already here, thinking I had rejected him? What if he didn't want to see me?

I pushed the doubt to the back of my mind before impatiently knocking on the door. Whether or not those things were true, I still had to get answers. I had to know for sure.

My palms began to get sweaty, waiting for an answer. His car was parked outside, so I knew he was here, just wasn't too sure if he was alone. I huffed to myself as I prepared to knock again, but as I did, the doorknob was turning.

He opened the door originally with an irritated expression, until he saw my face. I looked him up and down from head to toe, as he stood with a towel wrapped around his waist. His chest, neck and arms, were like his canvas, all filled with different and colorful artwork, glistening with drips of water like he had rushed out of the shower to greet the mystery person desiring his attention so late at night.

His face contorted into one of confusion before he spoke, "Bobbi? What are you-"

I cut him off quickly, "Did you mean it?"

My voice cracked a tiny bit when I asked. It was the same question replaying in my mind the entire way here.

He stood frozen, still taken aback by my sudden appearance.

"Did you mean what you said tonight?" The minute I blinked, a tear made its way down my cheek. My emotions from the entire night were hitting me without warning.

He swallowed hard before he nodded, reaching his hand out to me. "Every word."

Our hands connected and he pulled me slowly inside the house. I didn't take my eyes off of him for one second.

He closed the door behind me and I let go of his hand, as I started to pace a little, simultaneously running my fingers through my hair.

"I just couldn't do it anymore Don. I couldn't stay with him. I wasn't happy. I just wanted to be over you. But he couldn't do it. He couldn't make me get over you. And I'm just so sorry about what happened at the club and-"

"Shh, shh." he gently hissed, silencing me as he stepped closer and cuffed my jaw in his hands, forcing me to look up at him.

The tears were flowing at this point, and he softly smiled, wiping them away.

"Tell me what you mean when you say that you love me," I questioned, searching his eyes for sincerity.

He grinned, revealing the small dimple, and I internally counted the freckles that spread across from his left cheek over the brim of his nose to his right cheek.

"I mean that I don't want to live a life without you in it. I didn't find myself, until I found you. I'm tired of living a lie Bobbi. I'm tired of just wandering through life, acting like shit doesn't faze me when it does. Until you came along, I was used to how things were, I was comfortable. You came and made me uncomfortable. And I needed that." he expressed, as I took in every word.

"I'm not afraid to be uncomfortable. I'm not afraid of loving you. I'm not afraid to allow this to happen. I'm no longer afraid of the risk I'm taking. I love what I feel. I love the beautiful picture that has painted itself out. The image I see when I see us together. I'm not scared of it anymore."

I smiled looking up at him, before I gently kissed his lips that were inches away from mine, "I'm not scared anymore either."

EPOLOGUE

Bobbi.

Donovan and I sat on the front porch of my Aunt and Uncle's house one evening after Sunday dinner. I was sitting on the step below him, with his arms wrapped around my shoulder, and his chin sitting on the crown of my head. I rubbed his arm softly while sitting in a comfortable silence.

"It's such a beautiful night," he sighed happily, before placing soft kisses on my ear and then my cheeks.

I giggled a little at the affection.

We had been inseparable since the night of my birthday, spending every moment we could with each other. Being in a relationship with him felt completely different than anyone else I had called myself being with. With Donovan, everything came natural and easy, and expressing my love for him was an enjoyable experience.

"It is..." I cooed, leaning my head back into his chest, causing him to wrap his arms around me tighter.

"Makes me never wanna leave Cali."

His comment made my heart sink a little. Even with our new found love and relationship, he was still planning to move to Miami within the week. It took so long for us to even get to this point; the thought of him leaving was heartbreaking.

"I still don't even want to think about that," I replied softly, while dropping my head.

He gave a short sigh, before squeezing me tight and then releasing me from his embrace. I turned and looked at him strangely before he stood up and jumped off the porch to stand in front of me.

He clasped his hands together before searching for the words, "I've wanted to talk to you seriously about this Miami thing."

My eyes lit up, "You're going to tell me you're not going?" I asked hopeful, as he chuckled and shook his head.

"No silly. I have to go." My shoulders deflated with disappointment causing him to laugh.

"Come on, hear me out."

I rolled my eyes playfully before looking back into his, "Okay. I'm listening."

He reached into his back pocket and pulled out a rectangular piece of paper.

He looked at the paper, and took in a deep breath before speaking, "Baby, this last month with you has been nothing short of amazing. I've truly never been happier in my entire life. Like, it's crazy. And I don't want to lose that. Not this soon."

I furrowed my brows, "So what are you saying?"

He took in another deep breath before looking back at me, "I'm saying. I want us to really give this a chance. No distractions, no outsiders, nothing. Just me and you finding our own way together. I mean Miami would be a great place for you to start your photography, and hell, maybe even get your own company started. And you can be there every step of the way while I try to open this shop. You already said yourself you not really trying to work where you are-"

I cut him off. "Wait. Are you suggesting that I just up and move with you? To Miami?" I asked, with confusion clear in my tone.

"That's exactly what I'm saying."

He handed me the piece of paper as I slowly took it from him.

"That. That is a plane ticket to Miami a week after I leave. I wanna give you time to decide if it's something you really want to do or think you should do. Our whole relationship is based off risks that we were afraid to take, and now I'm asking you to just take one more. Give us a chance to really try and do this. Give something we've both been wanting our whole lives a chance. I know it sounds crazy and soon to move in with me so fast, but if you get down there and figure out your own way you can get your own place and everything. I just...I just don't want to lose you again Bobbi. I don't want any more distance between us."

I stared at the ticket, reading everything almost a hundred times over before I looked back up at Donovan.

"This is big," was all I could manage to say as his face saddened.

"I know it is. And it's something I wouldn't even ask of you if I didn't feel like it could be a good move. I'm not trynna pressure you and I'm not going to be mad if you don't come. I just at least want you to think about it."

He shoved his hands in their respective pocket while looking at me with uncertainty. Everything in me wanted to accept his offer, and run off to Miami with him without looking back, I just wanted to make the right decision.

He leaned down to become eye level with me, before taking my cheeks into his hands with tenderness, "Aye, look at me."

I did as I was told while swallowing hard, "I love you okay? I'm in love with your crazy ass," he teased, earning a chuckle from me.

"That's why I want you with me at all times. I want to experience something new with you. New for the both of us. I understand you just moved, and I feel like you learned what you had to out here. Me and you both. Now let's write our story now. New place, new scenery, new people. If you come and don't like it, cool. At least you tried, ya know?"

I nodded taking in his words. He smirked a little before placing a sweet kiss on my lips. I kissed him again, loving the way his lips felt against mine.

"I love that you suggested this, I really do. Lets me know how committed you are to this relationship. I just need some time to process everything and make sure this is something I want to do as well. The thought of you leaving kills me, but the thought of me coming out there and we don't make it kills me even more," I confessed, while receiving a look of understanding.

"Trust me baby, I get it. All of this is eating me up. But at least if you don't move, you can come visit. We can christen the new crib properly," he flirted, while biting his bottom lip as I giggled.

"You always gotta take it there," I laughed softly, shaking my head.

"Shit, I'm a man girl. My mind always there," he joked, while standing up straight to stretch.

I looked at the ticket again, thinking about the dates and the move.

Could I seriously see myself taking one last leap of faith?

Donovan.

"What do you think of this one Mr. McCall?" Rachel our realtor asked, breaking me away from looking at my watch for the hundredth time that morning.

We had been looking at different lofts and spaces for our future parlor. I had already fallen in love with one prior to her showing me the few today. The one I liked was just slightly over budget, but I was willing to make up the difference.

"Huh? Oh, it's cool," I shrugged while glancing my eyes over the place, causing her to let out a laugh of disbelief.

"You're not making this easy today. You've said that to every one I've shown you this morning. And you can't break away from your watch, or your phone."

I sighed as she looked at me, awaiting an explanation for my rude behavior.

"I'm sorry Rach. It's just my girl's flight is supposed to get in within the hour, and I honestly have no idea if she's even on it. Just looking out to hear from her, that's all."

Her expression softened. I told Bobbi not to tell me if she was coming to live or even to visit. I wanted to be surprised, so I gave her to the address to the beach right outside of my house, and instructed her to meet me there. I was regretting my decision because now it was bothering me.

"But, as far as this place goes, just the location itself is a no. Most importantly, we're looking for something on or near the strip. There's no point to open up a new spot that's not going to generate any revenue or buzz. We're aware of the pricing for that kind of location, and we're willing to kick up the budget a little for it and adjust numbers elsewhere. It'll level out with all of the business we'll receive after being here for a few months," I explained, getting back into professional mode and the real reason why I wasn't interested in any of these places.

"Okay. Did you speak with Shane about the place you liked yesterday?"

I nodded.

"Alright, I'll put in an offer. Just didn't want to before you saw anything else you could possibly like."

"Well the space we saw yesterday is one that Shane already liked while we were in California. So seeing it yesterday and it being on Ocean Drive was perfect. Make an offer, and get back to us when you can," I told her, as she nodded with understanding.

"I'll be in touch. Go get your girl," she winked, pulling out the keys to lock the place up.

I tapped her light on her shoulder before I swiftly made my way out of there and back to my car. I wanted to get home and change into something more comfortable before her arrival just in case she did come.

I arrived at my complex and took the elevator up to the fifth floor, walking the halls briskly, making sure I wasn't late to the meeting time put in place. I fumbled with the keys before opening the door and nearly tripping over myself heading to my bedroom. I threw on a pair of Levi cargo shorts, with a white t-shirt, Jordan flip flops and a matching snapback before quickly rushing out of my house.

My heartbeat steadied as I strolled calmly along the pathway, leading to the beach, searching every which way for a familiar face. My steps slowed to a stop, posting up next to the bicycle rental shack before looking at my watch for the time.

She could arrive any minute.

"Where are you baby?" I sighed to myself, shoving my hands deep into my pockets, ignoring all the lustful stares from women.

It amazed me sometimes how much I had changed since falling for Bobbi. The attention I could receive no longer mattered; I only wanted hers.

As more time passed, I felt myself become more saddened at the thought of her making the decision to stay in California. It was growing hard for me to accept that she didn't even want to visit me so soon, knowing how much I was missing her with each passing day.

I let out a deep breath after an hour had passed, and kicked at some sand before turning on my heels to head back to my house. The high I had been on all morning was starting to come down, and the anticipation was turning into regret. I was regretting asking her to move out here with me so soon, without allowing our relationship to develop. I laughed bitterly at myself for even thinking that she would yes to an idea so crazy.

My chin was sunk nearly to my chest while walking blindly back to my complex. I cursed to myself the minute my absentminded state caused me to bump into a small figure, causing her bags to fall at her feet.

"Oh shit, my fault..."

I allowed myself to look up, catching the beautiful brown eyes I had fallen in love with. A smirk instantly pulled at my lips, realizing exactly how we met so long ago had repeated itself. Except a scowl wasn't resting on her face this time; peace was.

She let out a heavy sigh while staring lovingly at me. "My flight was delayed..." she stumbled before scratching her head, revealing an unsure expression.

"Does this make me crazy?"

I shook my head before scooping her up into my arms and holding her tight while hiding my face in the crook of her neck; feeling relieved at her very touch knowing this was real.

I was never letting go.

ABOUT THE AUTHOR

Tiffany Campbell is a 26-year-old African American author born and raised in the thriving city of Columbus, Ohio. At the tender age of eight, she wrote her first short story and has since gone on to write and produce screen plays, mini TV series for her church, and drama presentations. At 24, Tiffany took her first major step into the world of published literature when she self published her first edition *Scared of Beautiful* while living in Chicago. It was a transitional time period for Tiffany and she knew it was time to reanalyze and focus on what it was that she truly wanted in life. There she discovered that the root of her passions and what made her happiest was writing, and she wanted to finally utilize the gift that God in-trusted her with.

She has since republished her debut novel in its second edition with Kenerly Presents in the summer of 2015. This upcoming year, Tiffany plans to release her sophomore novel, "*Don't Disconnect*," which she anticipates to be impactful to every reader she encounters. Tiffany's goal as a writer is to change lives, one word at a time with each title she publishes.

Tiffany prides her self in developing characters that not only she, but men and women can easily relate to in some form. Like herself, her characters are both going through or have transition themselves and are learning to let go of everything that has held them back in the past and push forward.

She only wants to motivate her readers to do the same; to follow their passions and their dreams, and to allow love to find them on the way.

CPSIA information can be obtained
at www.ICGtesting.com
Printed in the USA
LVHW041821040319
609437LV00001B/125/P